REVOLUTIONS

An Anthology of Speculative Fiction Set in Manchester

Editors
Craig Pay
Graeme Shimmin
Eric Steele

Assistant Editor
Luke Shelbourn

manchesterspeculativefiction.org

First published in Great Britain
in 2015 by Manchester Speculative Fiction Group

Introduction © Graeme Shimmin, 2015
Individual contributions © the contributors, 2015

The right of Manchester Speculative Fiction Group to be
identified as the editors of this work has been asserted in
accordance with sections 77 and 78 of the Copyright Designs
and Patents Act 1988.

ISBN 978-1518701351

Typeset in 16pt. Exo and 11pt Candara.

Version 1.0

To Madlab, thanks for all your help.

CONTENTS

INTRODUCTION

Graeme Shimmin

22 October 2015

I'll keep this short, as no one wants to read long-winded waffle about short stories.

Manchester is a terrific setting for speculative fiction. It's a steampunk city for one thing, full of what-ifs from its Victorian golden age. But Manchester also witnessed the birth of the technological era – the atom was first split in Manchester, and the first computer was created here too.

At the same time, if you look at it differently, it's not hard to see a dystopia. Manchester's astonishing ascent was built on the exploitation of the starving, diseased and down-trodden workers, and Friedrich Engels was so appalled by Manchester that he invented communism.

Some people say Manchester hasn't changed much since, and it's true there's still a darker underside to the city. Manchester does things differently, and that's reflected in this eclectic group of stories.

They fall into five categories:

1. **Comedy:** *Once Upon A Time in the Northwest*'s pie-gladiators, and *Gasoline Alley*'s Manc-Scouse war are surreal and fun.

2. **Future Dystopia**: there are no zombies, but down on the streets the future is grim in Sarah Jasmon's excellent *The Uncertainty Principle*, eco-dystopias, *No. 5 Passage*, and *Bridgewater*, and future-noirs *Cold Metropolis* and *Wrath and Duty*.

3. **Horror**: Die Booth's brutal *Maketh the Man*, Eric Steele's thrilling *Earthsong*, and the chilling *The Attic of Memories* all push the right horror buttons.

4. **Sci-fi:** Craig Pay's *Traveller* and Katya Fawl's *Waterways* are classic sci-fi ideas with great Manchester twists.

5. **General Weirdness:** *Please, Please Let Me Get What I Want*, *The Last Drag Show On Earth*, *Toil and Trouble*, and *Until Further Notice* all defy classification and show prodigious imagination and storytelling skills.

So, I'll just say, take it from me, there are some fantastic stories here!

Best Wishes,
Graeme.

THE UNCERTAINTY PRINCIPLE

Sarah Jasmon

It took me more than a week to track it down.

The arches were the best places to try, but the pop-up stalls never stayed put for long. Those dark spaces, under the railway bridges or tucked down by the canal, would sprout lights and shelves and endless boxes of junk, and the word would go out on the whispering network. Often, the bureaucrats would get there first and nothing would be left by the time I got there other than the white notices taped to the lamp posts or discarded, sodden, on the ground.

I found it in the end along Market Street. It was on one of the trays the old hawkers used. Most of the guys were alert, raucous, shouting out the improbable treasures you could find in their stock. The one I stopped at was silent though, his head resting on his chest and his eyes hidden behind a fall of grey hair. He had four trays, arranged in a semi-circle around his slouched body. The slim, cardboard box was hidden under a pile of unopened coffee pods, caramel flavour. When I held out the money, he looked up at me with a milky, sightless gaze.

Just as I walked away, a pair of policemen came around the corner from Cross Street, their boots kicking out at the first hawker on the row. The others started to scramble to their feet, sweeping their wares into bin liners and disappearing into the empty shops behind them. I glanced back at the blind man. He sat there, zen-like, ignoring the chaos around him.

I closed my fingers over my find and hurried away.

I'm taking my time in opening it, holding my breath and letting my hand rest on my belly before I break the seal. Part of me can't believe that something so simple can work, or that its function can survive for so long after the use-by date. The forums I've been following assure me that it will. I stumbled across them years ago, a community of women trying to keep some element of personal control over their bodies. As soon as I found them, I knew that it would be the way I wanted to find out, an old-fashioned moment of discovery, away from the speed and hustle of the scan clinics. I can go and do that tomorrow. Tonight it's just me. I don't even want Matt to be here.

He should be home soon. I've been planning for this ever since I met him. The door will open. He'll walk in with his late-night stubble and loosened tie. I'll hand him a champagne flute and a stick with two blue lines. It'll be us and the future.

I have shown him the blue lines and he has reached out and taken the glass, but all he does is stare at the bubbles. They force their way up, appearing with a final burst of velocity from behind his fingers, but the empty look in his eyes has turned the anticipation I've felt in my belly all afternoon into an empty space, the beginnings of the baby pressed to one side as if it shouldn't be there.

'Matt?' My hands shake as I put down first the stick and then my glass. 'What is it? What's happened?' Because it must be something outside, at work, that's making him be like this. He's always agreed how much he wants this to happen, how our baby will be perfect, a blonde and brown-eyed darling who will have the best of everything.

'Matt?' I give his arm a shake and his head jerks. He looks about as if wondering where he is before finally stepping forwards. But he's not coming to hug me. He drains his glass, refills it, then crosses to the sofa and sinks down, head resting in his free hand.

I pick my own glass back up and take a sip, sourness tracking down my throat. My voice only wobbles a bit. 'So, we'll need to access the New Child insurance data. I've got an appointment booked for tomorrow.'

That's when he finally looks me, his face an odd shade of grey. 'It's gone, Mia. I'm so sorry.'

I'm in the Citizen's Advice Bureau now, my head buzzing from my sleepless night. I lay awake for hours, thrashing around for possible options, but this was the only achievable one I could come up with. Matt was still in his chair when I left, staring out as if the view of the city was still visible from our windows. I didn't speak to him, and now I touch my swollen eyes with one of my lemon-scented wipes. I'm finding it hard to think. The smell goes some way towards keeping the sickness at bay. I'm glad somehow to have the nausea with me, even though a small part of my brain is telling me it would be better if the pregnancy test was wrong. I have the stick safe inside my curled hand, hidden in my coat pocket. Matt's explanations are circling round my head in an endless loop – the gambling debts, the demands, how he'd planned to replace the policy, he really, really had. I can feel the imprints of his hands where they'd grabbed at me as I'd screamed and tried to hit him. His glass had arced through the air, smashing into a thousand crystal pieces.

The floor here is a dull, speckled rubber, curving up the walls for a hand-span on either side of the corridor. If I could have chosen, I'd have gone out to Levenshulme, where the bureau has just been reallocated a new building that is supposed to have a library attached. Our postcode means I have to come to Spinningfields, though, to one of the old glass towers. The library might just be a rumour anyway. The view from here must have been amazing, back when windows were still being cleaned. I've seen the pictures of men in little cradles, swinging slowly along the edges of the buildings. Now the grime outside is thick, forcing the light to bounce away, showing me nothing but my pale reflection.

The screen to my right is running one of the news channels. There is no sound, just the usual run of new data announcements and graphs detailing percentage rises in the World Climate Exchange. A newsreader's face replaces the infographics, a close-up of her grave expression cut with images of the latest detention of migrants. Figures flash up: they were apprehended 148 nautical miles off the coast of Greenland. A thousand bodies packed into containers. A map now, showing the maze of plastic masses that caught the ship.

I close my eyes to be rid of the women's faces, captured in the middle of their pleas. I don't want to think of them. Instead I will marshal my facts: I've paid into my New Child policy for my whole working life; this baby should not be classed as a drain on the state; none of this is my fault. There must be a way, I say to the consultant in my head. This can't be happening to me. The cubicles are in a line to my left. Two of the doors open simultaneously.

One lets out a woman so buoyant with relief that she is fighting to keep her feet on the rubber. The other discharges a young man carrying a plastic bag that drags down at his hand. He doesn't try to conceal his reddened eyes. I dig my nails into the fleshy part of my palm. The first door. Please call me to the first door.

Behind the second door, the cubicle is airless and smells of sweat. The screen on the far wall is blank and I hesitate, not sure if there is something I'm supposed to do to verify that I'm here. I can't see a scanner, no dancing red line ready to read my data. The walls are white, with scuffmarks and dints peppering the dirty surface. A plastic chair rests at an angle as if it has been pushed out of the way with force. I pull it back and sit down, holding my bag on my knees. The screen has the shape of a hand imprinted on it. I can see the slash of the lifelines, even the whorls of the fingertips. They seem to glow an angry red against the dark surface of the screen, suggesting that the light behind it has only just gone out. As I gaze, the background jerks on again, and a face replaces the hand.

She's older than I expected, the resolution of the screen stretching and magnifying her pores and wrinkles. There's a mole on her jawline, dusted with a crust of powder too orange for her skin tone. I sit up a little straighter.

'Number.' She doesn't look up, and I can tell that her fingers are busy just out of view. I was expecting her to want my name and so I stumble over the digits. She gives an irritated sigh as I try again and carries on with her questions with her face still down. 'And you are here because?'

Her tone tells me to keep it short. I take a breath, reminding myself that I am allowed to be here, that my rights as a citizen allow me to explore my options, to appeal against any decision this woman will make today. I need her on my side, though.

'It's the New Child insurance.' A wave of nausea stops me, and I feel a drop of sweat run down my spine, vertebra by vertebra. 'I've only just found out about the pregnancy and my husband…' My voice is blocked by the ball of anger and disbelief that rises in my throat. 'When I asked my husband for the insurance papers, he…he…' The bastard. I press my fingers into my eye sockets.

Through the sparkle of multi-coloured lights jostling on my eyelids I picture his face, his mouth moving in its meaningless apology. I force myself to drop my hands and carry on. 'I know I should have kept track, but when we changed to a joint policy it just seemed easier for him to store it.' It had been in the grey time, before the Data Act made the Joint Safety Programme into an obligation.

She doesn't want to hear it, has sat through this before.

'All my money…' My voice is getting faster, rising into the high-pitched babble where actual words disappear.

Her hands make swiping gestures punctuated by the little jabs that tick boxes. She still hasn't made eye contact with me. I realise that the handprint, still just visible on the screen, is positioned right across her neck. I listen to the rustle of her clothes as she comes to a stop and finally positions herself to face me, her gaze resting some degrees to my left. Her tone is bored and monotonous.

Briefly, her eyes flicker to my stomach, still hidden behind my bag. 'It is possible to backdate the insurance at the higher rate if you have the resources immediately to hand to cover the reintroduction fee?' She looks right at me, her eyebrows raised in query.

I shake my head.

Her gaze slides away. I know what's coming. 'As you know, a fine will be imposed as a result of pregnancy without insurance. Termination is available at many of the healthcare drop in centres.' She is matter-of-fact, reciting from a well-rehearsed script. The handprint at her neck glows and my fingers twitch. But she is leaning in, pausing as she flicks a glance to one side. I think I see a flash of some strong emotion cross her face. 'There are other options.' Her voice lowers and speeds up. 'Not the Available Fathers Network, you have to be unmarried for six months for that.' Her fingers dance. 'There's adoption, of course, but that would involve compulsory sterilisation.'

I swallow, trying to decide how much I can trust her with. 'I thought… Isn't that for the second instance?' If I could cross my fingers without her seeing, I would. I think of my baby being carried away, a small and faceless white bundle.

She looks at her screen and gives me a quick glance. Is that sympathy I see, fellow feeling? 'This isn't your first time, though, is it?'

She knows. They know. It's not supposed to be in my records. It happened before the laws came in. I was young. I was attacked. I am rigid with the sense of betrayal.

The woman reaches out a hand towards the camera and I find my hand lifting in response, leaving my own print superimposed as we touch. Without any words, our relationship has changed.

'Right.' She sits back. If we still used paper, she'd be shuffling it now, gathering the stack together and tapping it into a neatly aligned pile. 'Are you a homeowner?'

I nod.

'And is that ownership solely in your name?'

I shake my head this time, squeezing my fingers together in a linked grip that presses bone to bone.

She hasn't waited for my confirmation, has anticipated my reply and is already tapping away, her expression intent. After a few moments she stops and gestures to the side with one hand, her other cupping over the microphone. I can still hear her voice, though. That must go to another feed. She leans in, her voice a fast-paced mutter. 'If your husband should be unfortunate enough to meet with an accident before your pregnancy is officially recorded, you'll be granted a compassionate exception, and the process of assigning your home to you alone will be expedited.' She watches my reaction. 'You must bring the data tomorrow. Quote the reference number when you book in, it'll bring you back to me.'

The screen goes black.

I reach the street in a daze. My nausea has returned with renewed strength, and its making it hard to think. I should probably get something to eat, a small decision that should be easier than the large ones I've just been presented with, but even that seems beyond me. Every time I pass a café, I hesitate for too long and end up walking by. They're scruffy places around here at the best of times, hiding at the bottom of the mostly empty offices that have been packed in so tightly that they block out the light. I'm feeling hyper-noticeable, my thoughts spelling out in the air around me, and I want to become invisible. But the cafes are empty, and I don't want to be by myself right now.

The building has an air of emptiness. I stand for a moment, listening to life carrying on behind the other doors along the corridor. That was me yesterday. Maybe there have been evenings in the past when a desperate neighbour has paused before their home like I am now. Did they stop to listen to the normal, everyday noises inside my walls as they fought to settle on a decision? It's not the sort of subject that comes up at dinner parties, or when you're waiting for the lift. I let the sounds surround me as I lift my hand up to the scanner and wait for the door to swing back. That's when I realise that the low-voiced murmur that makes up one layer of the background buzz is coming from inside my flat.

They're in the living room. I hold the door as it closes to keep it silent and step out of my shoes. These flats were built for young professionals, with all of the tired design quirks that city living was supposed to require. So the hall curves around as it reaches towards the front facing rooms, the dividing wall sweeping down as it opens up the main space with a flourish. I suppose the idea was to have the view from the glass walls unfold as you approached. Now, I ease my way along until I get to the point where the top of the wall is just above my head.

Matt is sitting with his back to the glass, his face hidden in his hands. I wonder how much of the world he is actually managing to block out. The others have their backs to me, two heavy, square outlines, both with an air of waiting for an answer, and not patiently. I draw back so that I can no longer see them.

Matt begins to talk, his voice muffled. 'The only thing I have left is this place. And that's borrowed against to its max.' He's using his whining voice, the one that can't believe how the universe is treating him. It's not the approach I would have taken. I think of the immoveable bulk of the men, and shiver.

'It still has a certain value.' It's the man on the left who has spoken. I was expecting hoarseness, a foreign accent, but his tone is clear, reasonable even. 'We have given you time, but there are certain... limits.'

Matt says nothing, and the pause stretches out.

'And your wife.' He leaves a space for Matt to reply, but there is nothing. He carries on as if his question has been confirmed. 'There are measures we can take, as I'm sure you will understand. We are patient, but the data must be unlocked.'

In the old films, men like this would carry a knife, a shining cosh, a needle. I imagine the steel of a gun barrel pressed hard to my temple, an anachronism to be sure, but one that makes me want to whimper aloud. I need to move, to get away from here, but my legs have no strength. I try to swallow, praying that the sickness stays away. I don't want them to drag me away on my knees, retching. I wait for Matt to protest, to beg them to leave me, us, out of the equation, but again he is silent.

Finally I manage to back away. I am followed by the sound of Matt's voice. 'She's not here, though.' He is hardly able to force out the words. 'I don't know where she is.'

That could be seen as a defence of sorts, I suppose, a stalling tactic at the very least, but I suspect that the trembling voice is signalling his readiness to do whatever it takes to save his own skin. The woman's words from this morning come back to me: *If your husband should be unfortunate enough to meet with an accident.* I have been battling the idea all day. I have asked questions I never thought existed, tracked down offers and possibilities that just pushed me further into that endless walk of indecision. I'd come home with my mind made up. I couldn't do it. I'd returned with the intention of telling him that I'd decided on the termination, but that it would also terminate our marriage.

I wonder how long Matt took to come to his decision.

There isn't much time. The nausea agrees with me, pushes me into making a move. I'm glad it's there, reminding me of what is to come, of what I have to do if I want to get past this moment and feel my baby transmute into the fluttering, physical presence of hands and feet, pushing from the inside of my skin. I spread my palms out over my abdomen, sealing our silent agreement and apologising for even considering its end.

The bedroom is a mess, with drawers upside-down on the floor and clothes scattered everywhere. Did the men do this, or was it Matt? Maybe they stood over him, forcing him to rake out my underwear on his knees, taunting him for his eagerness to please them in the face of their violence. But there's something wrong with that image: Matt knows where the Datascreen is. The chaos in here is just window dressing. They needed me here, with my handprint on the screen next to Matt's, unlocking our data records. It will be so much easier for them if they have the codes. They can say it was a legal transaction, and who will be there to contradict them?

It's hidden in a stupid place, and not one they'd have missed if they'd really been looking. We got it one summer, when the vintage markets were still allowed up in Piccadilly Gardens. It looks like an old-style poster in a frame, a black and white image of a couple kissing in the rain. There's a sensor on one of the long edges, and when you hold a finger over it for a count of five, a drawer slides out with a space just big enough for a Datascreen. I don't realise that I'm holding my breath until I see that it's still there. My hands are shaking as I take it out, and I nearly drop it. Just as the empty drawer slides back, I hear feet in the corridor.

There are no hiding places in an old city-centre apartment. They were planned for minimalist living, for sharp lines and space. I would feel ridiculous, standing behind the bathroom door trying to blend with the wall, if I wasn't so scared. I keep my eyes closed, a child invisible in a game of hide and seek. The feet turn into the bedroom, and a message tone sounds. A voice I haven't heard before answers it with a grunt. It must be the second man. Then feet shuffle close by and the door swings shut, leaving me exposed.

Matt and I stare at each other, and I wait for his mouth to open. His gaze drops to the Datascreen, which I have in a tight grip against my chest. My hands are slippery against it and I know I won't be able to keep hold of it if he tries to take it. But he doesn't need to try. All he needs to do is say a word and the men will do it for him. On the other side of the door, one of their muffled voices carries on with his call.

This is the end. I have no chances left. Everyone knows what happens to the unfortunates with no home, no data. I wonder if Matt is thinking the same thing. Once I thought we shared every thought. Now I smell the sharp acid of his fear and wonder who he is.

The voice in the bedroom stops. I tense, waiting for the door to swing open. Matt moves towards me. I flinch. He steps past me and turns on the taps. For a moment I am transfixed at the sight of the water swirling. Matt reaches for me. I tighten my grip on the Datascreen.

Matt's hand stops just in front of my belly. I feel a strange, almost magnetic pull from my skin to his. He takes the Datascreen from me. I don't resist. He has to guide my hand, placing it on the screen. I feel the tremor as he places his own next to it. Our thumbs touch as the screen gives out its light.

The man outside is still talking, but I can tell from his tone that the end of the conversation has come. Adrenaline spiders my veins. But Matt is pressing the screen back into my hands. He leans in close, his hair brushing my cheek, and reaches a finger to flick to the settings. I can't follow what he's doing because my eyes are blurred with tears. I blink them away to see that the system is asking for confirmation. Matt lifts my hand again and places it on the middle of the screen, alone. *Transfer confirmed,* says the screen. *Joint account terminated, assets transferred.*

He looks straight at me and, for a second, we are back at the beginning and he is the man that I love. He is saying something but his voice is barely audible. I'm reading his lips rather than hearing him. 'Tell our daughter… when… when she asks what I was like… lie to her. Tell her I was a good man. Tell her I loved her.' He smiles at me, though he is crying, and then he is gone.

I sink to the floor of the bathroom. Raised voices come from outside. Something thuds. Glass smashes and the alarm begins to wail. A voice I don't recognise starts swearing. Rapid footsteps. The front door opens and then slams closed.

After a moment, the alarm stops and there is silence.

I crawl into the bedroom. There's no one there. The windows to the Juliet balcony are broken. I peek over the safety railing. In the courtyard, three people are standing beside a body.

On the wall above my head is our wedding photo. I reach up to take it off the wall and smash the glass against the corner of the bed. A pen is poking out from the clothes strewn on the floor, and I pick it up. It is silver and machined in a complex of whorls.

My hands are shaking so much that it takes several tries, but I manage to pull the photograph from its frame. I take a moment to breathe, and then I write:

Your father was a good man and he loved you.

MAKETH THE MAN

Die Booth

There's a smell in the air, or should I say an aroma? I can't tell if it's cheeseburgers or dog shit. Whichever, it's turning my stomach and making me feel butterflies of excitement at the same time. These city-at-night smells. I feel on edge. The smells you'd usually find repellent – stale beer, sweat, hair – when you're out after dark and a few drinks they become something vital, something affirming. After days thinned by office air con and trammelled by rules, it's like being let out; like an animal let out. Born of the night.

It's that rosy light of late evening in early summer when black bricks throw back the day's heat lazily. The sun's setting behind concrete and parched trees and I turn to see, just for a moment, the sunset reflected in every window of two blocks of flats; blazing as if they're on fire. It's beautiful and then it's gone, and it leaves behind this fruit-salad sky, all yellow and orange, peach and pink and bruise purple along the horizon.

'Alright, Jamie?'

I'm expecting him, but he still surprises me. He has that effect on most people. He's wearing black patent brogues and sprayed-on red jeans and he's getting looks from everyone who passes – the guys, who hate him, the girls, who want him. He's pure loving it, and part of me thinks he looks a prick and part of me is jealous, because I wish I could pull that look off. Red jeans. Not scarlet red but the rich, saturated red of a nosebleed on a white linen hand-kerchief. "Clothes maketh the man", as he would say. Fashionista little bitch.

'Where are we going?' I ask.

He taps the side of his nose. 'You'll see.'

This is Eddie. He's a legend.

I met Eddie a few months ago at a White Rose Movement gig. Just after the second support band, we're both hang-ing over the black, iron guardrail of the fire escape, having a crafty fag. He's wearing this Adam and the Ants t-shirt, you know the one with the stiletto print on the front? The collar's torn out, but not in a shop-bought way, in a 'this happened by accident in the mosh pit of a band who're too underground for you to have heard of, but I still wear it 'cause I don't give a damn' way.

I say, 'That's cool,' and he says, 'I'm Eddie,' and sticks out his hand – chipped black nail polish and this big brass ring on his pinkie finger – dead pretentious, but on him somehow effortless.

And we shake and flick our filters sparking into the night street and we go back inside and he's dangerous in the second row for a little skinny guy.

Sometimes we go out to gigs and sometimes to clubs, but mostly we just drink or do pills. Sometimes I have reserva-tions: some of the people Eddie scores from look worse for wear. After a while, you start to notice them in the street, these invisible people, invisible like the homeless guys in doorways with mittened, curled fingers and dogs on string. Junkie-invisible, they drift like ashes down busy streets, wafting in-between the suits and shoppers, who either don't see them or pretend hard not to; I'm not sure there's a difference.

Eddie always scores. Even though I recognise the dealers now, I can't bring myself to do it, so I let him. This one girl, Eddie gives her the silent, film-star eyes and she floats over to him. He scoops an arm around her waist and kisses her, this grey-ashes girl. He dips her backwards like she's Scarlett O'Hara, with his velvet pink lips on her bloodless cracked ones and his eyes sliding closed – as if this lank, frayed chick is some pneumatic Vivienne Leigh – as he slyly tucks a tenner into a pocket of her jeans. That's how they pass the gear on, see? He waves her goodbye and then when we're round the next corner spits out a cling-film wrap into his palm, trailing a shiny clear tail of spit, and he grins at me. Somehow when we score, I'm always more bothered about traces of the dealer's spit still being on it than I am about touching Eddie's. She looks sick and, like I say, that gives me reservations, but Eddie's been doing it a long time and he doesn't look sick and as I figure it, we're just social users. You only live once, right?

Eddie says, 'I've got something for you: *coupe poudre,*' and he chops me out a line. I ask what it is and he says, 'The decline of Western Civilisation,' and starts laughing. I bend close to the mirror and inhale, and it tingles: it's like breathing electricity; coke, but cut with something.

I hardly remember that night. I swear I slept through Sunday. See, I've started to lose the odd hour here and there and that's not happened since I was a student. I first realise this when I wake up on Eddie's couch with new hair. Now I remember coming home at about three in the morning and I vaguely remember pizza and I definitely re-member Eddie waving around this blunt fucking pair of kitchen scissors – scary – perched on the couch with his legs tucked under him, me sat on the floor between his knees and him hacking away with sodden inspiration. But this morning I look in the mirror and there's this wicked bleached streak in my fringe as well and he says, 'We did that last night after your haircut, don't you remember?' and I don't. But it's okay, it looks cool. Not as cool as Ed-die's hair, but still boss and all's well that ends well and all that jazz. But in general, the losing time is… it's kind of bad, because it means I miss stuff. The crazy good laughs, stuff that we do all this for.

Like, for example, I ask, 'Isn't Michelle in?'

Michelle's one of Eddie's housemates. He lives in this sketchy student place, a four floor, Victorian townhouse in Rusholme with a basement and black damp crawling the walls and all-night parties five nights a week. This, de-spite the fact I know he's not a student anymore and he's well older than the rest of them. But I've never known him to have a real job so I suppose it's all he can afford. Any-way, Michelle's pretty fit, in a how'd-you-type-with-them-nails kind of way. I like her, Michelle, in a three-pints-of-courage-maybe type of way.

Eddie says, 'Shell's not speaking to us at the moment.'

That puts me out a bit and confuses me a bit too. 'Eh? How come?'

He gets that grin where his eyes go all wide and you can see the whites of them and he looks a bit tapped. On anyone else that expression would have people calling the men in white coats, and to be honest even Eddie's cut-ting it fine. He always looks on the verge of bursting into laughter does Eddie, a bit manic. He says, 'Mate, she's mad at us for filling her Soda Stream with minestrone.'

'You what?'

'We got back from The Attic. We were trying to make fizzy soup. You don't remember?'

'No!' I wish I could remember. 'Did we wreck it? The Soda Stream?'

Eddie's smile smears to a smirk across his teeth. 'Not gonna lie – we gunked it up a bit. I told her though, better soup than what you wanted to try in it.' He does a *Carry On* mime of weeing and then drinking it and I lose it for good-on five minutes.

It cracks me up to hear about all the mental stuff we get up to when we're out of it. Although, sometimes he says things like, 'So, no regrets about last night then?' and my stomach sort of echoes hollow, like the bottom dropping out of a big drum and I have to ask, 'Why? What did we do?'

His eyes are big and brown and round and innocent. 'You got down on your knees and begged me to let you suck me off.'

I can't even say anything. I just sort of inhale in horror, a hot, horrible flush swarming instantly across my skin, while Eddie says with sincerity, 'I'm sorry man, I was drunk. I wasn't going to turn down a blow job!'

I can only imagine what my face looks like, all flabby and sweaty, aghast, because then he can't keep up the pretence anymore and the skin round his eyes all crinkles up and he bends over double laughing. When Eddie laughs he doesn't make much sound, but his shoulders shake like he's crying and sometimes he does, he cries with laughing.

'You sick bastard! You had me going!' I'm laughing too, although mainly from relief, because I know now he's only messing and he doesn't know too much after all. And it's funny I guess, but it does make me wonder if I can really, properly trust him.

So we're walking through the part of the city with all the old high-rise warehouses on either side. They're all smash-ed glass, and chicken wire over the windows, and you can hear a distant shuffling inside from the rats and the junk-ies and stuff. Then there's a whole expanse of nothing, just the silhouetted skeleton of the railway viaduct over-head and a couple of girls who look like prossies clinging to the wall of the last warehouse and this one big building slap bang in the middle of the intersecting roads, as if eve-rything round it got bombed in the war but somehow this one survived, survived like a cockroach.

I follow the tapping of Eddie's Cuban heels across the road and round the side of the building, taking our place in the queue. If there weren't people lining up outside, you'd never guess the place was a club – it looks derelict, the windows blind, tar-painted boards and the drainpipes bursting with weeds.

Eddie says, 'They done a film here once. There's a swimming pool on the roof.'

I peer up at the sooty bricks of the wall next to me. I'm too close to it and looking to the roof makes me feel dizzy, like I'm going to topple over backwards. I can't imagine a swimming pool up there, but when Eddie says it it's like magic; it seems like anything could be possible.

My life unfurls like a dream these days.

Now we're in this club and I don't even know what it's called. There's an out-of-order jellybean machine in one corner of the bar. A handwritten sign sellotaped to the front reads, 'FUCKED'. A mirror ball in the middle of the ceiling is sailing circles of light across the heaving dance-floor, a twirling whirlpool of glitter that's like being inside a glass of champagne and makes you just as light-headed.

We're on the balcony looking down, and from here it looks like some kind of Heironymous Bosch vision of Hell: a mesh of twisted bodies and lurid colours. There's electro-clash playing with a really insistent bass-line that you can feel in your throat.

I look sideways at Eddie, at his Adam's apple bobbing as he swigs from his bottle of lager. Discs of reflected illumination slide across his skin. His eyes catch the light the most, depthless glossy black. He says, 'Look at it. Dissolution. The degeneration of a generation.' He looks excited, animated, like he's almost getting off on it. He says, 'We're like the last days of Rome, but poor. Can you imagine the sin going on down there? "The curtain of the temples was torn in two from top to bottom. The earth shook and the rocks split. The tombs broke open and the bodies of many holy people who had died were raised to life."'

It makes me laugh, even though I suppose he's right. 'You reckon they're all going to Hell?' I ask.

Eddie smirks and sticks his fingers in his mouth: it's this thing he does to get girls, says it makes him look all sweet and mischievous. I've tried it, it works. He shakes his head, his shaggy hair flicking round his shoulders. 'There is no Hell. This is all we got. We've become so corrupt and decadent and jaded; anything goes. We do things just to prove they can be done. Hey, Jamie?'

I raise my eyebrows. 'What?'

'What you want to happen to your body when you die?'

I've rehearsed this one in my head. You think about it;

burial versus cremation, what song you want at your funeral, all your exes gathered around sobbing in stilettos and pencil skirts and those little mourning veil things. Seems almost a shame you won't be around to enjoy it. I say, 'Cremation. It's got to be more hygienic, innit?' Eddie gets the giggles bad when I say 'hygienic'. 'And it takes up less space – gotta think of the ol' carbon footprint. And I want,' I'm warming to this subject, pardon the pun, 'that thing where they run the Crem heating off of the furnaces. So I can do everyone one last favour and keep them toasty for the service. I think that's nice, y'know, environmentally friendly. Death-powered central heating.'

He's still in stiches and I get a funny little glow of something in my belly. It makes me feel strangely proud that I can make a guy like Eddie laugh like this.

'And I want The Doors *Light my Fire* played. No, wait – I want Kool and the Gang, *Celebration*. No, hang on… that Lionel Richie one, they're having that street party in the video, what's it called?' I wrack my brains, resist the urge to get my phone out and check. I don't want to spoil the moment. '*All Night Long*?'

Eddie leans back on the balcony rail, looks like he's trying to balance his beer bottle on it, which isn't a good idea. He looks at me from under his fringe and says, 'Cremation's so permanent though. What about reanimation?'

I laugh, and somehow it sounds louder than the music, tinny and forced.

He carries on. 'Seriously. It's a thing, reanimation, people do it. It's illegal to make a zombie in Haiti, you know. I mean right now, proper law. It's seen as murder, even if the zombie's still got a job and a family and everything.'

'Yeah, right.'

'For real. A *bokur*, yeah, is a sorcerer. They make a powder neurotoxin from puffer fish venom and they give it to whoever they want to be a zombie and the person goes into a coma. All their body functions slow down so's people think they're dead. Then, when they've been buried, the bokur comes along and digs them up and gives them another dose of toxin – this one's made from plant extracts – and it puts them into this trance state where all they can do is obey orders.'

I look down at the backs of my hands, out of focus clutching the balcony rail. The warm feeling in my belly is spreading like liquid, getting hot and then cold. Everything's a bit hazy, like maybe I've drunk too much or maybe I've been spiked, even. There's a club stamp shaped like a top-hatted skull melting into the skin of my left hand. I lick my fingers and rub at it. My skin looks dull, grey, and it's not the ink. Yeah, I reckon I've been spiked. Should I be more upset? 'So they're not exactly dead then?' I say, to keep up the conversation. I'm starting to sweat, but I try to ignore it. I don't want to look like a lightweight.

Eddie says, 'Deprived of free will; it's worse than death if you think about it. Just imagine: trapped in the shell of your own body. But that's not all. Sometimes they do die. Sometimes they come back. And sometimes they just don't realise they're dead.'

It's probably whatever I've been slipped that's affecting my mood, but this topic of conversation is starting to make me feel proper uncomfortable.

Eddie's off on one, to be honest he's starting to rave a bit. 'Anthropodermic bibliopegy, you know what that is?' He shouts over the music, shaping his words in the air with his hands. 'It's binding books in human skin. Imagine that as immortality – being made into a book. I reckon I'd like that, what d'you reckon? The Nazis, yeah, they made lampshades from human skin. They just didn't give a shit; they'd experiment on people just because they could. They were well into the occult too, shut people down, switch them back on...'

This girl passes us, pretty with bottle-red hair, and shoots us a filthy look. I say, 'For God's sakes, Ed, stop going on about Nazis.' I pass the back of my hand across my face and it comes away damp with sweat, my hair slicking to my forehead. 'Mate, I'm not feeling so hot.' My legs shake beneath me; I can barely hold my own weight.

Eddie drops his empty beer bottle over the edge of the balcony, and he turns and he says, 'Let's go.'

I can't even remember the walk back to his.

'You should eat something.'

'I'm not hungry.' I realise that I'm really not, although I'm not sure when I last ate. I'm sure that's a sign of alcoholism or something. All this cheap vodka pickling me – it's practically embalming fluid.

Eddie brushes a scatter of crumbs off the kitchen counter with the side of his hand and picks a shrunken tangerine out of a plastic carrier bag sat there. He throws it to me.

I only just catch it, too many late nights screwing up my coordination. 'Cheers.' I should eat. The tangerine is shrivelled, juiceless, the white pith stringy and dry. It kind of tastes of nothing and when I've choked it down it seems to sit really heavy in my stomach, like I feel *too* full. And I'm sitting on the couch and Eddie sits down next to me and I'm thinking he's sitting closer to me than I'm comfortable with but somehow I can't get the words out to complain.

Eddie says, 'You ever done that thing, you know, when someone says to you, "remember to breathe"?'

I know this one, but it works every time. You only have to think it, 'remember to breathe', and suddenly you're purposefully doing something you'd normally never consciously consider, and you're guaranteed to be short of breath. It's just the sort of thing he'd say to someone who's tripping; head-wrecking. He can be fucking cruel sometimes. Actually, a lot of the time.

But this time, I'm not short of breath. It suddenly hits me – I'm actually not breathing. 'Eddie...' I take in an exaggerated big gulp of air and feel my dry lungs inflate like paper bags, 'Eddie, shit, Eddie...' And I'm starting to panic, to hyperventilate. 'Fucksake... Eddie, I'm not breathing!'

He's laughing his doubled-up laugh at me, but he stops laughing then and looks at me like... worried? Not worried. Curious. Like he's studying me. 'Don't be soft.'

'I'm not... joking.' I wheeze air in, gust it out. 'Eddie, am I breathing?'

'Of course you're breathing, you spaz. You're just wasted. If you weren't breathing you'd be dead. Keel over, wouldn't you?'

Sometimes, I wonder why he hangs out with me. I'm such a dick at times. I'm just uncool. I stumble to the mirror and stand close to it and wonder 'am I breathing'? Maybe it's one of those weird philosophy things like 'if a tree falls in the forest will it make a sound?' If you don't think about breathing, are you still doing it? People don't question it because it doesn't occur to them. But you're supposed to see breath on a mirror if someone's conscious. I huff on the mirror and it fogs up. Question answered, but I don't feel as relieved as I'd like to. My breath smells really bad; I should lay off the booze for a bit, probably. As the glass clears, I lean in and peer. 'What the hell is this?' Studying my face, I rub this purplish blotch along my jaw-line thinking maybe it's club stamp ink; but it doesn't come off. It looks like a bruise, but it's definitely not.

Eddie comes up behind me, and I can see both our faces reflected side-by-side. Him almost girl-pretty. Me, I look like death.

'What does it look like?' I watch his lips moving in the glass.

'It looks like a fucking KS lesion! I'm going to A&E.'

'No, you're not.' He says it quietly, definitely. 'You're not going anywhere.'

I turn round, trying to focus on the hallway door, trying to will myself past him and out, but this all-consuming exhaustion has me. I collapse like a sack of marbles, slumping untidily into Eddie's arms. He staggers under my weight, but holds me up. Then I suppose I pass out.

I come to in the spare bedroom. Everyone in the house calls it "the gimp room" because it's pretty much just this cupboard with a slanty roof and no windows and a mattress. Crash space, right? Party accommodation.

Eddie is outside the door. I can hear him speaking but I can't quite make out the words. I try to sit up, but my entire body aches. I try to reach out and bang on the door, but every muscle is so stiff I can't move. I turn my head, and my neck makes this sick, cracking noise that makes me throw up acid stuff into the back of my mouth. It dribbles out the side, which makes me gag worse. I feel like my entire body is seeping, like my entire body is the hot-cold feeling in my guts. Looking down, I can only see my bare shoulder, pale on top and sunset bruise-purple underneath where I'm lying on the mattress.

This is a bad trip, obviously, but that doesn't make it any easier and outside the door, Eddie is saying, 'The first part's known as Somatic Death.' He recites it like his speech back at the club, like he's pored over it in some book and learned it by heart. 'You had all that a while back, man, but you slept through it. Your brain, heart and lungs shut down. But your skin cells and stuff: still alive. They can be revived. Primary flaccidity – it don't sound too glamorous, does it?' I actually hear him laugh a bit at that.

'Algor Mortis. You reach room temperature. You feeling cold, man? Rigor Mortis. You stiff?' Another laugh, bubbling low. 'Your blood settles, gravity, yeah. Makes all the lowest parts of you look bruised, especially if you're lying on something, but the rest of you's nice and white. Your muscle cells are oxygen starved, so they make extra lactic acid which is what makes you go stiff, like a full body cramp – you feel that starting in your face? You can look forward to that for a day or so, and then the bacteria and chemical stuff will break the acid down and you can relax again. Then, right, it's putrefaction time...'

It's like I'm hearing him underwater, droning tonelessly on like one of those town-centre preachers. On and on, I don't know how long; it loses all context and his words have no meaning.

He says, 'How long can we retain our humanity, Jamie? Does it sit in the heart, or in the mind?' His voice buzzes outside the door: a swarm of flies trying to enter.

Eventually the words dissolve and all I can hear are sounds.

PLEASE, PLEASE LET ME GET WHAT I WANT

Katy Harrison

I was wired on the 142 Magic Bus shuttling me down the Oxford Road Corridor: Manchester's major artery, the busiest bus route in Europe. An ever-updating Instagram account of life as I knew it.

I pressed my forehead against the damp, mouldy-smelling window. Jumping out at me, streaked by crepuscular pink but poisoned by orange street lighting, were things I'd seen a hundred times and yet still seemed fresh. The large fin of Sainsbury's Fallowfield, Revolution, Mr Bubbles Laundrette, then hitting the Curry Mile, a rush of sari shops, Middle-Eastern corner shops, shisha bars, milkshake bars, a bank-turned-betting shop, then past Whitworth Park where a forgotten king stood with a pair of blue Y-fronts thrown over his head. Past the Manchester Royal Infirmary, McDonalds, Costa Coffee, and finally arriving at the university, where a mixed salad of students alighted with me, tight-skinned and perky, in skinny jeans, baggy jeans, split jeans, with dyed green hair, piercings, hipster glasses, Oxfam pin badges, boys with topknots, girls wearing the hijab. They carried iPads and Marvel backpacks. Some pushed, some huddled into themselves. I merged with them and then parted down a side street as they went to better themselves and increase their debt.

With each step, my body became heavier. If I was doing a degree, even a diploma, I wouldn't be stuck with this all-consuming wretched thought that burrowed like a tapeworm into my personality.

When the sliding doors to the building sighed open, my tapeworm crystallised.

I hated my boss. It was that simple. I hated my boss. I didn't dislike her, I didn't distrust her, I didn't feel uncomfortable around her. I hated her.

Annabel Morgan.

Everything about her struck me as wrong: morally wrong, emotionally wrong, psychologically wrong. Just wrong, wrong, wrong. But the things she did, they were so petty that I felt embarrassed mentioning them. Little things, you know? The way she'd not acknowledge junior members of the team, but kiss arse to anyone her grade or above. 'Oh, hello!' she'd coo when a member of senior management would enter her office. People who owned greyhounds and ponies and rented vines in Bordeaux and had medals for ballroom dancing. But she'd glide past our nest of desks all day, sealing herself inside her own private office whenever it became apparent we were stressed. She only deigned to come near us when she needed something doing. Or needed some information that she could shake glitter over for a meeting and present as her own work. Annabel didn't know the work she was supposedly in charge of. She didn't know what our jobs entailed. Hell, she barely knew what her job entailed.

The more work we had, the less she'd be around. How someone can be in a meeting every day for seven hours is beyond me. She was the last to arrive in the morning and the first to leave. We could go for days without her speaking to us. Even her e-mails were curt. No 'Hi', no 'Thanks', just:

```
>>>Colleagues
>>>
>>>Find   attached   the   report   on   the
>>>company's recent restructuring
>>>proposals. I expect your annotations
>>>by 4pm. Review meeting is booked for
>>>noon tomorrow.
>>>
>>>Annabel
```

I don't think I'd ever even heard her use the word 'Please'.

Our office, low-grade air conditioning, housed twenty workers, mostly women. On my section, discounting Annabel, we were four-strong, working in Admissions. Siobhan, my boss, was a friendly round-faced girl in her thirties who favoured jeans and primary colour blouses. She was the nicest person I knew and could find a good word for everyone, but even she hated Annabel. Kerry, somewhere in her forties, was angular like a penknife and moved her arms in snapping motions. She had a harder outlook on life on account of her last two boyfriends refusing to leave their wives for her. Pauline, a gentle, big woman with large glasses and oversized floral dresses was in her late fifties and kept two cats at home that she had photos of pinned up on her desk. And myself, the youngest, the junior. Twenty-four, living alone in an unheated bedsit in Withington and vaguely apathetic about things, which is one of the reasons I never finished college.

Annabel was our supervisor. She had a strong jaw line

and mannish features capped with a starched black bob that crowned her strangely asymmetrical looks. The look that pedigrees have; inbred to the point of brutally bland looks and miniscule intelligence. But graced with a powerful sense of self-preservation. That others, even those who save her arse countless times, are going down before she ever does. Rising from the shit storm a scented, protected peacock. The only nod to make-up was the mushroom-coloured lipstick that was too pale for her cottage-cheese skin tone. She also had a wide, low arse that I had to resist from kicking whenever it wobbled past me.

She drove Siobhan, Kerry, and I to drink (Pauline considered herself too old for pubs). The drinking culture at our company was well entrenched. Every Friday, Kro Bar, Jabez Clegg, and Big Hands would be deep with staff. Each pub was just under four minutes door-to-door so you could be on your first drink ten minutes after you clocked off.

After each week of Annabel, we three huddled around a table in Jabez Clegg, finishing drinks in four gulps, holding what we called Escape Committees. Within the gloom of dark wood, spilt beer, scuffed pool tables, and beaten-up speakers playing The Smiths, we dissected Annabel. Why did she do the things she did? Why couldn't she admit when she was wrong? Why did she treat us like shit? What we'd do if we ever got her outside the office. All the witty fuck-you sentiments that would make her blink then cry. How much better than her we all were. How much more intelligent, funny, compassionate, self-assured and grounded we were. What we'd do when we left the company. Because we would. We wouldn't stay there for another six months, no sirree, we were going to be stars. We would treat Annabel like a part of the furniture. We would tell her to go fuck herself. We would be smugly civil to her. We would steal her desk ornaments. We'd accept her flaws were not our flaws. We'd hack and crash her computer account. We'd take up yoga and evening classes because she was not worth the pain she put us through. We didn't live for this job. It was only paper and hell, why are we talking about this bitch? This is the longest possible time until we have to be back there and it's your round and yes, I'll have a tequila shot with that pint. Hell, bring the fucking bottle.

I was passive-aggressive in the way I dealt with Annabel. I hated her, but like a child getting bollocked in the staff room at school, I could never voice my feelings. I could never say, 'Annabel, you treat us with a great degree of disrespect and I find it unprofessional. So, let's be civil and do the jobs we're both paid to do. We don't have to like each other, but we do have to work together. So let's shake on it.'

Instead I waited until she went to lunch and then stole the crossword from her desk, filled it in and put it back. The only thing worse than that was that she never mentioned it.

In my kinder moments I tried to gain some perspective. Maybe she'd fucked up in the past and was now so terrified of putting a foot wrong that she used others to cover-up for her. Or maybe she had a personality disorder. With enough leave, I would reason that she was just a bully. And you deal with a bully in one of two ways. You confront them or you ignore them. I'd feel better with my conclusions. Then I'd return to work and would return to hating Annabel. Something, I felt, had to be done. She couldn't get away with herself any longer.

So I decided to kill Annabel.

It was simpler than I realised. She had two weeks booked off back-to-back, something we would never be granted. She was going to Turin to do something middle-class like look at the architecture or throw bread at peasant children. I had two weeks to end her life.

I knew she lived in a good part of town, one with a local paper. One phone call and debit card payment later and I had the following placed in the obituary columns:

ANNABEL MORGAN
AGED 56. DIED SUDDENLY ON HOLIDAY.
DESPERATELY MISSED BY ALL.
DONATIONS AND FLOWERS TO
KP FUNERAL DIRECTORS, SADDLEWORTH

I typed a letter from her next of kin, Mr Frederick Morgan, and addressed it to Personnel. He apologised for the formality of his correspondence, but felt a phone call at this time was too much. His wife, his partner, the love of his life, had perished on a rocky outcrop in Turin. The Italian medics had been wonderful, but sadly Annabel had been unable to survive the massive internal injuries suffered by the fall, attributed, in part, to poor footwear.

All work stopped for the morning when Pauline arrived in tears, clutching a copy of the paper. In silence we all read the little box in the obits.

'Oh, my God.' Siobhan covered her mouth. 'She's dead?'

'Shit,' I said and concentrated on keeping a straight face.

'Jesus. I mean, she was so, and we were...' Siobhan's voice trailed off and she looked at me. Guilt was written on her face and I prayed it wasn't on mine. I knew what

33

she was thinking. We hated the woman and now she was dead. Siobhan was probably giving herself a mental kicking. You know, that feeling when someone dies, that you wish you'd spoken to them more, known them more, or just been nicer. I saw it in Siobhan's eyes so I stopped looking at her.

But I didn't stop what I was doing.

I bought a shelf of condolence cards from Hallmark and filled each cloying fold of card with a different signature, a different sentiment, a different name of a retired and forgotten colleague. I spent a weekend on a bus pass traipsing to different parts of the city to send the cards back to the office from different postmarks. They came from Worsley, Failsworth, Sale, Stretford, Alderley Edge, Denton.

I spent a week's pay on a huge bouquet of lilies that made the office reek of death. The Principal Manager was unsure of what to do with it, how he could refuse it, so it was laid to rest on her desk, dripping first water, then thick clods of vermillion pollen that stained the carpet. A morbid tribute that I could easily imagine Annabel sending to a dead colleague's desk. A grief-ghoulling gesture to be seen, with the price tag probably still left on it. That week I ate toast and 15p lemonade for tea, but I didn't care because it was all going so beautifully.

The output at work slowed to trickle over the next few days as people stopped what they were doing, put their chin in their hand and sighed. Someone would notice them, ask if they were okay, and they'd tear up and women would crowd around with tea and tissues to talk about Annabel, but spoke more of the other losses they had suffered. Annabel was a catalyst, but she wasn't the focus. It was the acceptable face of skiving.

After several long days of lost hours, the Principal Manager saw fit to formally speak to us. He appeared from his office and gave a brief speech about how Annabel would be missed and how terribly sad it was and that the next few weeks would be hard on everyone, but that Annabel would have wanted us to carry on. She had always been efficient and dedicated, he said, and I had to bite the inside of my cheeks to keep myself from laughing. He asked for a moment of silence, which was interrupted from start to finish by a ringing phone that no one dared answer. Then the Principal Manager went back into his office and shut the door.

'I still can't believe it.' Siobhan shook her head and looked at me bewildered. 'I keep expecting her to walk in anytime now, but she won't.'

'She wouldn't have done anyway,' Kerry said. 'Her leave wouldn't have ended until Monday.'

'Shut up!' Pauline snapped. 'Stop trying to be so fucking clever!'

We looked at her in group shock. Despite the backbiting and casual plain speaking in the office, you just didn't swear at someone like that. It wasn't the way things worked.

'Sorry,' Pauline mumbled. Then her eyes misted up and she got up from her desk and walked out of the office.

'Pauline's worked with Annabel for over ten years,' Siobhan said. 'This has hit her really hard.'

Michael popped his head up from the desk. Aspie Michael we called him. He rarely spoke and never joined in group conversations or ate in the office. In a room full of women, he'd adapted to being an office eunuch, seemingly oblivious to talk of clothes sales, smear tests and menopause. So it was a surprise when he opened his mouth and it wasn't about work.

'The thing about death is, you know, you have to accept it. It happens to all of us, you know?' Michael said. 'The worst thing you can do is go one pretending everything's the same. It's not, but you have to carry on.'

Then he blushed, and having used up his quota of daily words he bobbed his head back down, curling it over his screen.

There were a few scattered murmurs. Then people returned to their work, taking on board Michael's opinion as gospel. I looked around, fearing my crimson cheeks would give me away. I was going to catch hell for this. I smiled.

The bouquet shrivelled up. Petals tumbled off in crisp brown curls. The stems withered to sticks and the pollen dried to stains that the cleaners couldn't get out of the carpet. Eventually, someone threw it in the bin and its smell was contained by the closed door of Annabel's office. The condolence cards bent from standing in the glare of the sun and fell in a soft domino line on the desk. The cleaners left them, unsure of what to do with them. We left them alone, not wanting to be seen as the person who threw them away. Flowers were okay, but not cards.

The Monday arrived. My skin prickled when Annabel walked into the office. I knew my cheeks radiated guilt. I could expect at least an utter management bollocking for this. I'd be lucky not to lose my job over it. I focused on my keyboard. But a delinquent part of me waited for the shocked expressions on my colleagues' face. I'd spent fourteen days waiting for this moment. People would be scared shitless. Annabel would be first baffled, then hurt. She'd realise things managed fine without her. That we didn't need her. That we didn't want her. She'd fall from grace, she'd be humiliated. People would laugh. They would get over it. They'd say she'd deserved it. They'd never know it was me. I would make everyone feel better. Except Annabel and I didn't care about her.

'Good morning,' she said and breezed through the office. I counted to ten in my head and then looked up.

People continued to photocopy. The phone calls went on, undisturbed. Someone cursed Outlook and a rapid tapping of keys could be heard as someone wrestled with Task Manager. The plastic lid of the Celebrations popped open as someone helped themselves to a breakfast of mini Galaxy Caramels and Mars Bars.

I felt her standing near me, hand on the handle to her office, doing her usual lioness of the pack routine, surveying the Savannah, eyeing up the crippled antelope.

'How've things been?' she asked.

No one responded.

'Has anyone else's Internet gone down?' Michael asked, popping his head up from his desk. A few people shook their heads and Michael popped his head back down.

Annabel narrowed her eyes in annoyance. She rummaged in her bag. She pulled out a box of Duty Free Toffifees that we all craved. She placed them on an empty desk that had a few bags of crisps and packets of wine gums on it. Kerry sidled up to the desk of treats. She opened the Celebrations.

'Are there any Maltesers left?' Siobhan called.

'Yep.' Kerry picked one up and threw it to Siobhan. She unwrapped it in one fluid motion and popped it in her mouth.

'Thanks,' she called.

Annabel returned to her doorway for a moment. Then

she went into her office and slammed the door.

A few long moments passed. The door opened. I turned around slowly. She glared at the office, a sample of the sympathy cards wedged between her fingers.

'Would anyone care to explain these?' she barked.

A phone on our section rang. Siobhan picked it up without moving her eyes from the screen.

'Hello, Admissions, can I help you?' she intoned. 'Annabel Morgan?' Siobhan cleared her throat and lowered her voice. 'I'm ever so sorry, but she's passed away. Yes. Yes, it was very sudden. Thank you, I'll pass that on. If you'd like to put any future correspondence for the attention of the Principal Manager and we'll see it gets sorted. Thank you. Not at all.'

Siobhan hung up and returned to her spreadsheet. A couple of people looked quickly over at her, then back at their work. This was old news after all. Pauline looked stricken, but then her computer pinged and she opened an e-mail that had just arrived.

I pushed a pen off my desk with my elbow. I bent down to pick it up and looked over at Annabel.

Her face was plum; her mushroom-coloured lips a pale slice in her face. I could just make out a vein pulsing at her temple. I picked up my pen and sat back down. I could feel her fury rising up the back of my neck.

'Is this some kind of joke?' Her voice was low and poisonous. The tone that turned us all to children. I held my breath. No one said anything.

She stomped over to Siobhan's desk. She folded her arms. She waited. Siobhan carried on working. She tapped a few keys. She opened a new window on the computer. Absently, she picked up the Maltesers wrapper, crumpled it between two fingers and dropped it in the bin. She belched quietly under her breath. She frowned at the screen and tapped the mouse a couple of times. Each muted click made the hairs on my arms stand up further.

'Siobhan, could I have a word?' Annabel asked, pushing her face into Siobhan's eye line. Her voice rose up at the end, quavering slightly. Siobhan blinked, but just removed a stray eyelash and blew it away.

'Siobhan!' Annabel barked. Her face was losing control. The fold of skin between her eyebrows twitched. The jowls slung low from her cheekbones quivered.

Siobhan looked over to the clock.

'God, today's going slow,' she said, to no one in partic-ular.

Kerry and Pauline murmured in agreement. The twitch between Annabel's eyes started to pulsate, seemingly beating in time with her enraged heartbeat. Then in a strong breach of office etiquette, she pushed Siobhan's shoulder. But she didn't just push it. She pushed it, held it back and left her hand there, trying to force Siobhan to turn her body toward her.

Siobhan flinched. Annabel jumped back and removed her hand. Siobhan rubbed her arms and shivered. I could see the goosebumps flare along her skin from where I was sitting. She caught my eye.

'You okay?' I asked, forcing innocence into those two words.

She nodded and looked quickly around the office. Then she bent her head towards me.

'It's like I can still feel her,' she said, quietly.

'Her?'

She blushed. 'Annabel.'

'Oh.' I decided more was less. The more I said, the

more I incriminated myself. I rubbed my arms discreetly, the hairs on my arms now needle-sharp.

'I know, it's stupid,' Siobhan said. 'I mean, I don't believe in ghosts and all that bollocks, but it's just so odd. You know that feeling you get, like someone's walking across your grave?'

I nodded. 'I suppose it's going to be weird.'

'Mmm.' Siobhan shivered again. 'I guess it's not really sunk in yet. I suppose maybe because she was due back today. But actually she's never coming in again. That she's gone. That she's dead. It just feels, I don't know, weird.' She lifted her hands helplessly then dropped them back to the desk.

'Right.' I looked towards Annabel. Her face was a mask. Frozen in fear. Incomprehension. Her jaw hung slightly open, a quiver just underneath her left eye. Like she'd had a complete mental snap. I waited for her to turn her head, see me watching her and know. Realise the practical joke. She opened her mouth. I caught my breath.

'Why…' she started to say, but nothing followed. Annabel stared back at her office. I saw her take in the condolence cards. The rotting bouquet pressed into the bin. The utter ignorance of her presence.

With a shriek, Annabel ran from the room.

After a moment, I got up and followed her.

I pushed open the door to the Ladies' Toilets. A low groaning interspersed with sobbing rose from the floor, under the sinks. I took a step closer. Annabel was curled up on the moist, bacteria-ingrained floors, her hands over her head. I stood over her for a minute, frozen in indecision. Then I crouched down.

'Annabel, are you… okay?'

She whipped her head up and looked directly at me.

Then she pointed a shaking finger at me.

'You!'

Guilt grabbed me around the shoulders and shook me. Oh fuck, she found out. I decided to front it out as best I could.

'Yes, Annabel, it's me. Do you need a first aider? Can I call someone?'

Her eyes were huge, the pupils dilated right to the edges of the irises. 'You can see me!'

'Um, yes, I can. Is everything okay?'

She dropped her hand abruptly and stared at me, her chin quivering.

'I'm dead, you know,' she said, softly.

I blinked. 'I'm sorry?'

'I died. That's what everyone's saying.'

I swallowed a thick knot of bile down. 'They are?'

'Don't try and pretend!' she hissed.

'Then how come I'm talking to you, Annabel?' I asked. 'You sound crazy.'

Her face fell into a dull mask. 'It isn't crazy. I'm dead,' she said, flatly.

She pulled at her hair and a thick swatch of black, grey at the roots, came away in her hand. She looked at it blankly. I looked first at the hair, then back at her head. Her scalp was starting to bleed.

'Jesus, Annabel! Look what you're doing!'

She looked up at me then dropped the hair to the floor. 'It's not real anymore,' she said.

I returned to the office, feeling cold in my fingertips and toes. The same feeling I got as a kid before I was about to get caught out for something. I hovered at my desk, straightening the pens and highlighters, trying to

41

get my breathing to relax. But they were talking about Annabel. She was today's hot topic, outstripping X Factor and Celebrity Strictly Come Dancing.

'Well, I never liked her,' Kerry said, through a mouthful of corned beef sandwich.

Siobhan looked at Kerry, shocked. 'You can't say things like that.' She looked around the office quickly and checked that Pauline was busy photocopying and wouldn't hear over the noise of the machine. 'Have a bit of compassion.'

'I'm not saying I'm glad she's dead, but I never liked her.' Kerry chewed thoughtfully and swallowed. 'I've been thinking about it a lot. I think we should be consistent in our views. It's such a cop out to say how great someone was just because they died. Don't get me wrong, I'm sorry she died the way she did. I mean, it's a terrible way to go, but when your time's up, that's just it. You live a mean life, you can't blame people for thinking you were mean.'

I couldn't stand it any longer. 'She's not dead!' I blurted out.

The office stopped. A sea of faces looked at me, each mouth open in a shocked o.

'What?' Siobhan looked at me askance.

'Annabel. She's not dead.'

'Tara, what are you talking about?'

'She isn't dead,' I said, my hands trembling. 'I just saw her.'

'Where?'

'In the Ladies.'

'Must have been someone else,' Kerry said. 'Joan in Accounts has the same haircut.'

'No, you don't get it. I spoke to her.'

'You spoke to her?' Siobhan asked carefully.

'Yes! She isn't dead. It was all a... mistake.' I almost said, 'joke'.

'Oh my God.' Kerry covered her mouth. 'So, it was some other poor woman in Turin?' But she didn't sound upset. More ghoulish. Revelling in the horror. Or worried that Annabel really would be coming back.

I nodded vigorously. 'Has to be. Mistaken identity.'

A buzz of chatter ripped open the office and I stood in the middle of it. I had done it. If I could convince them she was alive, then it would convince Annabel. She would exist again.

'No, wait. Stop!' Pauline's voice brought us up short. Her cheeks were red, her glasses beginning to fog up. 'I'm sorry, but Tara's wrong. Remember, Fred wrote to Personnel. It was Annabel.'

I opened my mouth and then shut it. How did I explain that to them?

'Oh, yeah,' I said, weakly. 'I forgot about that.'

People's eyes flicked away from mine. They studied their hands, their paperwork, their paperclips. Siobhan stood up and rested a hand lightly on my shoulder.

'Tara, come outside for a minute.'

'Why?'

'Just to have a word.'

She led me out of the office out into the corridor. Just before the door closed, the office exploded into whispers.

Siobhan folded her arms and cocked her head at me. 'Listen, Tara,' she said. 'This is hard for all of us. It's very odd. And you... well, maybe you should take some time off.'

'I don't need time off. I need you to understand that Annabel isn't—'

'Dead. Yes, I heard you the first time. I'm sorry you're having a hard time getting your head around it and I don't know why that is, but you've got to accept it and move on. You're unsettling people, just when they're starting to get over it.'

'I'm sorry,' I said, in a small voice.

'You know you can talk to me if you need to, don't you?' Siobhan said.

I stared over her shoulder and I saw Annabel. She stood some way down the corridor watching us, her hair wild, damp stains on her blouse from the floor of the toilets.

'Yeah.'

'Okay, then.' Siobhan rubbed my shoulder. 'Why don't you get yourself a cup of tea and come back in when you're ready.'

'Okay.'

Siobhan went back into the office, leaving me staring at Annabel who stared at me. I shivered. Someone wasn't walking over my grave. I was walking over someone else's.

During the afternoon, the Toffifees remained unopened. The Celebrations tin became rapidly depleted. I felt deeply unsettled. Probably because Annabel had followed me around the office and was now sat next to me on a spare chair, staring at me like I'd just shot her puppy. I kept my head turned away from her. It was freaking me out.

A couple of the porters arrived with sturdy brown boxes and began packing up Annabel's personal effects.

'Does anybody want the Van Gough prints or can we just toss them?' Barry called from Annabel's office.

'Toss them,' Kerry said, not moving her eyes from the

screen. Barry shrugged and dropped them in the bin.

Annabel moaned and put her head in her hands.

When the porters had filled the boxes and carried them through the office, there was a gentle hush, like watching a funeral procession. Soon the office would have to be reclaimed. No doubt there would be a morbid battle amongst managers who were sharing offices and now could have their own space.

Pauline started crying. She was typing out an e-mail, but tears kept leaking out from behind her glasses and bouncing off her chin. She wiped them away and blew her nose into a tissue.

'Pauline, really, why don't you go home?' Siobhan said. 'You're not doing yourself any favours. Trying to be at work when you're thinking about Annabel, it's not easy.'

Pauline sniffed and took off her glasses. She rubbed her eyes. 'It's not that. It's Fred. Poor man. He must be going through hell. He doesn't deserve this. He's such a wonderful man.' Then her face coloured and she pressed her glasses back on her face.

Siobhan looked at me. Then she cocked her head at Pauline. 'Are you saying... you're not, are you? You and Fred?'

Pauline looked at her miserably. Then she started crying again.

'For God's sake, she's barely cold in her grave!' Kerry snapped.

'No, you don't understand.' Pauline blew into her tissue, then rolled it up in her fist. 'We've been seeing each other for over a year.'

Annabel's mouth dropped open. I had to avoid looking directly at her. I picked at a hangnail on my thumb instead.

'I said to Fred,' Pauline continued, 'I said, "We should

just tell Annabel, come clean." I said that was the least she deserved. But he said, "No". He promised he'd leave her. When the time was right, you know? But he hasn't called me. I've left a bunch of messages, but he won't talk to me.'

Kerry patted her shoulder. Most women know it's bad news to fall in love with a married man, but still sometimes it happens.

Annabel's eyes misted over. But she was my friend, she mouthed, unable to get the words over her tongue.

'Oh, Pauline,' Siobhan said. 'I had no idea.'

'I just, I miss Fred and I feel so guilty now Annabel's dead and it feels just, just wrong.'

'Siobhan's right, though, Pauline,' I said. 'You should take some time off.'

Siobhan looked immediately grateful. Beside me, I heard Annabel sobbing.

'Maybe,' Pauline said. She sniffed. 'Yes, I will. If that's okay, Siobhan?'

'Of course. Take the time you need.'

Pauline blew her nose and switched off her computer. She gathered her things and left the office under sympathetic glances.

'Fuck,' Kerry said.

'That's putting it lightly,' Siobhan said. 'She must hate herself right now.'

I could hear Annabel muttering to herself. I could just make out one word, over and over again: 'Why? Why? Why? Why? Why?'

It was full dark by the time I finished work. I was the last to leave the office, everyone else crying off early on grounds of grief. I switched off the printers and photo-copier and signed out the keys at the front desk.

Annabel was sat on a bench outside the main entrance, under the chestnut tree. It was raining. It rains a lot in Manchester; I blame Morrissey.

In the low lighting spilling from reception down the path, I saw her hair was patchy, the scalp white and scabbed in the torn places. Her make-up had run and found its way into the wrinkles on her face. Her blouse and skirt were grubby. She looked like a bag lady. Actually, what struck me was, she looked human. Approachable. More real to me than she'd ever been.

I sat down next to her. She turned her head slightly toward me. I sat there for a moment, staring up into the oily blackness, the pearly clouds drifting by.

'How are you?' I asked finally.

'Not great. I'm dead.'

I sighed. 'Yes, I know.'

'Why can you see me?' she asked. 'You didn't even like me.'

'That's not...' I stopped myself. 'Okay, maybe I didn't. But we're talking now.'

'For what's it worth.'

'I'm sorry,' I said, after a moment.

'What for?'

'I don't know. The way things have turned out, I guess.'

'It's just been such a shock.'

'It has been for all of us.'

'I suppose you think the world would stand still if you died. But not even the office did. And Fred...' she trailed off. She stared at her hands. I noticed her nails were chewed down to the nail beds, swollen and red.

'The office did stay still,' I said. 'People were really upset for ages. For days people barely got anything done.'

'Really?' She looked slightly hopeful, then the expression flickered and died. 'No, they weren't really. Everything's carrying on without me. I shouldn't be here.'

I couldn't say anything to that. I didn't have any answers for her.

'I have to get going,' she said, but didn't get up. She balled her hands into fists in her lap and lowered her head.

'Where will you go?'

She shrugged and bit her lip.

'I don't know. Heaven?'

I fought the sudden, hysterical laughter that surged up my throat. This was unreal. It was like I'd taken hold of the darker side of humanity with both hands around its throat.

'Do you believe in Heaven?' she asked.

'No,' I said, honestly. 'I don't believe in an afterlife. When we're done, we're done.'

'So why am I still here?'

I shrugged. 'I don't know. Maybe you haven't accepted it yet.'

'Maybe.'

I stood up and buttoned up my coat. It was getting cold.

'Bye, Annabel.'

She didn't reply. She stared at the ground between her feet. I walked away towards the main road. When I turned back, she was still sat there, her outline indistinct in the tree's shadow. As I watched, the lights in the main building began to switch off, one floor at a time, until they were all gone and the building was in darkness and I couldn't see Annabel anymore.

The next day, Annabel didn't come into work. People stopped talking about her. I didn't see her again. And it was like something vanished with her. Not like having the heart ripped out of us, but like we'd recovered from cancer after beating huge odds and weren't quite sure what to do next. How to live life after such a poisonous growth had been removed.

My commute on the 142 became grey. I noticed less and less people, less and less of the outside world of Manchester, whose heartbeat had seemed to cease.

We all need a nemesis. When we have an enemy, something to fight against, somehow it justifies our lives. We are doing something worthy. We are the underpaid, overworked, unappreciated underdog. And we like that just fine because then we'll always have an excuse about why things didn't work out the way we wanted. I could have done it if I'd tried. If only I hadn't had a bitch of a manager I'd be climbing my way up the greasy pole at this company. Without Annabel, we were aimless. We had nothing to hate, so we had nothing to focus on. Days blurred into one another, a gentle zephyr of monotony. Our drinking stabilised. Jabez Clegg closed down. No Escape Committees. No back-stabbing. We were content. And I hated it.

I killed her. Annabel is dead. I got what I wanted.

And yet something is missing.

Dare I say it, but I think I miss Annabel.

BRIDGEWATER

Bryn Fazakerley

Three years they had been apart. Any marriage would feel the weight of those years. He was at least as jittery now as he'd been on their first date. That too had been at the Bridgewater Hall, seeing the Hallé back when they were students. He'd been so nervous he'd barely heard a note.

The summer city hadn't changed much in three years. Few people were about under Manchester's midday sun and the streets were vast plains of mirror-baked tarmac over which the dry air warped. Unburdened by traffic, little disturbed the stillness of those streets – only hulking Metrolinks that rolled along, near empty, propelled toward what had once been G-Mex by their clean-burning coal engines. Between the rolling thunders of passing trams he fancied he heard the scrabble of bird claws in dry dust, faint and distant.

He reached the Ishinka Touchstone. That streaked marble sculpture had stood sentinel outside the Bridgewater Hall his entire life and he pressed his hand against it before turning to head down the steps. As a boy he'd called it 'The Pebble' and remembered the huge stone, rain-slick and shining under streetlamps. That had been a time when people prayed for the arrival of Manchester's brief snap summers. It seemed a very long time ago.

The low-slung canal dazzled at the bottom of the

steps, its dark waters thick and soupy, reflective as oil. He squinted until he reached one of the café's shining metal chairs, draping his greatcoat over it to soak up the sun. That was a relief. He'd sweated under the charge-cloth's weight; that the fabric powered his cell proved little consolation. The material trapped vapours as efficiently as the multihued dew-catchers stretched thin across nearby roofs. Although, unlike those rubber tarpaulins, blue and brown and red, deformed and dipping where weighed down by stones, no buckets waited to collect his perspiration.

Slowly he settled into another of the table's metal seats, this one half-in and half-out of shade unlike the chair occupied by his coat. He winced and shifted his weight. Five patrons occupied chairs outside the café: two couples and another alone like himself. On the wall a simple LCD showed BBC News, an ostentatious cable tethering the screen to a nearby solar dish. Green credentials were worn on the sleeve these days but – despite all the reasons they should – he still wasn't sure people cared much more than they ever had. Maybe if lip service was paid long enough the idea would permeate, the people absorbing it by osmosis.

Then again, one could care too much. As the waiter approached he looked away from the screen, the anchor's voice announcing: 'Yet another case of brutal eco-terrorism.'

'What can I get you?' asked the waiter.

'Just water please.'

When the water arrived the waiter settled a glass beside the carafe and returned inside the café.

As he poured water into the glass he savoured the clean, freshwater scent that jumped into the air. They said water was odourless, but that wasn't true. You could taste it on the air. A taste of absence. A cool scent free of dust, free of salt, free of the dryness that seemed everywhere. One deep draught seemed to swell the cracks in his lips, revive the coarse tissue of his tongue. Unable to resist that first deep gulp, he resolved to sip the rest.

He pulled his screens from his breast pocket and put them on. In the sun's glare a ghost of his own eye overlaid the glasses' display. He thumbed a rubber bullet earpiece into his right ear and tugged thin force-feedback gloves onto his hands. Doing his best to ignore the television, his fingers tap-danced the air, dialling. The earpiece buzzed steadily. A beep cut short the seventh buzz. Voicemail.

'Hi Olivia, it's Nathan. I just arrived. Sorry I didn't get here straight away, had something I needed to take care of. Some work. It's done with now. I'm waiting at the café so make your way. The show isn't for another hour. Well, I'll see you here anyway. Love you.'

Nathan rubbed his cheek, the glove rough against smooth skin. He'd thought it would feel cold without the beard but, a cool sea breeze missing, it felt much the same. Warmer even. Three days onshore, the longest land bound he'd been in three years. Three long years on tugboats, seeding the seas with ferro-filings, hoping to make the oceans bloom.

Before that, the Sahara solar farms. And before that, geothermal plants across Yellowstone. Seven years in total, nothing more than a few weeks here and there with Olivia. And now he was back for good, a thought that should have made him ecstatic. Yet the question niggled at him – as it always did – had it been enough?

The lone man at the table across from his was staring past him. Nathan gritted his teeth, turned in his seat, and followed the man's gaze up and up to take in the glittering solar cell façade of Beetham Tower. An impressive sight. A grand gesture. But how much energy did it really produce? Just enough, Nathan suspected, to make everyone feel better when they looked up. Not enough to make a difference. Same old problem, same old Malthusian dilemma: too many people, not enough resources.

Same old, same old.

Olivia always said he did too much. He'd always felt the opposite. Morris had agreed with him, for whatever that was worth. Strange to think of Morris as he was then, as they'd all been then.

University thrust them together. Time and again they'd been side by side at rallies and events, in charity groups and committees, all three of them dedicated to the fight. Not that they'd been unique: the climate change scene had become very active back then; once Manchester stopped raining it became clear something had gone very, very wrong. Cyclonic, circling the same cause, their lives tangled together until, after graduation, they found themselves working together. They'd helped build carbon coffin catacombs under the warehouse district, now the repository of Greater Manchester's dead. The idea had been to take the deceased out of the carbon cycle, something he'd later realised could, with the right materials, be done anywhere.

Another grand gesture.

Morris had been the first to realise the hollowness of such gestures. He'd gone off to 'make a real difference'. Unsettling television images stared into Nathan and he amended: 'the wrong kind of difference'.

When Olivia started wanting to settle down and start a family, Nathan hadn't been ready. There'd been so much more he needed to do. And she'd supported him in that. While he went off on one scheme or another she'd stayed here working on the city council's sustainability schemes, waiting on his promise to come back and start a family.

Nathan sat upright and hissed through his teeth, feeling guilty.

She'd wanted a boy and a girl. Then five years ago the global one child policy ended that dream. With 9.5 billion people subsisting on an increasingly arid world it was too little too late. He'd cost so much of her time and hopes. The right thing would have been to let her go. But he couldn't – he wouldn't. He'd given up years of his life to do what he felt was right and he deserved his cut of happiness.

'Aren't you going to say hello?' Olivia asked.

She was standing beside him. How long had he been staring into space?

She laughed: 'You were a million miles away.'

'Sorry.' Nathan stood. Slowly. For months he'd imagined this moment, pictured himself leaning in to kiss her long and slow. Instead he wrapped her up in his arms and held her, tight and close.

'Are you okay?' she asked, her voice squashed against his chest. He nodded, feeling her dark hair bunch and scratch against his jaw. He'd forgotten how much he'd missed the smell of her: the sweet lilac and honey perfume, the gentle bite of sweat beneath.

Finally he let go. They kissed, soft, slow, gentle. It went on for some time. He could feel the baking sun on his skin, the warmth of her in his arms. He wanted this to be a perfect moment and found himself thankful for the carafe. Without it his parched lips, those osmotic vampires, would have drained Olivia of all moisture.

They sat. Olivia's draped her charge-cloth shawl on the chair beside his greatcoat. The shawl was thinner, better adapted to this climate than the coat he'd worn at sea.

'Are you alright?' she asked.

'Yeah,' he said, waving away concern. 'Hurt myself when we got into port. Funny, I spend all that time at sea without a scratch, then scupper myself the day we hit land. I'm probably going to be clumsy while I get back my land legs.'

'So, do you think it's worked?'

'The iron fertilisation? It should, in theory. We'll just have to wait and see. If the phytoplankton bloom in a big way, well, then we'll know.'

'Carbon capture, oxygen production, marine food chain... this is the big one, Nathan! Are you happy?'

'I should be, shouldn't I?'

'Yes, you should.'

'I feel like I should be doing more. That I haven't gone far enough.'

'Don't talk that way. You sound like him.' She flicked a glance at the television. 'What is it this time?'

'Oil workers lynched in Texas.'

'You think it's Morris?'

He shrugged. 'I'm not like him.'

She laced her fingers with his. 'No,' she said, 'you're not.'

For that moment, looking into her eyes, he considered telling her the truth. She deserved to know. Then the moment passed and that look in her eyes just made him more afraid to lose her.

Fear and the guilt weighed his jaw down. 'I'm sorry,' found its way through his teeth.

'What for?'

'You've waited a long time.'

'Oh, it's okay. It's been worth it. I love you.'

A smile forced itself onto his resisting lips. A genuine smile. It surprised him.

'I love you too.'

She looked over at the Bridgewater. Like with Beetham Tower, the glass across the building had been replaced piecemeal. Photovoltaic panes caught the clear blue of the sky; cerulean, beautiful, wholly self-sufficient. A blue impossible for the old grey weather. That might have counted for a silver lining had there been any clouds left in the sky to count. These days black clouds didn't seem too bad at all.

'So what are we seeing?'

'Beethoven. The Hallé.'

Olivia sighed, 'That'll be nice. But just once, I'd like to go see something electric, something non-acoustic.'

'It's got to the point where people do something just to show they're doing something. You can't put the genie back in the bottle. But then again, maybe it's best people do something, anything, even if it's not ever enough.'

Uncomfortable with that ad-lib epiphany Nathan pushed back his chair.

'Come on,' he said. 'It's almost time.'

He left cash on the table, grimacing at the flashing price on the table readout. Even with the dew-catchers fresh water seemed to cost more every day.

As they made their way over to the entrance, Nathan did his best to limit the limp and wondered if that was what he had done: something just to show he'd done something, even if only to himself; an attempt to put the genie back in the bottle.

He'd got the vasectomy the moment he'd got into

port, at some cheap, chop-shop surgery. Reproduction would be his one last sacrifice – one he'd volunteered Olivia for by proxy, without asking her, without telling her, because he was a coward.

He needed her.

She'd waited for him, for the family he had promised, for the thing that she needed. But there were far too many needs in the world already. The decision had to be made. It was right. It had to be.

By her side, he limped in toward the show.

THE LAST DRAG SHOW ON EARTH

Matthew Bright

They come out of the dark to Tallulah's. Alone and in groups, they make their way along the street, follow-the-yellow-brick-road amongst the cracked and rancid cobbles. The fairy lights are lit in the trees, just like they used to once-upon-a-time, in flagrant disregard for the regulations – not that they need tell-tale lights as targets to drop the bomb these days, or like any of them believe the regulations really have anything to do with safety. Regardless, it doesn't matter tonight: tomorrow this street will be gone, sealed away for decontamination by the machines from the South. This is the final hurrah, the swan song of the last speakeasy in Manchester.

And of course it's here, on Canal Street. Of course it is.

One by one – far more orderly than a Friday night crowd has any right to be – they present themselves to the bouncer. There's all manner slinking through the wreckage to join the queue tonight: a kaleidoscope of hairstyles; a barrage of outfits – they've outdone themselves for the occasion. There's representatives of all the genders, in every configuration of grouping imaginable – although it's so hard to tell these days, when you can never be sure what's really written on the skin underneath.

The bouncer shines her torch where they indicate – a neck, a hip, one smart aleck who bends over and points at his podgy left buttock. In the incandescent beam the glamour-tech ripples and shorts, and you can see clear through to the pink lipstick triangle on the skin – tonight's secret sign, passed in whispers around the city.

The tiny bar is nearly full to capacity. Tallulah has outdone herself. She's stripped out all the threadbare old tech and taken the bar right back to how it was at the turn of the century – this is beyond retro and into historical. Behind the bar, men in old-fashioned tank-tops are handing out drinks – no charge tonight – bottles of the kind too obscure for even the hipsters to get their hands on these days. WKD, Bacardi, VKs – even honest-to-god Coca Cola. How she's procured them is anyone's guess.

The crowd jostles and press against each other impatiently – looks are exchanged and assets are assessed, but there isn't the usual frisson of sex in the air that any other night at Tallulah's might have carried with it. Not that Tallulah's on a regular night was all about cruising for sex, because there were better places for that; anyhow, it was so difficult these days. Half the time if you pulled a cute guy into the cubicle for a quick fumble, they'd drop the glamour and you'd find yourself with an entirely unexpected set of genitalia on your hands.

You can screw with the glamours still on, of course. But that's only for the real perverts with no regard for health and safety.

In the tiny cupboard she calls a dressing room, Tallulah finishes strapping on the ninth layer of quick-change dresses, and sits to apply her makeup in the ancient mirror surrounded by a rectangle of doddery lightbulbs.

'The place is full, Hunty darling,' Shiva tells her from the door. Tallulah presses her face close to the mirror, inspecting her make-up, turning it side to side to check the contouring.

Spectacular. Even if she does say so herself.

Tallulah raises a lumpish hand, points a single lacquered nail into the air decisively. 'Play something to get them in the mood. Let's get a little nostalgia flowing, shall we?'

There's an encouraging cheer from outside – they can glimpse her through the open door. They're waiting.

'Play something old,' she says. She touches up her lipstick. 'They're not ready for me yet.'

They come out of the dark to Tallulah's. The dark waters of the canal awaken, and release those who sleep in its eddies to walk the street. Brackish water trails their footsteps. They say no words to each other – it is not clear if they even see each other. Perhaps they do not even see the street as it is now; perhaps instead they see it as they remember it.

Aloysius Coal was an officer in the war – but probably not the war you're thinking of. He wrote poetry while he served, page after page in a notebook he was given by his spinster aunt the night before he set sail. She had kissed him on the cheek, and reminded him that he should remember who he was at war, because men often forgot. And she, better than anyone knew who he was, after she'd caught him with – well, it didn't need to be said out loud, did it?

The book was lost – not dramatically in a bomb, or a fire, or anything like that. Just sometime in the last few days before victory was declared – gone. He didn't miss it too badly. Instead, he returned home to his wife who, with trembling lip, showed him the child in the crib that could plainly not be his. He kissed her on the forehead, and then did the same to his new son.

Some months later, on the way home to his wife and children he took a detour down a street he had heard of, but never visited. There weren't many bars then – although of course there was Tallulah's decades before it was called Tallulah's. Sipping whiskey in a quiet corner, he was approached by a man. Older, and gentle, they fell to talking. The man told him he was a poet. Aloysius did not tell him about the lost notebook.

Under the bridge by the canal, the poet turned Aloysius around and yanked his trousers down around his thighs. A little while later, when Aloysius turned to try and kiss him, he startled and lashed out. The cold stone received Aloysius' temple with a wet finality. The poet ran, and so did Aloysius' blood.

Tonight, the bouncer doesn't even give him a second glance.

The crowd are getting impatient, albeit in a jovial, benevolent way. They're stomping for Tallulah, despite the best efforts of Shiva MaTimbers doing her routine bit on stage with the torch.

Ezekiel Hodge is a boy tonight, and he's caught the eye of a silver-haired gentleman by the bar. Ezekiel likes the distinguished type, although he's not quite as sold on the man's husbands lolling on either side of him. They look rather gauche, and Ezekiel can't help feeling that they're unlikely to appreciate the true significance of tonight's entertainments. They wouldn't know drag if it popped an inflatable breast in front of them – no sense of heritage.

Still – if it's a package deal. He approaches the man and introduces himself. The man shakes his hand. 'My name is Magnus,' he says. A good name, thinks Ezekiel. Rich, like something from a storybook.

They talk a little, of this and that: of how the bar isn't what it was when Magnus was young, and how youths like Ezekiel couldn't begin to imagine it, no matter how many photographs or movies they've watched. Ezekiel smiles politely.

On-stage, Shiva gyrates the torch, issuing gargantuan chortles whenever the beam ripples the façade of her outfit enough for the punters to glimpse that, just maybe just maybe, underneath it all, she's a man. Ezekiel bites his lip. Glamour-tech, however expensive, isn't real drag.

Shiva's torch-beam rakes suggestively across the audience, and Ezekiel catches a glimpse of the flesh beneath Magnus' glamour. It is youthful, in first flush. For all his talk, he can be barely twenty. 'You young'uns wouldn't remember, would you?' Magnus says to Ezekiel, and the words ring as false as his glamour.

Ezekiel backs away, recedes to the shadows, sets his sights on someone else. There by the door: in a war uniform – though probably not the war you're thinking of – with impeccable attention to historical accuracy. A long way from the reaches of Shiva's torch, where the beam could not possibly catch him, and there is no chance of the man in the ancient uniform catching sight of the sag of ten decades that hangs beneath Ezekiel's own glamour.

Failing singularly to appease the thickening crowd, Shiva ducks into the cupboard-cum-dressing room. 'Tallulah, they're waiting.'

Tallulah shakes her head. 'Not yet,' she says. 'They're

not ready for me yet.'

Elizabeth Bennett, fully cognisant of the absurdity of her name, had never read a book to the end. Instead, she painted – from the day a paintbrush was first thrust into her chubby infant hand to the day she died, although it has not been a straight line in between.

When she was ten, she painted pictures of her back garden. Sometimes, the girl from next door leaned over the fence to watch her. Sometimes she did not. Nevertheless, the girl appeared in all of her pictures.

When she was fifteen, she plumped up her breasts, and conned her way into Coyotes. At nearly 1am, after sipping three sweet cocktails that were better named than they were flavoured, she was surprised to find herself sat opposite the girl from her back garden, grown up but unmistakable. She was deep in conversation with another girl – a woman, really – but she caught Elizabeth's eye and smiled. The woman asked Elizabeth's neighbour how old she was, and her neighbour answered 'eighteen', and gave Elizabeth a conspiratorial wink.

When she was twenty-five, the national newspapers declared Elizabeth the foremost painter in the UK. After she conducted a couple of interviews, they started to call her the foremost lesbian painter in the UK, and the extra word never disappeared.

When she was twenty-seven she put on her second exhibition. She hung paintings in pairs next to each other: one from the awkward childhood drawings she had rescued from her mother's attic, hung beside a new, repainted version. 'Improved', she thought. In a breathless gap at the opening, she looked at the collection and thought to herself, when I have a daughter I'll give her all my paintings and she can copy them, and we can hang this exhibition again, in reverse. It'll be a sensation.

And then there was the girl from her back garden, stood with her head cocked, looking at the twin visions of herself in watercolour. Elizabeth drew breathlessly near. 'Excuse me,' she said. 'I couldn't help notice you looking.'

The girl turns and smiles, and introduces herself – an Elizabeth too, though she goes by Lizzie. Elizabeth is smitten.

When they were thirty, giddy with the novelty of a change in the law, Elizabeth and Lizzie were married in celebration. Elizabeth's mother was not present, but Lizzie's was. A world-famous photographer took the pictures.

When she was forty-seven, Lizzie died, and at eighty-six, Elizabeth followed her. She was found after a month, in her studio above Canal Street, surrounded by hundreds of paintings, a platoon of portraits of Lizzie at aged fifty, sixty, seventy, a hundred, and at aged ten in a quiet back garden in Manchester.

The bouncer is stooping to inspect the pink triangle on the ankle of a stilettoed biker bear, and doesn't notice her slipping quietly into Tallulah's.

Emmeline Panic – for such is her chosen, if not God-given name – is a rock-chick of the most subtle variety. She eschews the obvious choices that glamour-tech place before those of the sartorially rebellious nature: no plastic androgyne, no physics-defying piercings, no choreographed tattoos. Instead, she cleaves tight to the old mother's saying: 'we are all born naked, and the rest is drag.' Every breath from our very first is a performance, and Emmeline Panic's more than most.

Straight out of university she had conned her way into

a contract with a major publisher, and since then her whole life has been a performance, each year sub-divided neatly into the chapter of the eventual book.

At first she'd started impersonating the obvious ones – she'd been Marilyn for a year, and Gaga. Easy, and ostentatious. When, in her tenth year, she'd essayed the Mona Lisa, she knew she'd found her groove: the elusive women of great art.

Tonight is a first outing, a test-run in the dead days between Christmas and New Year when the publisher's dictadrones are off duty. Time to smooth out the rough edges in the performance. And it was fitting anyhow, to appear here tonight on Canal Street, as her.

On stage, the drag queen is failing for the second time that evening to amuse the crowd. Poor woman, thinks Emmeline. An average performer, quite frankly. Despite the towering wig and wafer-thin heels, she just doesn't commit to the role.

Then she notices the woman watching her – an old woman, haggard in the way that old women aren't any more. Like she's from the history channel. She has white hair, shoulder-length. She's wearing a nightie, of all things. Still, Emmeline thinks, who am I to judge?

The woman approaches her, and Emmeline shifts uncomfortably. Looking closely, she wonders if maybe the woman isn't all-natural, without a trace of glamour-tech. There's a few like that going around at the minute – if they weren't careful it'd become a fully-fledged movement.

'Excuse me…' says the woman. Her voice is barely there, as if it has been swept away the second it leaves her mouth. 'I couldn't help notice you looking.'

Emmeline simpers sweetly. 'Hello, dear,' she says, unsure what else to say.

The old woman cups her cheek. Her touch is cold, which it shouldn't be, not at the amount Emmeline's glamour cost.

'Lizzie...'

Emmeline's face lights up. 'Yes!' she says. 'I'm so glad you recognised me! I've been so worried! I thought she might be a little too obscure, you know...'

She might be mistaken, but there are tears in the old woman's eyes.

In the dressing room, Tallulah silences Shiva before she can even speak. 'Nearly, darling, nearly.' She casts a scarlet smile back over her shoulder. 'Do your three-legged can-can routine – that always goes down a treat.'

The door closes, and Tallulah stands, smoothing her skirts in front of the mirror, adjusting her bosom. 'They're nearly ready for me,' she whispers to herself.

At 5.30am, Alex Dale threw himself from the bridge into the cold waters of the canal. Although the coroner later placed the time of death anywhere between 5am and 6am, the time could be stated exactly: zie jumped the moment that the notification symbol popped up on hir wrist, and she knew it had been published. No backing out now.

Then zie was gone.

On hir desk at home, a screen was left awake, and beside it the glamour-tech strap, with its shattered stinger. Four months saving – this stuff is new, and expensive if you want the ones that support the hacked outfits – and gone in one swing of an angry fist.

At 5.30am the screen pings.

It doesn't bear repeating the contents here. The majority of it was for hir father. Some of it was for the world at large, although, in the swell of history, it would turn out that the whole thing would be for the world, in a way.

There are phrases that jump out. There's the ones the campaigners use: Not a choice. Neither one nor the other. Not a phase. Then there's the ones that no-one seems to notice: Sorry. Love. Daddy.

That last one especially.

Daddy, they're not ready for me yet.

They call it Alex's Law, but it doesn't make any difference to the canal.

You're not ready for me yet.

So they come out of the dark to Tallulah's – not just these three, but all the other ghosts: the mollies in their frock coats, the happy drunks who slid into the water instead of another man's bed, the old and the young, the men blackened by lesions with the skin loose on their bones, the women who loved loudly, and the women who loved secretly. The bouncer doesn't see them – or perhaps just pretends not to.

And anyway, the show's about to start.

Shiva is panting. She's never had to work so hard for so little applause. It's Tallulah they want – and, it seems, it's Tallulah they're going to get.

She pats her hair. 'I'm ready,' she says. 'They're ready.'

Shiva crosses to her, embraces her like a mother. 'There's more ghosts than bloods out there,' she says. 'I've never seen it like this. Not that most will even notice...'

Tallulah breaks the hug. 'Once the morning comes, it'll make no difference,' she says. 'We're all ghosts now, really.'

Shiva licks a finger and dabs a spot of errant make-up on Tallulah's face. 'Knock 'em dead, bitch. The last true drag queen on earth.'

Tallulah fingers her corset. 'And don't I just feel it.'

There's an impatient cheer from outside. I Am What I Am has started, and most of them know that's Tallulah's song, the one she comes out to every night.

'I'll do the honours,' says Shiva. She turns to the door, primps herself.

'Is zie out there?' asks Tallulah quietly.

Shiva doesn't look back at her. 'I don't know,' she says. 'You'll have to go out there and find out.'

Then she flings it open and prances out. The crowd roars appreciatively. Her voice booms, barely muffled by the thin walls. 'Right then, you horrible lot, are you ready? I said are you ready? Yes? Then it's time to introduce her... the one, the only, the incontinent... Tallulah Trout!'

When it's all over, and they've all gone home – even Shiva, whose battery runs low in the last ten minutes, reverting her to a portly thirty-year-old in ill-fitting underwear – Tallulah returns to the dressing room and locks the door tightly behind her. She sits in front of the mirror, and begins to meticulously remove her make-up.

It doesn't take long, stripping back layer-by-layer, lipstick swiped away to reveal the thin, cracked lips beneath, the removal of contours transforming the rounded full cheeks into sharper, masculine forms. Then the eyebrows, and the eye-lashes and she's left with her ordinary face. A pedestrian, unremarkable face: a brother, or a father, perhaps, but one easily forgotten.

When the light-bulbs switch off – accompanied by the sound of all the electricity in the bar shutting down – she knows the machines are near.

The last dress of the quick change is dark blue with military insignia, like a naval captain. There's a bit that goes with it – sweeping up the most bearish man she can find in the audience to do a gender-swapped Officer and a Gentleman. A good captain always goes down with their ship.

And so they come out of the dark to Tallulah's – for these days, even the mornings are dark. The machines, and the men in the masks, with their seals and their fire. The flames reflect from the black waters of the canal where Aloysius, Elizabeth, Alex and all the others silently watch as Tallulah's vanishes in smoke. The men with the machines don't see them – or perhaps pretend not to.

When she closes her eyes, Tallulah can't feel the blistering heat anymore. Instead, she imagines she's sinking into black waters, swimming free towards the others up ahead of her, the last true drag queen on earth.

No. 5 PASSAGE

James J. Ridgway

'Any person born outside the United Kingdom shall be deemed a foreign national liable to immediate deportation by the appropriate authorities. Dependent citizens may remain in the UK at the discretion of their legal guardian.'

The Emergency Depopulation Act, 2065.

I woke to the whine of a drone passing overhead. The prop blast forced the tent walls down and in, turning it into a claustrophobic cave. As the walls snapped back into place, the announcement came. 'This is a population control by the UK border agency. Please have all passports ready for inspection.'

Beside me, Yoyo rolled over in his sleeping bag. 'Jesus, again? What time is it?'

'Early.' It was cosy inside my bag. The thought of standing on the cold riverbank waiting to be scanned was too much for my brain.

The Babylon repeated his announcement. This time I recognised Welky's voice. I wasn't the only one.

Yoyo cracked an eye and glared at me. 'Is that your mate?' His bloodshot stare said it was my fault he was awake.

When the announcement bounced off the riverbank a

third time, he rolled on his back and filled his lungs. 'Give it a rest, I'm trying to sleep here!'

Outside, some of our neighbours laughed. Others joined in, shouting rebellion or obedience depending how scared they were of getting deported. With a great shush of plastic and buzzing tent zips the riverside homeless presented themselves for inspection.

Still half asleep I opened the tent flap and stuck my arm outside. It was so cold I got instant goose bumps, but at least the rest of me was still warm in the bag.

A shadow darkened our tent entrance. Welky stamped his foot on the ground. 'Knock, knock. Mind if I come in?'

Before we could answer he'd unzipped the flap. Straight away all the warmth escaped out the hole. He squatted down and stuck his head inside. 'Morning boys. Cold enough for you?'

I shivered in the sudden chill. 'It is now you twat.'

'Why don't you piss off?' Yoyo suggested.

Grinning over us in his uniform, Welky grabbed Yoyo's arm and waved a scanner over the passport chip embedded under his skin. 'That's no way to treat a friend.'

Yoyo snatched his arm back. 'Friend? You threw my family out of the country and nationalised Munch's house off him. You're no friend of mine, officer.'

I willed him to bring it down a notch. Friend or not, these days the wrong word to the wrong Babylon could land you in a French refugee camp before you could say 'illegal deportation'.

Welky looked hurt. 'That wasn't me though was it Yoyo? In fact, I seem to remember I told Munch the raid was coming, so maybe you should get your facts straight before you start mouthing off, yeah?'

Yoyo pulled his sleeping bag over his head. 'Whatever.'

Unable to stop shivering, I dragged some cleanish jeans out of my rucksack. 'Ignore him, he lost his job last night.'

'Shut up, Munch.'

Welky made a show of looking round our water-stained tent. 'I can't believe you're still in this shed. River living's for suckers, boys. You're citizens, you should get land-based.' He did something to the police camera on his chest. 'It just so happens Uncle Welky might be able to help you out. You still working at Cleveleys Avenue allotments?'

'Yeah.' I remembered something. 'Shit.'

'What?'

I looked around for my specs. 'What time is it?'

'Five past eight.'

'I'm late for work.' I pulled on my coat. 'I've gotta bail.'

As I tried to push past him, Welky stopped me. 'Hey, I'm giving you a heads-up here. You want to get off the river? Cleveleys Avenue, ten pm.' He winked. Then he clicked his camera on and left.

Looking around for my specs I noticed how messy the tent was. 'Yo? Can you take my bag today, I haven't time to pack.' I felt guilty leaving him to tidy up on his own, but he had no choice. My job fed us both now. I pulled out my ration card and flicked it so it clicked. 'Here's my card. Come meet us about four. Soz for the mess, okay?'

'God, okay. Just shut the bloody flap.'

Tents filled the muddy path that separated the upper and lower riverbanks. It had rained overnight and the Mersey was high, just two feet off the path. Another downpour and we'd be searching for another place to camp tonight.

I could tell how late it was from the number of people

out and about. Upriver, they were already packing up their tents. Downriver, they mostly stood round cooking stoves waiting to be scanned by Welky and his Babylon mates.

I found my specs in my coat pocket, but they were flat. That's why the alarm hadn't gone off. I propped them on my head to charge and picked my way between the tents. The shortest route to Jan's allotment was up to the bridge and along the tram tracks to Chorlton Park Farm, but if people were packing up here, Southern Cemetery would be emptying too. Quicker to go through the woods. As I joined the crowd heading that way I hoped Jan would be cool about me being late. With Yoyo jobless we needed the food she paid me more than ever.

As soon as my specs reached one bar, I called her.

'This is the voicemail for Janice McDougal...'

'Shit.'

'...please leave a message.'

'Hi Jan, it's me. Look, sorry I'm late. Yoyo got laid off last night and they cancelled his work permit before he could get back to the checkpoint so I had to pick him up— Oh, I think that's you.' I blinked up the incoming call. 'Hi Jan.'

'Where the hell are you?'

'I'm on the way now. Yoyo got laid—'

'Do you know anything about this?'

'Err, what?'

'The police are here.'

'What, why? Are you okay?'

'I'm fine. Just hurry up and get here.' She rang off.

I pushed through the crowd. Something serious must've gone down for Jan to get so mad. It wasn't her style to get caught up in anything dodgy, so if the Babylon were there she'd been done to, not the other way round. I needed to hurry, but Beech Road was one solid pavement jam. The stink of unwashed bodies pressed in around me, overheard conversations shifting between food shortages and when the rainclouds would open.

I'd been right about Southern Cemetery. The queues for the water lorries filled both sides of Barlow Moor Road. I pushed through mums and street kids carrying bags of empty plastic bottles and presented my forearm to the alley's entry sensor. Behind the turnstile, two massive bouncers watched me over their morning coffee. The bigger one raised his chipped 'Democracy Now' mug in recognition.

The alley doesn't have a name. On the specs map it's just a public footpath that joins up all the avenues branching off Sandy Lane. But when you see it, well … With the bylaw against sleeping near a road and most public spaces reserved for growing food, the alleys and passageways around old terrace houses are one of the few places people can build a permanent home. And man what they've built! At ground level you're walking under metal pipes and wooden planks, but above that there's enough floodproof rooms for hundreds of people, all made from scaffolding and chipboard and those foil blankets the ration stations hand out.

I hurried past desperate-looking people haggling over cauliflowers and homemade pickles. At the end of each avenue a razor-wire fence kept out non-residents. If you want in you've got to bleep yourself through a turnstile, or bribe a bouncer to do it for you.

The allotment entrance is halfway up the alley. Through the turnstile I could see the Babylon's bicycle

parked outside Jan's polytunnel. Worried, I bleeped myself in and ran past the busy gardeners. Soon as I got inside I saw we'd been burgled. There was a slash in the
polytunnel wall big enough for a man and dirt all over the
floor. Worse, all the plants were missing. A summer's
worth of growth, all our trade produce, gone. The bastards had torn them out by the roots.

Jan was over by the workbench, rummaging through a
drawer. Nearby, the Babylon was talking to a little
handheld screen. Jan would've only come up to his chest
but you'd be wrong to mistake her for just another old
lady in her tatty gardener's fleece and bobble hat.

Seeing me, she came over.

'Bastards.'

'Innit. You okay?'

She huffed. 'I'm fine. At least they didn't get the roots.'
She nodded at the raised beds. The roller shutters I'd installed looked intact. 'Thank god you put those shutters
in.'

She was putting a brave face on it. In reality, barring
the root veg we'd lost our whole crop. We wanted to be
self-sufficient. Now we'd have to rely on government
handouts to get us through the winter.

The Babylon came over. 'Right Mrs McDougal, that's
about it for now.' He looked at me. 'Are you Mr Mujid?'

'Mujid's my first name.'

He pointed his handheld at me. 'Oh yes, sorry. You'll be
happy to hear checkpoint W-15 confirmed you were picking up Yoyo Mahmood when the burglary took place.' He
printed out a slip of paper from the handheld and gave it
to Jan. 'Here's your incident number. Your insurance company will want to see that. My contact details are also on
there if either of you see or hear anything else relating to

the case.' He slid the handheld into a pouch. 'I'll see myself out.'

'Thank you, officer.' Jan folded the paper and put it in her fleece pocket.

I pointed at the mess. 'Are we allowed to tidy up?'

'Why wouldn't we be?'

'Dunno... evidence?'

She laughed. 'Yeah right.'

'So that's it? A pensioner gets burgled and all they do is give you a case number? They took all our food!'

'What would you have them do, stop and search everyone in Chorlton? There's a hundred thousand people living on our doorstep. By now everything they took is probably in someone's belly.'

'But... our whole crop!'

'It's only theft, no one got hurt. Imagine how desperate they must have been to steal food in the first place.' She went back to searching through the drawer. 'Ah, here it is.' She held up a roll of tape. 'Help me fix this hole, will you?'

About midday it started raining, and I mean monsoon style. It got dark enough to see the fire flickering inside the stove and then the heavens opened. I thought of poor Yoyo waiting in some queue or other for food that'd probably run out before he got there. Then I remembered how high the river had been. No way would we be sleeping there again tonight.

We'd spent all morning cleaning up the mess, sweeping the dirt into pots and preparing the beds for replanting. It was heavy work, digging out ripe compost and wheelbarrowing it back, and around eleven I keeled over. One minute I was pushing the barrow, the next Jan was kneeling over me asking when I'd last eaten. When I told her she got really angry and made me sit down while she cooked me some porridge. I was finishing it off when someone knocked on the polytunnel door.

'Hellooo, Janice? Are you there?'

'Hi, Cheryl. Come in.'

A posh woman in a clean overcoat and flowery head-scarf came in. 'Ooh, it's nice and cosy in here.' She shook off her umbrella and noticed me. 'Oh, hello. I don't think we've met. Cheryl Martinez, chair of the resident's association.' She offered a bony hand covered in rings. It was like shaking a bird's wing.

'I'm Mujid. Hi.'

She wrinkled her nose; it was a while since I'd had a proper wash. 'Not interrupting am I?'

'Not at all,' Jan said. 'Fancy a cuppa?'

'No thanks, I just popped round to make sure you're alright. Francis told me what happened. Terrible business.' She took in the empty beds, the taped up wall. 'Did they take much?'

'Everything that wasn't nailed down.'

'Oh dear. Any idea who it might have been?'

'No. Whoever it was had no idea what they were doing. They tore everything out by the roots. All I've left is potatoes, carrots and onions.'

Cheryl followed Jan's finger to the raised beds. 'What are they?'

'My root beds. Mujid installed roller shutters over them so we can lock them up at night.'

'How clever.'

'He put in the stove too. It used to be electric, now it burns just about anything.'

'Really?'

'Yes, useful guy to have around this one.' Jan gave me a 'get involved' look. 'Tell Cheryl what you told me earlier.'

I'd only told Jan about Welky's warning because I wanted her to keep me on. With only a few months till winter the new harvest would be half what we'd expected, perhaps enough for Jan on her own but not for two. This wasn't contracted work, it relied on her goodwill and a heads-up about a raid was leverage Jan could use. But I didn't know this Cheryl.

Jan nodded encouragement. 'Go on.'

'A friend of mine told me there's going to be a raid on Cleveleys Avenue tonight.'

Cheryl looked surprised. 'Really? When?'

'Ten o'clock.'

'Do you believe your friend?'

'He's a Babylon, but I've known him since primary school. I don't think he'd steer me wrong.'

Cheryl raised her hands as though thanking the sky. 'Finally.'

'Finally?' I remembered Yoyo on the pavement outside our house, one Babylon kneeling on his back while the others marched Mum, Dad and Gran into the snatch wagon. I'd never seen anyone so angry. They'd taken Yoyo's folks away nine months earlier, that's why he came to live with us. If they hadn't Tasered him I think he could've killed someone that night.

'Yes,' Cheryl said, missing my tone completely. 'The scaffolding flats have become terribly overcrowded since the last raid. It'll be nice to spread out a bit.'

I stared. 'Do you know what they do with deportees? They give you a torch and a pack and make you walk through the tunnel to France. If you try to come back, they shoot you.'

Cheryl looked away. 'I don't believe those stories.'

'Mujid, I'm not sure this is the time—'

I talked over them both. 'My Gran was eighty two when they dragged her out of our house. It used to take her five minutes to get from her chair to the toilet. How well do you think she's doing in the refugee camps, with a billion people all desperate for food?' I pointed outside. 'Whoever's on the Babylon's list tonight, this raid is like a death sentence. And all you can think about is how much space you've got—'

'Mujid!' Jan threw her big ring of keys at me. I caught them easily. 'Go and get the seeds from my flat please. They're in the cupboard on the left hand wall.'

I felt betrayed. 'They won't let me in.' She knew my passport wouldn't open the passageway gate.

'I need to talk to Cheryl alone.'

'But it's pissing down.'

She gave me her no-nonsense look, so I pulled up my hood and headed out.

The rain was nuts. My jeans were soaked before I got halfway to the allotment turnstile. From there, the scaffolding flats rose up like a wall, three and four storeys high in places. Through the lit windows I could see the triple bunks and layered hammocks people squeeze into those tiny rooms. There's so much demand for shelter some people sleep in shifts.

I understood Cheryl's obsession with space. Everyone wanted to upgrade where they lived. Folk camping in tents wanted a scaffolding flat. The alley residents wanted into the safer gated passages that run along the backs of the terraces. Everyone preferred bricks and mortar to chipboard and scaffolding. That's what Welky meant when he'd said to "get land based". I got it, I'd just seen the flip side. To free up space someone had to get deported. That's why me and Yoyo still chose to camp.

Cleveley's Avenue was starting to flood. I turned right out of the allotment turnstile and splashed along the alley, grateful for the planking over my head. Jan's flat was on passage number five, which ran along the backs of Cleveley Avenue and the next street over.

The entrance was blocked by a tall, iron gate and a bouncer so big I wondered how much the job paid for him to afford so much food. Standing next to him, wrapped in a foil blanket and shivering hard, was Yoyo.

'Munch? Jesus, where've you been? I've been trying to ring you for the last hour!'

My specs must have gone flat again. 'Soz, it's been a crazy day.'

'Tell me about it.'

The bouncer eyed Jan's keyring. 'Hey, where did you get those?'

Yoyo waved him down. 'It's okay, he's my cousin. Munch, this is Bull. We used to do the door together at Prime.'

'Hi.' I noticed Yoyo only had one rucksack with him. 'Hey, where's the other bag?'

His face fell. 'Yeah, I was just telling Bull. About an hour into the queue for the ration station this protest march turned up. Well, it suddenly kicked off. Babylon drones turned up and started spraying that microwave shit.' He looked at Bull. 'What did you call it again?'

'Active Denial.'

'Yeah, that. Well you know what it's like. My skin felt like it was on fire, and with the screechers going off all I could do was cover my ears and run. That's when I dropped the bag. I went back after the crowd left, but...'

He looked at me. 'Your bag's gone, the tent too.'

I had all my clothes in that rucksack, my sleeping bag, my soap and toothbrush, all our emergency food. And the tent gone too.

'Fuck, Yoyo, where we gonna sleep?'

His blank look confirmed we were in trouble, but before he could say it an old geezer in a Barbour jacket and fishing waders turned up behind the gate.

'Barry, what's going on here?'

Bull straightened himself. 'Oh, hi Mister Perkins. Just some friends dropped by for a chat.'

'Hmm, well, you know the residents association rule about loitering, especially outside the gate.'

'Yes, sir.'

The old guy waited.

Bull sighed. 'Sorry guys, you'll have to do one.'

'But I have to pick up Jan's seeds.' I jingled the keys to show I had permission.

The old guy cleared his throat.

'Not gonna happen, kidda.' Bull held out his fist. 'Yoyo.'

Yoyo bumped the fist and shouldered our remaining bag. 'Yeah, laters.'

I took Yoyo back to the polytunnel. We had nowhere else to go.

Jan was alone inside. As soon as she saw Yoyo she put the kettle on. After he'd changed into dry clothes and his wet ones were steaming on the stove, he told his story.

While she listened Jan stood at the bench filling seed trays with compost. When Yoyo finished she said, 'You must be famished. Do you want some porridge?'

'Sure.'

She started measuring oats into a pan.

'You can't keep feeding us,' I said.

'I've nothing else to pay you with.' She pointed at the empty beds. 'So, what are you going to do?'

Yoyo shrugged. 'Dunno.'

She looked at me. 'What about your house?'

Yoyo gave a humourless laugh.

I said, 'It's not our house anymore, they nationalised it after they threw us out.' I'd been fourteen when they came, too young to own property. I was a ward of the State, and the State's always going to act in its own interests first.

'I thought you found a solicitor?'

'Nah. Anyone who didn't want cash up front expected me to sell it and give them half. Besides, there's like five families in there now – we've nowhere to go.'

Yoyo looked around the polytunnel. 'What about here?'

With last night's burglary, security around the allotment would be tight. We'd have to hide in the dark with no stove to give us away. I imagined trying to sleep on this cold floor with only a foil blanket for warmth.

Jan shook her head. 'I can't, I'd lose the allotment, maybe the flat too. Sorry boys, I'd let you sleep at mine but we're not allowed visitors. They're terrified of people claiming squatter's rights.'

We fell silent. The spoon knocked against the porridge pan. Rain hammered on the roof.

I caught Jan's eye. 'What happened about the raid?'

Yoyo was already shaking his head. 'No way, I won't take advantage of some poor bastard getting deported. I'd rather get arrested.' He looked across at me. 'It'll be cold again tonight. A dry cell might be our best option.'

Jan smiled. 'No, I have a better idea.'

At ten o'clock, Jan stood over me with her big 'Democracy Now' umbrella. The waterproofs she'd lent me were too big and not very warm, so she waited with me as I sat shivering on the doorstep of number eleven Cleveleys Avenue.

We'd been busy since Yoyo turned up. Taking the shutter off one of the raised beds and fitting it over the front door took the whole afternoon. The sun had set and the streetlights were bright before we got around to the padlock.

'They'll be on a clock,' Jan had explained when she told us the plan she'd cooked up with Cheryl. 'They only get thirty minutes to clear each house, so if you can hold them up for longer than that you'll press on their schedule. We know which house they'll go for.'

The Lings were long gone, probably already in the boot of someone's car heading for the Scottish border. My job was to stop the Babylons coming in the front so the new residents of number eleven could nationalise the house through the back.

Suddenly, the thump and scrape of furniture I'd heard all afternoon ceased. A tiny voice spoke in Jan's specs. She looked down at me. 'A police drone just flew round the back.'

That was the signal. Behind me, the house grew very quiet. Then someone shouted and it came alive again. Voices and music burst out like some kind of party.

Another drone hummed over the rooftops in front of us and a black snatch wagon sped down the avenue, blue lights flashing.

Jan touched my arm. 'Good luck.'

She walked away to join the small umbrella-wielding

crowd who'd gathered on the pavement to watch.

The snatch wagon doors burst open and eight riot police splashed out. They'd come dressed for war: Tasers, armour, helmets, battering rams; everything black. As they pushed the crowd back, one of them peeled off and approached me. She lifted up her visor and bent down to my eye level, a Chinese woman with a Scouse accent. Presumably the translator for the Lings.

'Hello there. Can you tell me your name?'

Water dripped off her helmet. She was beautiful. I looked into the lens of her police camera and said, 'This is a peaceful protest against England's immoral deportation laws. I have no other democratic way to register my objection to these laws.'

Her expression changed. She stepped back and scanned me.

'Okay, Malik Mahmood, British Citizen. How's your English? Is that all you can say?'

I saw the way she looked at me. 'I speak like a native.'

'Mister Mahmood, you are obstructing the legal enforcement of a warrant. If you don't move aside and allow us to enter I can detain you by force.' She unclipped her Taser.

The chains around my wrists were too tight. I had to pump my fists to keep them awake. 'I'll happily get out of your way if you cut me free. I want you to. My arms are killing me and my ass has gone to sleep, so please, cut me free.'

I looked over at Jan. She circled a thumb and finger to signal she had my request for aid on camera. When the translator looked round to see what I was looking at, Jan made a point of straightening her specs.

The translator tutted and pushed me forward to inspect the chains. The padlock was clamped between my forearms, its keyhole filled with builder's putty.

She triggered her radio. 'Dave, we've got a lock-on at the front. We may have to go in through the passageway. Over.'

Half the Babylons peeled off and disappeared down the alley.

'Is there anyone else inconveniently attached to this property?'

'Just tell it straight,' Jan had said.

'My cousin is blocking the gate to passage number five. They're nationalised there so you'll probably need a separate warrant to move him.'

Her radio bleeped. 'Yep. Yeah, this guy just told me. What?' She looked me in the eye. 'About eighteen minutes. Okay, wait one.' She turned the scanner on the house and studied the readout. 'No signal from the Lings. I'm seeing twenty passports, all legals. A.L.U says they're all locals, vicinity residents, four-weeks-plus. Okay. Understood. Out.'

The Babylons walked back from the alley and started climbing back into the snatch wagon.

The translator looked down at me. 'Right, Mister Mahmood, first we're going to unlock you, then you and your cousin are coming with us.'

They held us in Didsbury Police station overnight. I didn't see Yoyo after they took us out of the wagon.

In the morning they charged me with obstruction and let me go with a fine of one week's rations. If Jan didn't keep her end of the bargain I'd be getting hungry pretty soon.

It took an hour to walk back through the crowds to the alley. Inside, Jan was waiting at the passageway gate with Bull, the bouncer.

'Here he is.'

'Have you seen Yoyo?' I asked.

She nodded. 'He got back about an hour ago. Hey, good work last night. Number eleven got a letter through this morning. They've been added to the national register.'

Bull grabbed my arm and bleeped me into his scanner. 'Congratulations kidda.'

Jan smiled. 'Let's get you settled in.'

She led me down the narrow passageway. The high garden walls and wood planks overhead made it feel like a tunnel. Jan stopped by a scaffolding ladder bolted to the wall. Light shone down from an open hatch.

'Here you go.' She pointed down the alley. 'Toilets are on your right, showers on the left. I think you've earned a day off.'

I didn't know what to say. Without thinking I hugged her. 'Thanks.'

'Ha, it's alright son.'

Up the ladder, the flat smelled of incense and strangers. It was maybe seven foot square, with windows in opposite walls overlooking the terrace gardens and gaps in the paint where they'd taken their bunk beds. Yoyo lay on the carpet inside an arms-and-legs sleeping bag I'd never seen before. As I climbed up, he smiled sleepily. 'Hey, how you doing?'

'Okay. Tired.'

I let the hatch slam too loudly. Behind it, I found a little beer barrel stove and a car battery wired to a desk lamp. Charging cables snaked down from the ceiling.

Yoyo waved a sleeping-bagged arm. 'Not bad huh? Hey, check it out, they left us presents.' He pointed to a heap of stuff in one corner. 'That lot's yours, I'm keeping this. No more cold nights for Yoyo.'

Rooting through the gifts I found a towel and a fresh bar of soap. Sleep could wait... I needed a shower.

EARTHSONG

Eric Steele

'Let's move, people!' The Assistant Director's voice cut through the chill air. 'We've only got thirty minutes' of light left!'

Keith shrivelled up inside his gabardine, which barely shielded him from the biting wind. The fire-gutted tenements funnelled the cold air through the courtyard in an angry protest at their presence. Technicians were busy unloading equipment from the van. Atop the vehicle, a huge satellite dish perched a like a gigantic barnacle. Cables snaked parasitically out of the van's belly and slithered like some obscene beast into the open doors of Nixon Street Day Care Centre.

The grey, concrete building looked more like a fortress than a community centre, with its narrow windows and razor-spiked railings to deter vandals. He surveyed the rest of the estate. Angular brick and concrete stared back everywhere he looked. A dog sniffed around some refuse in an alleyway. Keith heard a crunch and looked down to see that he had trodden on a broken beer glass, no doubt launched the previous night from the squalid pub across the road.

It reminded him of the terraced streets of Miles Platting. Gone now. Some enlightened urban planner had put them out of their misery, leaving only empty grassed areas watched over by distant office blocks.

Ever since their arrival in Hattersley, he'd been reminded of those days – days he'd worked hard to forget about in his journey from student to office junior to newscaster. Now the rows of dilapidated terraced houses welcomed him to familiar territory.

He found himself hating the locals for their lack of education, their poverty. Worst of all he hated the familiarity of it all. His own childhood had been spent in an estate just like this one. Thankfully, his family had moved away while he was young, but he still remembered the cramped, claustrophobic little terrace they had occupied with its concrete rear yard. He caught a glimpse of children running barefoot past some houses. The stereotype that every garden had an old sofa or a burnt-out car in it had proven depressingly true. Worse still was the all-pervasive, sweet odour of household garbage. Refuse overflowed from choked litter bins on every street corner. It spilled forth from tattered plastic bags that formed rotting mounds in the alleyways. Had the refuse collectors simply given up?

Something rustled in a pile of rubbish nearby.

'Keith! We're ready!'

The Assistant Director hopped over the broken concrete flagstones, a picture of amoral, carefree glee amidst the human tragedy in her enormous floppy hat, sensible shoes and woollen tights.

'It stinks here,' he said.

'Of course it does, dear, it's a council estate,' she said. 'But it's also pure prime-time material with great follow-up potential.'

'And I thought you were educating the masses.'

'The masses don't want educating, dear. They just want a good story.' She regarded her shoe with disdain as if contact with the ground had tainted it. 'Besides, it's about time they got rid of these god-awful places. Were just speeding up the process.'

Her smile faded when she saw a cameraman haul an expensive video camera inside the Centre.

'Julian, not the good camera! Save it for the exteriors. We don't want one of the little hooligans breaking it.'

Keith smiled as she stumbled off after the cameraman, although it felt more like a grimace in the bleak wind.

When he'd first started working in TV he had been full of high ideals. He was the boy from Manchester, proud of his roots. He was going to be the crusading force who would reveal to a shocked public the true extent of the urban neglect of the 'Eighties.

But his morals had dissipated with each pay cheque. There were enough bright, young things ready to stab him in the back and grab his spot – the role he'd worked so hard to create for himself. So he ignored the depressing social stories, choosing instead to grill the politicians who trotted before him every week, eager to prostrate themselves before the god of television. He was the TV interviewer they all dreaded. Unafraid, intimidating, ruthless. So why did he feel like a small boy again? Maybe it was these surroundings.

'Are they ready for us yet?' the A.D. shouted over to Denise, a harried Junior Researcher with Coke-bottle spectacles.

'The manager won't agree,' Denise said, embarrassed. 'I tried to tell her it would do some good but she kept going on about privacy and how she can't trust the press.'

'Oh, for goodness sake,' the A.D. snapped. 'If you want

something doing...'

She swept past the young woman, who flushed bright red, and disappeared inside.

'Don't worry,' he told Denise. 'She's an arsehole with everyone.'

They decamped into the Day Care Centre.

'I think the work you do here is phenomenal! Just phenomenal!' the A.D. was telling the manager, a slightly overweight woman in her thirties with a perpetually stressed expression. 'I don't know how you have the patience. It must take a special kind of person to look after them, day in, day out. But don't worry; after we've finished, we'll make sure everyone in the country knows what you have to put up with.'

'I'm only doing this because we need the publicity,' the manager told them, unimpressed by the A.D's arguments. She glared straight at Keith. 'Just don't misquote me, that's all.'

'Of course,' he said with a noncommittal shrug.

'Perhaps you could introduce the little dears, one by one,' the A.D. said, leading the woman toward the day room. 'Just the terminal ones. And say what they're suffering from. It'll sound better that way.'

They walked into a room filled with comatose and catatonic faces. Doting relatives with resigned expressions accompanied some of the children. Keith felt nothing but revulsion for them and their sickness. He wanted to get away from this miasma of suffering.

'This is Paul,' the manager said, wiping the boy's chin with a towel. 'He has cerebral palsy. We're holding a raffle to buy him a new wheelchair.'

'Can't you get one on the NHS?' the A.D. asked.

'We've already been waiting six months,' the manager

told them. 'They say we'll be lucky to get one within a year. And then it'll be one of the old manual ones.'

She moved over to a ten-year-old who was vomiting into a cardboard cup held by a young woman who did her best to smile.

'This is Christian. He was born without a bowel. We try to keep him comfortable. And this is Jemma.' The manager brushed the hair of a fragile-looking blond child who stared into space. 'She's just celebrated her twelfth birthday. She has a brain tumour. The doctors haven't given her long. It's okay, she can't hear us.'

'See?' the A.D. whispered in Keith's ear with an air of satisfaction. 'Everyone wants to talk to the press when there's something in it for them.'

He fought down the desire to run out of the place, screaming, and followed the manger into the kitchen. The cameramen and crew trailed after them like some obscene centipede. As they stepped through double doors into a large kitchen a strange, zoo-like smell assaulted his nostrils. It was out of keeping with the rest of the place which, though bare and antiquate, was clean enough.

'This is all we have to prepare two meals a day for the children. As you can see, it has next to no equipment, especially for the more specialised needs.' The manager peeled open the empty cupboards. 'We're basically running on a shoestring so... Jesus!'

The scream jerked Keith out of his daydreams.

The manager backed away from the cupboard. She looked as pale as the peeling white emulsion on the mouldy walls.

A tiny, furry body fell out of a gnawed hole in the back of the cupboard.

'Christ!' the cameraman yelled.

Dozens more followed. A brown rain poured forth from the cupboards into the washbasin. Triangular heads poked over the metal rim. The sink brimmed with dark muzzles until the rats squirmed over the lip of the basin. They dropped onto the floor in a living carpet that swept directly toward the Assistant Director.

The look of terror on the A.D's face was one that Keith would always savour as the tide of vermin flowed over her sensible shoes, ropy tails whipping around her ankles. She gaped at them, open-mouthed.

Then the screaming began in earnest.

'Hattersley, a council estate that has long been the over-spill from many of Manchester's poorest areas. For years, the residents' plight has been ignored. Far enough away from the city centre to be forgotten about, some of them have been living in what can only be described as medieval conditions. But today that word takes on a new significance. Because today Hattersley is officially suffering from a plague of rats.

'The images you are about to see may be upsetting to some viewers...'

They didn't have to wait long for a reaction. Phone lines jammed with complaints. Councillors protested that they hadn't been allowed to watch the film before it had been broadcast and that many of the houses were perfectly clean and habitable. Opposition MPs denounced the atrocious living standards. Thousands of residents were re-housed. Tabloids ran front page stories. For two weeks Hattersley enjoyed unparalleled notoriety as both right and left fought to blame each other for decades of neglect.

Then, the rats were gone.

An explanation followed; the local council had employed a specialist to clean out the rats using high-tech equipment. Urthona Enterprises, a new company who had come all the way from some Scandinavian country, had used the latest methods in pest control. They were so secretive they had done the job and gone again before anyone knew. A glimpse of their featureless white vehicles appeared in one brief segment. Within days the estate was declared habitable once more.

Over time, papers and public lost interest in Hattersley. Keith received a nice salary raise, and the A.D. became current affairs producer in her own right. The news reports became less frequent. Finally, they stopped altogether. Researchers began to scrabble around for more stories.

That was how Keith found himself back in Nixon Street, looking up at the battered Day Care Centre shutters. His former A.D., now his producer, had sent him to put together the promised follow-up story after all.

He offered to take her with him but she declined.

'Once was enough, dear,' she had said, flicking cigarette ash over the manicured lawns outside the news building. 'I've learnt my lesson. Never go any further North than the Watford Gap.'

So he took the cameraman, Julian, who had expressed some interest in seeing how things had changed, and his senior researcher, Denise.

'It'll be nice to see how the place has improved,' she told him during the train ride from Victoria.

'Don't get your hopes up,' he said. 'These places are like human sewers. They never get any better. They just drag you down along with them.'

'Didn't you come from somewhere like that?' she asked.

He cursed the accuracy of her research.

'Yeah, I was one of the lucky ones. I got out. And I had the sense never to go back.'

'Until now,' she replied.

He said nothing.

They got a hire car from Manchester and drove through a grim collection of decaying suburbs, passing row after row of shuttered shop windows, until they came to a more rural section of the city. But the greenery was just an illusion - the fields soon gave way to a cluttered sprawl of council houses and twisty alleyways.

They dropped Julian off at the only hotel nearby and headed for Nixon Street. There were fewer people around than usual. But other than that, the place looked the same. At the Day Care Centre they found the corrugated metal shutters dropped.

'Do you have a phone number for the manager?' he asked Denise. She checked her bulky Filofax while he peered through the letterbox-sized gap in the shutters.

'If you're hoping to get another interview, you're too late.'

The Day-Care manager was standing behind them, carrying a large cardboard box.

'It's shut,' she said. 'Nothing could keep it open once people saw the rat problem. I just came back to get the spare toys.'

She opened up the shutters and led them inside. Again, he could smell the stench of mould and mildew. He stared through the glass doors into the abandoned day room. His stomach sank.

'Sorry about your place,' he said.

'The estate's dying anyway,' the manager replied. 'The ones who've moved out aren't coming back. A lot of people complained about headaches after they killed all the rats. Maybe it was something the council used to kill them, I dunno. They're knocking down the tower blocks now. Maybe it's for the best.'

An hour later, he and Denise sat in the car eating a greasy burger and drinking a chemical-tasting milkshake concoction from the nearest fast food outlet.

'You know, when you get past the buildings, it's not all that bad,' Denise said.

He followed her gaze. Some of the tower blocks had already been demolished. For the first time he could see the pleasant, rolling hills surrounding the estate. Keith nodded. He supposed that his own viewpoint, like everyone else's, had previously been obscured by all the trash.

'I'd like to stay for a few more days,' Keith told the producer on his mobile. 'They say the estate's being emptied and people are complaining of headaches. I'm wondering if it might be connected. Julian's set me up with an interview with a local Councillor tomorrow.'

'Absolutely not,' came the reply. 'Keith, darling, this month's budget simply won't stretch that far.'

'What if I'm right? What if they're covering something up? Wouldn't that be a good story, too?'

'For the papers, maybe. But it's too involved for television. All we need is a quick human interest segment.'

'This is human interest!' he said. The producer went quiet on the other end of the line. He forced himself to calm down. 'Look, what if someone else gets hold of this after we pass on it – the newspapers, for instance. How would it look that we'd ignored the chance to investigate? And think of how good it'd make us look if we did find something? We'd be the news channel that really cares.'

More silence.

'All right,' the producer said. 'But be quick. Nothing good ever comes out of places like that.'

He lowered the phone, smiled at Denise and gave her the thumbs-up.

Clive Thacker, the councillor in charge of planning and development, saw them for lunch at an Italian restaurant in nearby Manchester city centre. After a couple of glasses of wine and some schmoozing, Keith figured the councillor was loosened up enough to divulge some information. Denise had joined him and, at Keith's prompting, was wearing a top that was low-cut enough to arouse the councillor's interest.

'So, it must have been hard, getting rid of the rats,' Keith said in a casual tone.

'Ha, the rats were easy,' Thacker said, as his Bolognese arrived. 'It was Paulsson who was the problem. His firm's a nightmare to deal with. I mean, I know they've got some funny ways in Sweden or wherever the hell he's from, but even so...'

'Funny like what?' Denise asked.

Thacker's stare lingered over her.

'I really shouldn't be telling you,' he said.

Denise leaned forwards, smiling that sweet smile of hers. For once, Keith felt a little ashamed at having put her up to this. 'All we want is the facts,' she said. 'It can't hurt now that everything's over, can it?'

Thacker hesitated, stuffed some spaghetti into his mouth, and wiped his greasy lips on a napkin. 'You're right. Well, we paid him quite a lot, as you can imagine. National media coverage and all.'

They nodded in sympathy.

'But the funny thing is, the bill came to about eight million…'

Eight million pounds? Keith's mind reeled. That amount of money could have built a hundred Day Care Centres.

'Now that in itself is nothing. But Paulsson insisted on being paid in gold.'

'Gold?' Denise asked.

'Bullion. I mean, what kind of business is that? Of course, the gold standard being what it is, we offered to pay cash instead. But he refused. Said no, only gold would do. Anyway, he's come unstuck. Our lawyers took one look at the contract and said it would be laughed out of court. Now, you know what legal fees are like. By the time any court case is over, Paulsson won't get one penny out of the council. Serves him right for being greedy.'

The councillor slurped down another strand of spaghetti and grabbed the bottle of wine. 'Care for a top up? It's all on the expenses bill. Totally above board and all.'

Keith managed a grin and held out his glass for a refill.

They returned to the hotel to find Julian in a state of excitement. Urthona Enterprises had called. They had heard about Keith's meeting with Thacker and had offered an interview of their own with their CEO, Paulsson. The only stipulation was that it had to be today.

Denise said she needed a shower, so he and Julian raced to a nearby business park in their hire car to Urthona Enterprises's temporary base of operations. It was a nondescript building, completely white and block-shaped. Inside, the building was devoid of desks or chairs of any kind except for a sole, white-suited receptionist. Had to be a Swedish thing, Keith wondered. They liked their furniture minimalist.

The receptionist stared with intense blue eyes and a severe expression while they explained their mission. Without a word, she gestured to a white door behind her. They went inside and entered an office.

The room behind the door was also completely white. And sparse. White leather chairs surrounded a white plastic desk. The only thing out of place was a small, black, rectangular case on top of the table.

'Ah, Mr. Woodgate,' Paulsson said, materialising beside them and shaking their hands in turn. 'Please take a seat and tell me how I may help you.'

The CEO of Urthona Enterprises wore an immaculate, collarless white suit. His eyes were an indescribable milky blue. Tall, with swept-back, platinum blonde hair. He was of indeterminable age. His face gaunt and insubstantial as a mask.

'Do you mind if I film this?' Julian asked, awestruck.

'Absolutely not,' Paulsson said. 'We're here to help.'

They sat down while Julian set up a small camera on a tripod.

'I'm so glad you came,' Paulsson said in lilting, foreign-sounding tones. 'We really cannot negotiate with the council on the point that payment must be made in gold. They knew this when they contracted with us. But our laws are not your laws, it seems. We hope now that you will let us put forward our side of the story, so to speak.'

'I don't mind doing that,' Keith said. 'But I would like a little information first.'

Paulsson waited.

'How did you solve the rat problem? People say they

just disappeared overnight. I was hoping you'd tell us a bit about your methods.'

Paulsson interlaced his fingers into a steeple. 'So are my competitors,' he replied. His voice seemed disassociated from his face, as though it did not emanate from those immobile lips of his.

'But you must be able to tell us something,' he pressed. 'The public really do have a right to know. And by not telling them you just invite suspicion. Surely you can reveal your broad operations without giving away any trade secrets.'

Paulsson considered.

'Very well, Mr. Woodgate. You are a very persuasive person. Tell me, have you heard of ultrasonics?'

Keith caught Julian's arched eyebrow over his camera eyepiece.

'Over seventy-five percent of a rat's senses are devoted to hearing. Their squeaks convey so many meanings that they even rival human language. Our equipment produces high-frequency vibrations that confuse the rats and drive them out, where they can be destroyed en masse. There was no need for traps, poisons or searches. As for the final extermination, it was quick and clean, I assure you.'

'That sounds a little extreme,' Keith said.

'Extreme problems call for extreme solutions. Also, we had certain equipment we wanted to test.'

'And has this equipment been checked out. I mean, is it safe?' Keith asked.

'Safe?'

'I'm told many residents complained about headaches after you moved in. Could that be your equipment?'

Paulsson's face tried to simulate a smile. 'If there is any

residual energy capable of affecting human brains, it is perfectly harmless. Human brainwaves operate at a very different frequency than those of rats.'

'I see,' Keith said, though he didn't, really. 'Could we take a look at your equipment? It might put the public at ease.'

'My equipment? But of course. Here.'

Paulsson bent down and picked up the case. He opened the silver clasp. Inside was a strange, elongated device, with numerous keys. It seemed to be made entirely of gold. The light shimmered on it so hard it hurt Keith's eyes. Paulsson's long fingers crept over the instrument like spiders.

'What's that?' he asked.

'My equipment,' Paulsson said. 'It's really quite simple. It works on the principle that all molecules resonate at their own speed, producing vibrations. A kind of frequency, if you will. Now, imagine whole universes, all occupying the same space but vibrating at different speeds. Think of it: whole worlds all around you, invisible to the human eye, unless you too could vibrate at the same frequency. Then you would see it all. Now, what is the key to unlocking those vibrations you ask? What enables us to control those hidden harmonies of the cosmos? What else, but music.'

'I see,' Keith said. He couldn't take his eyes off the flute-like device.

'Perhaps, in return for publicising my plight, you might allow me to give you a gift,' Paulsson said.

Keith tore his eyes from the instrument. 'You mean a bribe?'

Would Paulsson really be that stupid? Maybe this was how things worked in Sweden.

'I was thinking rather of showing you something, a demonstration of sorts. Would you not like to see what my music can unlock?'

Keith hesitated. The room was growing brighter. At first, he thought it was the flute in Paulsson's hands. But now he saw that Paulsson had put the device to his lips and was playing it. It was a simple melody, but somehow it hurt his ears. The white light was emanating from another door at the rear of the office behind Paulsson. He had never noticed it there before. The light filled the doorframe, scintillating, coruscating. It hurt his eyes. His head ached.

'Keith,' Julian said. The cameraman looked fearful.

The room thrummed. The light was intense, almost hiding Paulsson from view. Keith got to his feet. His temples throbbed.

'No, thank you,' he managed to say. 'I think that will be... be...'

The music ceased. Paulsson stopped playing.

'All?' Paulsson volunteered.

Keith nodded. The light was so bright. Where was it coming from?

'What kind of equipment do you have back there?' he asked.

'Back where?' Paulsson asked.

Keith blinked. The light was gone. Paulsson replaced the device in its case, snapping the box shut. The door was no longer there.

'Well, I have to go now,' Paulsson said, standing and ushering them to the door. 'I have places to go, people to see. It was nice meeting you, though, Mr. Woodgate. And please, don't forget about our arrangement.'

◈

'I saw Jemma Davies' parents last night,' Denise said, when Keith had re-joined her back at the grim hotel at the edge of the estate. She was fresh from the shower, sitting there in a towel, her sleek arms jewelled with water droplets. 'The girl with a tumour? They're moving out. They say they can't sleep since the rats left. They've all got headaches.'

'All of them?'

'As has every family we interviewed. Virtually everyone who was on the estate when Paulsson carried out his cleansing or whatever it was has constant migraines.'

He remembered the way Paulsson's instrument had played on his field of vision. His head was no longer throbbing, but his mind – it felt almost bruised.

It was dark outside. Denise had spent the rest of that day trying to find Urthona Enterprises in various company directories, only to discover it didn't have any business premises or officers listed at Companies House.

She had then contacted the Swedish Companies Registration Office with a similar lack of success. So they weren't Swedish either. Keith realised he had never asked Paulsson where he or his company were actually from. So much for the great interviewer. An internet search had thrown up similar negative results.

Another call to Clive Thacker had yielded nothing useful. However, Thacker had revealed another point the council was going to raise if the case went to court. Apparently, Paulsson had approached the council, who were so eager they chewed his hand off. But afterwards, when they'd checked his credentials, they weren't satisfactory

'So now they're refusing to pay him eight million in gold and are offering him only two million in regular cash until he shows them his accounts,' Denise said.

'Paulsson was very specific.' Keith replied.

'The council won't budge. What if Paulsson is responsible for these headaches? Would they really let something like that loose around so many people?'

'I read that, in the Sixties, the government poured pneumonic plague virus into air shafts on the London Underground to see how many people got sick,' he said. 'I wouldn't put anything past anyone in office.'

He frowned at his own words. Something Paulsson had said had unsettled him. All that talk about vibrations being the key... to what?

Denise was staring at him.

'What?' he asked.

'You,' she said. 'You really care about this story, don't you?'

'Of course. I'm a professional.'

'No,' she said. 'I mean you care about these people. You pretend not to, but you do.'

He stiffened. Years of guardedness about his past readied him to be defensive, to deny his upbringing. Poverty was so unattractive.

She slipped her bare arm around him. 'You're so not like the others,' she said, pulling him closer. The towel slipped, and her lips locked onto his.

Faint notes drifted through the walls. He pulled back.

'What is that?' he said. 'Do you hear it? That sound...'

'I don't... yes. What is it?'

'It sounds like music.'

The hairs on his arms were standing up. The sound crept in, delicately at first, then intoxicating. Soft, melodious chords surrounded them in a warm blanket of vibrations.

Vibrations. The key to the universe.

He thought back to Paulsson and his flute, and remembered another story, an older story of rats and music. A strange, dreamlike feeling descended upon him.

'Where's it coming from?' she asked, covering herself up with the towel and going to the window. She peered through the curtains.

'Keith!'she cried, her voice filled with awe.

He joined her in staring down at the estate below.

Something that resembled an enormous snake was winding its way through the estate; a strange procession of dozens of children, all no more than eleven or twelve. The somnambulists walked slowly down the middle of the main road, one after the other, toward an old church that stood on a raised hill.

'Look,' Debbie pointed at one little girl who absently dragged along a teddy bear.

'It's Jemma Davies,' she said. But Jemma had been unable to walk even when Keith had first seen her. Denise pointed to another child. 'And that's Paul Brackenridge. Remember? He had cerebral palsy.'

A lone figure before the church gates caught Keith's attention. He knew that figure with its white suit and white blond hair. It swayed to the music, playing a golden flute like some eerie nocturnal bandleader.

Our laws are not your laws.

'It's Paulsson,' Keith said. 'That's how he killed the rats. He charmed them with music. Don't you remember the story of the Pied Piper?'

'Yes, but I don't see how…'

'Remember how the story ends?' he told her. 'Remember what happens when he doesn't get his gold?'

She laughed. But his seriousness appeared to unnerve her.

'The children…'

He nodded.

'You go, I'll follow,' she said, grabbing her clothes. He cupped her face in his hands and kissed her. He didn't want to go. Didn't want to break away from her. But he had to, didn't he? He had to know the truth.

'I'll see you downstairs,' he said.

In less than a minute he was racing along the road in pursuit of the procession. The children had moved on now, the last of them disappearing through the church gates. Paulsson waited at the end of the column, then turned to follow the children inside the grounds.

'Paulsson!' Keith yelled, but his voice was lost in the music. It seemed to be everywhere, drowning out his voice.

The figure disappeared through the gates.

Keith ran after him. He stumbled up to the churchyard entrance and doubled up, out of breath and panting. The night was no longer dark. A shimmering pool of light emanated from a small chapel that stood in the midst of the graves. The children were disappearing into it, one by one. He watched as they vanished into the light, heads descending out of view, each subsumed by a blinding glow.

Still Paulsson played.

'Paulsson!' he shouted.

The man turned to face him, and Keith felt his knees buckle.

Paulsson had no eyes.

In place of those fleshy orbs were two radiant pools of light, as if Paulsson's face and the whole of his humanity had been nothing more than a mask. Paulsson lowered his flute and extended a gloved hand.

'Mr. Holdgate,' it said with a voice like static. 'Join us.

There is room for another.'

'Where to?' he asked. He was in a dream. He had to be. And just like a dreamer, he was not completely in charge of his own actions.

'To where there is no death, no disease. Where no-one ever knows pain. We can help them there, even the sick ones. But they can never come back. They must stay with us, always and become beings of the spirit, like ourselves. For we are only brought here through music, and for too short a time.'

He stared into the light. The beautiful light. He had to see, didn't he? He had to know what lay beyond the veil. It was his job.

'You were not ready before,' Paulsson said. 'Are you ready now?'

The Paulsson-thing reached out toward him. That light was beautiful beyond words. It drew him closer. Elation filled him.

Then he heard his name being called. Denise was standing at the entrance to the churchyard with about a dozen other adults – presumably the children's parents. They looked frightened and haggard.

He hesitated. 'We must go now,' the Paulsson thing said. 'If I had more gold, I could keep the gate open for longer. But it takes so much effort. And there are so many. We can only take a few at a time.'

'I... can't,' he murmured. 'You understand?'

The thing nodded sadly.

'Then perhaps we shall meet again, when it is time,' it said, and stepped into the light, descending like a melting icicle, until the shimmering glow flared, closed, and winked out into oblivion.

He came to in Denise's arms. Other, rougher hands grabbed him. Clive Thacker loomed close, his red face hysterical with fear.

'My son!' the councillor yelled. 'My son was with them! Where's it taken him?'

'Gone,' Keith said. 'You should have paid him.'

'That bastard! If he thinks he can... I'll have him for this! I'll have every penny... I'll have his company! It's blackmail! Kidnapping! He won't see a single cent from this council! My son...'

He heard more adults shouting and cursing, trying to make sense of it.

Denise hugged him close, protecting him from the world. But Keith doubted he would ever forget the terrible longing that had filled him.

'You saw it, didn't you?' she said. What was it like?'

'Like Paradise,' he said and shivered in the chill air.

She nodded. He had never noticed before, but her eyes were milky blue. And in just the right light, they reminded him a little of Paulsson's. He no longer felt the bitterness of the wind. She smiled at him, and her smile was like the sun. He kissed her hand and let the others rant and rave around him. If Paradise was not for him, at least he knew that he had found the next best thing.

GASOLINE ALLEY

Steve Palmer

Sergeant Perceptival Wroobab was not a man to ignore a looming crisis. When the Liverpudlians appeared in his sights, he cocked the hammer on his revolver and waved up a company of hollymen. But he did not know what next to do.

The day had been warm and wearisome. In the western reaches of Eccles, where the ruins of Patricroft railway station lay beneath a hundred tubular outliers of the invading city, he and a tiny band of men had halted the automated construction of a dyke. But they had sustained considerable losses. As he lay on his stomach amidst pools of scarlet Liverpudlian ichor he recalled the battle of the day. Then came a splash and a grunt at his side as somebody lay next to him.

'Report, Sergeant Wroobab!'

Perceptival turned to see his superior, Captain Rouger. 'Looks very bad, sir,' he said, pulling off his ear muffs. Gesturing with his revolver he continued, 'Over there the tentacle outliers have pulled down a whole row of buildings around the railway station. We couldn't hold them back. The Manc edges here are ragged and weak, and the Scousers are too strong.'

'But they've over-extended! How can they be beating us?'

Perceptival sat up, pulling his binoculars out and looking to the north. 'See that huge bulge of metal swathed in rubber tubing?'

'Yes...'

'I reckon that's the local Scouser command post. You can see Scousers trying to spy out our positions.' He waved his revolver to the west. 'They're trying to penetrate Eccles. They want to reach the breast-shaped hill.'

'Well they bloody well aren't going to,' Captain Rouger muttered. 'How many men are you down, Wroobab?'

'About twenty. Mostly crushed when the Scouser and Manc tentacles battled it out. Beetles everywhere—'

'But you had a platoon of hollymen!'

'Yes, sir. But the Scouser machine is just too strong, and most of the hollymen were half-ruined. We're exhausted.'

Captain Rouger uttered a groan. 'Word from above is there's no more men to contain this advance.'

'What about this Project Nash rumour—'

'Shh! Don't say that name in public. Anyway, it's just army gossip.'

'Yes. sir.'

Perceptival turned his gaze to the east, where the looming defences of his home city reared up like so much mechanical jungle. Grey ichor dripped from ruined stanchions, splashed scarlet with the fluids of Liverpool, as the muted shrieks of metal scraping against metal echoed down Cromwell Road.

'What are we going to do, sir?' asked Perceptival.

'Defend. All we bloody well can do.'

Captain Rouger stood up, but ducked as half a dozen auto-rifles shot at him. Bullets clanged against weary Mancunian buttresses.

'Now see here, Wroobab,' he said. 'You'll do as I order. This line is not to be conceded. Nelson Street and Lewis Street will never fall. D'you hear?'

'Yes, sir.'

'Good. Chin up, old lad. I've got faith in you. Gonna be a quiet night, I hope. You might get a decent kip, eh?'

'Sir.'

Captain Rouger crawled away.

A few quiet minutes passed. As the sun fell and the air cooled, a thousand steel and carbon fibre battle-tentacles creaked, contracting in unmelodious symphony. The Liverpudlian scouts he had observed earlier had vanished into the warren of flooded tunnels beneath Liverpool's ragged edge. He sighed.

'Better use the last light to check them out,' he muttered to himself.

He glanced over his shoulder. The remainder of his unit, a dozen men and half a dozen hollymen, lay beneath a Mancunian bus stop, above them a huge buttress of steel set with razor wire. He put his binoculars to his eyes and scanned the opposition outliers.

There was something odd about that command post...

He thumbed the magnification dial on his binoculars to max. Usually there would be hordes of beetles crawling over a high security deck. It was in the right place, it was the right size, and it was covered with the rubber tubing that carried red Mersey ichor. Yet where were the beetles?

He looked again. He could see people inside the deck.

He gasped. He recognised that fall of blonde hair – that insouciant pose. Surely not...

'Miss Shellak!' he whispered.

It was her. A former beloved. So she had been captured, as the rumours suggested. He fought back a cry of dismay. The Liverpudlians would imprison her, even execute her. Again... he did not know what to do.

'There's something funny going on here,' he told himself.

He watched. Some kind of scene was being played out by Miss Shellak and two Liverpudlian officers. In their lantern-lit room they prowled around one another. He could just see their faces, though distance and dust-clouded air faded them to sepia and grey.

Determination overpowered him. This was a chance in a thousand that he could not waste. Night would soon fall. He turned over and waved at the nearest group of Privates.

Three of them crawled over, their faces splattered scarlet, as if with the blood of their enemies. 'Man this post,' he told them.

'Yes, sir,' said á Toe, the oldest and wiliest of the trio.

'Do not move for any reason,' Perceptival continued. 'This post is not to fall.' He glanced westward, then added, 'Not that we're likely to see any attacks at night time.'

'Yes, sir. Where are you going, sir?'

'Never you mind, á Toe. You just do as I say – and you two lads. Follow my orders to the letter. I'm relying on you all. Watch the Scouser city edge like a hawk. There's scouts about. They might fly Mr Kites to our side – to attach wires, you see? Watch the ground and the sky.'

'Yes, sir.'

'I've... I've got a small mission to accomplish, Tom.'

'Good luck, sir.'

Perceptival handed over his faxola machine. 'In an emergency, use this to contact me.'

'Thank you, sir. We'll be okay here 'til you come back.'

Perceptival crawled out of the foxhole, splashing into the maze of channels that surrounded this section of Cromwell Road. He reckoned he could crawl through the rubble and tubing that filled the shattered housing plots to the south without being spotted, but it would be a difficult undertaking, even in this evening gloom; the area was a matted conglomeration of metal, brick, rubble and melted plastic. It stank of the ages of industry. And there would be beetles about.

He halted. A single decent hollyman would be useful. But no… this was a mission for a man alone.

Beneath the remains of a Smiths-devoted youth club he halted. He lay quite high, atop a hillock, with a view of Nelson Street before him. Now that the sun had set, the night clubs, whore streets and neon-fritzed pubs of Liverpool, translated into this suburb along vivid, albeit stretched lines of cultural invasion, shone firefly bright against dark streets and alleys. And those bastard Liverpudlians had even translated Eric's to Eccles – upstairs and all. Perceptival ground his teeth together. It was almost more than he could bear.

He looked to the west. Like an autonomous rainbow, a flickering image of Lucy flew across the sky, as if following the flow of deep red ichor that sustained the invading city. He looked away, his heart thumping. He choked. He had to rescue Miss Shellak from this.

At Nelson Street he examined the front line, where city edge met serrated city edge. Grey Mancunian ichor pooled around him, but red Liverpudlian ichor also flowed from ruined stanchions spiked by the auto-spears and bullet sprays of the outlying Mancunian attack pods. The invaders had not gained more than a few yards.

But now he faced his most dangerous moments. The place where the invading city met the defending city was a narrow alley writhing with tubing and steel tentacles – each wall a hundred feet high. Scaffolding lay everywhere. But it was dark; with luck he would be as good as invisible. He looked through his binoculars, observing scout beetles, CCTV eyes, microphones and even a couple of human watchmen eating chips out of crumpled copies of the Liverpool Echo. Too much surveillance. But further south things looked better.

He spotted a mound of tarmac and mud along which one of the Mancunian pods had been dragged, a channel four feet deep gouged out, and filled to knee depth with ichor. It blocked the inter-city gap, disappearing into the darkness beneath Liverpool's edge. He crawled along the channel, then dropped a few feet into the mould-stinking bowels of the undercity. Throbbing bass riffs from Crucial Three songs resonated throughout the structure.

He pulled out his torch. He heard scraping. But there was nothing moving nearby. Still, there could be solo beetles about.

He oriented himself. The putative command deck lay about three hundred yards to the north, and high up. He needed to climb.

The compass on the torch held his direction firm in the gloom. He clambered through the groaning metal scaffolding, as dripping Liverpudlian ichor smeared his loose fit jeans and jacket.

Then he smelled the sea: port air. Albert Docks most likely, sent east to dismay the Mancunian defenders. But it meant he was near his goal.

The deck was a hundred-foot pod of steel and glass, from which Liver flags hung. And yet... no beetles. He clambered up to its oil-sheened underside, locating a trapdoor. He put his ear to it. No sounds from inside. He unscrewed the door and popped his head through.

'Oh, Perceptival!'

He turned around. Miss Shellak stood alone.

In seconds he was inside. 'Shh!' he whispered. 'Microphones—'

'None,' she said, placing a forefinger across his lips.

He took her in his arms, and for a while they hugged.

'I saw you—'

'I didn't think you would come!'

He stared at her. 'What d'you mean?'

'I wrote a letter so all the local beetles would zoom off to London. I—'

'You mean, you're active here?'

'Yes! And I know how to stop this madness.'

Perceptival pushed her away. 'You? How? The last I heard you were working for Special—'

'I am, you idiot! But, well, I didn't know you'd been sent into Eccles.'

Perceptival glanced around the pod. 'This is a trap. It must be.'

She shook her head. 'No, Perceptival. It's our one chance.'

'Then you were captured?'

'All part of Operation Factory. Getting a few of us girls into the forward pods. But I had a hunch... I thought I knew what the Scousers were up to. Their fluid lines are stretched to breaking point. Liverpool is losing thousands of gallons of ichor a day.'

'So what? They get it from the Mersey.'

'I know! Just like we get ours from the Manchester Ship Canal.'

'Listen, Miss Shellak, listen to me. I came here to rescue—'

'No! I needed a bit of muscle, that's all – you. We've got
to head south, to the river and the canal. And there we'll
stop this war in its tracks.'

'Us? How?'

'By blowing the Manchester Ship Canal to smither-
eens,' she said. 'So the red ichor of the Mersey and the
grey ichor of Manchester mix. Then there'll be no separa-
tion, no narcissistic glorying, no fake differentiation. Just
peace… at last.'

'But…'

'Because I know how to do that. I found things out.
Them and us… we're not so different after all.'

He gasped – that was tantamount to treason, if she
meant what he thought she meant. 'But… that's impossible.'

'Are you with me?'

Again Perceptival looked around the pod. 'Who were
those two men I saw you with?'

'Billy Shears and his lieutenant.' She laughed. 'Ha! I had
them on the go.'

Perceptival shook his head. 'We can't stop this war.'

She frowned at him. 'Huh. Not with attitude like that.
Now, are you coming with me? 'Cos this is a job for two.'

Through gloomy, rubble-choked alleys Perceptival and
Miss Shellak crawled, until they lay on their stomachs near
a ruined chippie where Lewis Street had copped a flying
tentacle – the place soaked red.

Miss Shellak pointed to an arch, behind which lay a passage. 'Gasoline Alley,' she said. 'It leads through Patricroft
all the way down to the Manchester Ship Canal.'

'Dangerous at night, so close to the invading edge. There's solo beetles about. I have heard them.'

'Don't worry,' she said, taking his hand and giving it a squeeze. 'I'm Gasoline Alley bred.'

He choked down his rejoinder. He felt uncomfortable. In the face of a crisis he needed a plan.

'What have you found out, then?' he asked.

She turned her head. 'Eh?'

'What have you found out about the canal?'

'Never mind that,' she whispered. 'Gimme a lend of your binocs, eh? I see a lamp down there.'

Perceptival took his binoculars and looked down the alley. Under medium magnification he saw a fuzzy pink light hanging from a barber's sign. 'I think it's a dead beetle,' he said.

'Gimme.'

'No! Stop pulling me. I'm looking.'

She muttered something under her breath, but left him alone.

'Listen,' he said, 'I'm in charge around here, under Captain Rouger.'

'That feckwit!'

'Don't you call him.'

'Just give me the binocs,' she said, taking the strap and raising it over his head. For a while she peered down Gasoline Alley. 'Yep, think you're right. There must be some volunteer defence down there – Manc locals I 'spect, banding together. I see razor wire and stuff.'

'Then we'll go another way.'

'No we won't. Lewis Street is no-go.'

'Then we'll head back into Manc territory, where it's safer.'

She snorted, throwing him a look of scorn. 'What did I

ever see in you? Nothing's safe anymore, now this rivalry has got so out of hand. We need speed. Got a spare revolver?'

'No. Just this one.'

'Hmmm... oh, well. Follow me.'

A hundred feet into the passage they stood beneath the glowing beetle. Spiny leaves and a few red berries lay on the ground, but none were trampled, indicating that the defence volunteers were likely far away. The alley wound on, dark as Curtis' last day, into the hunched stanchions of the Mancunian defences, the ruins of terraced streets, corner shops and chippies to either side of them, all lightless and silent. But then a sound.

'Shh!' Perceptival hissed.

They halted. A massive steel tentacle lay before them, blocking the alley, grey ichor dribbling from it; atop it the scythe-covered basket of a fallen Mr Kite.

'I hear sounds,' Miss Shellak said. 'Groovy sounds.'

At once Perceptival pulled out his Factory defence speaker. 'Keep calm,' he said. 'They usually only send the lesser beetles into enemy territory.'

'Grandmother? Eggs?' she said, grabbing the speaker from him.

'Shh!'

Perceptival watched as the light in the alley brightened. Then, from a few hundred feet up, the distance-reverberated sounds of Sgt Pepper washed over him, as the entire album floated like a WW1 dirigible overhead. Rainbow light flickered across the shards of a hundred shattered windows, and everywhere there were sitars and the cloying sweet smell of weed.

'Hide!' he whispered. 'It's too strong for us—'

'No,' she replied, grabbing his arm. 'Look!'

From the rooftops a hundred hollymen leaped up: Suzannes, Carrie Annes, but mostly, so near to Eccles, Jennifers. Their swirling, spiny green cloaks were like evening velvet and their berries shone like LEDs. Thirty seconds later the floating album had been pierced in scores of places. It sank, flabby and bass-heavy, as the hollymen soared out of the way. Hitting the ground with a groan and a final, apparently never-ending chord it gave up the Liverpudlian ghost.

Miss Shellak flashed him one of her looks. 'Never underestimate this city,' she said.

He had nothing to offer in reply.

She handed back the speaker, saying, 'I don't think Tony would have wanted this to be used. He was cool.'

Perceptival shrugged. 'Whatever. Now where? Gasoline Alley is blocked.'

'We'll climb over the remains and carry on.'

Having clambered over the punctured Sgt Pepper they stood for a few minutes in psychedelic shadow, pulling rubbery bits of the album off their clothes, fragments of which they stuck like used chewing gum onto the alley's walls. Then they moved on. An air of stolid defence lay around them, as if Manchester knew what it was doing, despite the odds against it.

The junction of Gasoline Alley and Trafford Road was a shattered site of rubble, metal and glass. Dead beetles lay everywhere.

Then Perceptival heard his speaker squawk. 'Damn!' he said. 'Message via the faxola.'

Beetles collecting on eastern Scouser edge: stop. Upper surfaces of Liverpool empty of beetles: stop. Moon lamps and spotlights focussing on Cromwell Road: stop. Suspect attack imminent: end.

He glanced up at Miss Shellak. 'I've got to go back,' he said. 'If Captain Rouger finds out I've gone AWOL…'

'Captain Rouger? What does he know about our mission?'

'Exactly! I can't just desert my post. He'll—'

Miss Shellak poked him in the chest. 'Who are you loyal to? Captain Do-It-By-The-Book or Manchester? We're a few hours away from stopping Liverpool in its tracks.'

'So you say!'

'Yeah! So I say.'

Perceptival felt his anger rise. His loyalties lay confused. 'I'm a soldier, remember? We have chains of command.'

'I'm an agent. I have commands too – from the same source as you.'

'Which I didn't hear.'

'You calling me a liar?'

He shook his head. 'That's going too far. You know me.'

She said nothing, but glanced away. He saw a hint of remorse in her face. At length, in a meek voice, she asked, 'So what you gonna do?'

Perceptival dropped the speaker into his top pocket. 'No choice. The lads need me. It must be an emergency.'

He took a step back, but in doing so bumped into a lamp post. Something light and dry showered him, like old feathers from pigeon nests atop the lamp. He grinned at her, then waved and turned to depart.

'Wait!' Miss Shellak said.

She ran forward to pick up a handful of the debris. Perceptival said, 'What's the matter?'

She looked at him, alarm showing on her face. 'Project Nash…'

He stepped up to her side, concerned at the fear in her voice. 'Project what?'

'So the info was true. The Scousers have found a way to decimate the hollymen. And already they've let it loose on our side.' She stared up at him, brushing aside a stray wisp of blonde hair. 'Every hollyman a goner, desiccated, weak. We heard rumours they might set it loose, but…'

'Set it loose?'

'You didn't bump into a lamp post, it's the remains of a hollyman, enervated by a disease tailored to do most damage to Mancs. Your men were right! There is an attack imminent.' She put her arms around him. 'Perceptival, we've got to head south now, before it's too late. Dawn will see a full scale assault, and the hollymen won't be able to defend us.'

Perceptival shook his head. 'Surely not. Besides, we've got reserves of mercenaries from the Wirral—'

'Perceptival! Use your brain! Can't you see the urgency? In a few hours this disease will spread to the city centre – to the breast-shaped hill itself. Then what does it matter about your chains of command? There won't be any!'

He tried to ignore the logic in her plea, and the urgency in her face. The voice of Captain Rouger echoed through his mind: You'll do as I order… I've got faith in you.

He sighed, and as he did the desiccated hollyman fell, crumpling into a long line of dust and a few dried berries that rolled into gutters like crimson marbles. From far off, the murmur of ancient Warsaw recordings warbled, but they sounded weak.

'Okay,' he said. 'But you've got to tell me what it is you found out that will stop this war.'

She shook her head. 'Tell you before we reach the canal? Not likely.'

He frowned. 'Why not? I'm following you now.'

'Why not? Because you ain't gonna like it.'

She spun on her heel and walked away.

They reached the southern end of Gasoline Alley as darkness began to retreat. The night grumbled to the noise of ten-ton tentacles rolling in random abandon over rubber-shod steam valves, which hissed in accompaniment. Beneath their feet desiccated berries crunched, and all the while, like anti-manna, dead leaves fell from former holly-men.

When they reached the end of the alley Perceptival looked out over a ruined landscape. The glutinous mess of the Manchester Ship Canal slopped a few yards away.

He grabbed Miss Shellak's arm. 'Supposedly the cause of the rivalry,' he said, nodding in the direction of the canal. 'So, what is your plan?'

She turned to glance at him, and for a moment he remembered more pleasant times, when they were lovers. Not now. She was as driven as he was, albeit in a different direction.

After a few sniffs of the air she replied, 'What do you suppose happens if you prick a Manc with a needle?'

He shrugged. 'Blood? A spot of grey.'

'A spot of red.'

He snorted. 'It's grey underneath the Scouser dye. We only have that dye because Liverpool is so close.'

'You actually believe that? Really?'

Her anger dented his poise. He shrugged again, looking away, annoyed with her and with himself.

'You're an idiot,' she said. 'You think Scousers have red

rain?'

'It's well known they do.'

'Nonsense! It's grey rain, like Manc rain.'

He shook his head, letting his scorn show. 'So... this rubbish is what you found out on the other side?'

'Everybody thinks the Mersey water and the Manchester Ship Canal water won't mix. They see two streams, and, yes, lots of pretty vortexes where the flows are in parallel down from the Irlam Docks. But if we demolish the whole thing, then the red would mix with the grey.'

'And that really is your plan?'

'Yes,' she said. 'It really is. You and the whole Manc army – and the Scouser army, come to that – you all believe a load of tripe. It's time to mix things up – the real world. And you're going to help me with the explosives.'

'You reckon?'

She walked up to him, glaring at him. 'I do.'

'I don't answer to you. I answer to my commanding officer.'

'Like a good little boy?'

He clamped down on his irritation. She must not get to him. After a silent count of five he said, 'It's how things are done. You've been fooled by the enemy. Grey rain? Did you really think I'd believe that? They're our enemy, and always have been. They're not like us.'

She shook her head. 'You coward,' she said. 'Too fond of duty to see the truth.'

He nodded. 'Yes. I will do my duty.'

'For a false dichotomy? Why?'

'Because that's how it is done. It's the law. You can pretend all you like that our blood is the same colour, but their culture is different to ours. It's got a different source, a different outcome. It smells different. It's the clash of cultures all over the world between neighbours. Us Mancs are no different… except us and the Scousers made our cities into our military bodies.'

'I'd rather follow the truth than any law in any book. Sometimes, Sergeant Wroobab, you have to stand up and do things yourself.'

Perceptival took out his revolver and pointed it at her. 'That's traitor talk.'

His swift motion shocked her. She stared at the revolver. 'You'd never shoot…'

'You think so?'

'… so why are you pointing that at me?'

'I don't like your attitude, Miss Shellak. I'm taking you in.'

'In? Where?'

He hesitated, glancing over his shoulder. 'Back to my foxhole for a start. Then I shall hand you over to Captain Rouger.'

'You'll do no such thing. I'm blowing up this whole canal, and if you won't help me shift the explosives I'll find a real man. '

'Quiet! Be quiet. You're coming with me, back up Gasoline—'

She turned and ran. He raised his revolver into the air and fired a warning shot, but she ignored him. He took aim for her legs, hoping to down her with a real shot, but missed twice. He cursed. He had to capture her now – no other option.

And then the beetles appeared.

The shot must have alerted them. From the edge of the canal he heard Miss Shellak scream.

'Perceptival! Beetles! Help.'

He ran, jumping like an athlete over the smaller beetles, dodging a large pink one. Miss Shellak lay on her back, writhing beneath a shiny crimson beetle. Blood everywhere. She screamed again.

She was a goner.

He ran. 'Oh, dear god,' he wailed.

The beetles followed. He had three bullets left. Extra ammo in his pocket, but no time to reload. He skidded to a halt, turned, then fired.

'Take that, you Scouser bastards!' he yelled. 'That's for Miss Shellak! You poisoned her mind!'

The beetles splintered into fragments of Norwegian wood – they were an older, simpler, hand-crafted species. But nearby he saw a phalanx of Polythene beetles, and those, he knew, because bullets bounced off them as often as not, were a bastard to kill.

The full horror of the cities' battle confronted him then, as he stood shaking in the half light. This was war. This was madness. What should he do? To mix the waters would be an act of treason, yet it could halt the war – save peoples' lives. He felt torn in two. Only minutes left now.

He hesitated. He saw the stack of explosives nearby, as yet untouched by beetles. He had maybe a minute of free time. Could he shift them on his own?

He ran over. The boxes were 12' wide, wired to a turntable and marked Blue Monday – heavy. They must have been carried down here by others involved with Operation Factory. He knew not what else had been planned, but there was a trailing wire and a portable record player.

Groaning, he pulled the explosives boxes to the edge of the canal. A blast here would destroy the whole area – Mersey into Manchester Ship Canal – full mixing. He grabbed the wire and the record player and ran off, stopping only when the wire was taut. He lay down on his stomach. He was too near maybe, in danger of flying hooks, but he had to try.

A copy of Blue Monday lay on the turntable. He wound the record player up, then raised the playing arm. As the stylus hit the vinyl the explosion roared.

Gasoline Alley was now a kaleidoscope of red dawn skies, dark shadows, mud and filth and shattered glass. He crushed the flesh and bones of Manchester beneath his boots as he ran, but his horror made adrenaline pump through his system, and soon he found himself at the junction with Lewis Street.

He halted, bent over, hands on his knees, gasping for breath.

Not far to go. One last effort.

But at the foxhole in Cromwell Road he found Captain Rouger with the three privates.

'Where the bloody damned hell have you been, Wroobab?' the Captain bellowed.

Perceptival glanced over his shoulder, then at the others. None of them met his gaze. 'On a mission, sir,' he said.

'A mission? Alone? Leaving these novices to defend a forward position?'

'It was important, sir.'

'It bloody well better be! Well...?'

Perceptival took a deep breath. 'Sir – Project Nash. It's real. I've seen the evidence.'

Captain Rouger stared at him. 'Project Nash? What are you talking about?'

'It's a Scouser weapon to destroy the hollymen, sir – and it's already being used. If we don't act right now the disease will spread all the way to the breast-shaped hill.'

'Wroobab! I've told you before about bullshitting nonsense in the presence of privates. How dare you affect morale with ludicrous stories—'

'But, sir! I've seen it. With my own eyes.'

'You've seen nothing of the sort! I have it on very good authority that Project Nash is a Scouser plot to reduce our morale before a major attack – which looks like it might happen today. Project Nash is imaginary – a ploy, intended to unsettle us. And you galloped off on some stupid mission? That's practically anarchism! Pull yourself together, or I'll have you cashiered before lunchtime.'

Captain Rouger stamped his foot on the ground, snarled, then saluted; and Perceptival had no option but to salute back. He glanced down at a shell hole, where he saw red and grey water mingling.

Miss Shellak's death was not in vain.

THE ATTIC OF MEMORIES

Quentin Van Dinteren

23 October 2014, Stockport Cemetery.

I was there. So was Amal.

We stood next to the bus stop in front of the cemetery, overlooking St George's Church. I reached into my pocket for my cigarettes. When I offered one to Amal, my hands trembled.

She pretended not to notice. 'No thanks,' she said.

I lit up and inhaled deeply. Just like they do on those commercials for breath mints, when some guy has climbed a mountain and breathes in the fresh mountain air that tastes of his victory.

I was silent. It seemed like my whole body started to tremble. The cigarette tasted foul, like rot.

'Are you alright, Dick?' Amal asked.

And I broke out in tears.

With effort, I forced my mind to return to the present and leave my memories in the past. I shook my head violently, as if there were some kind of nightmare creature hanging onto it. And maybe that was right; if so, the shaking didn't help.

I flicked the light switch at the bottom of the stairs that

led up to the attic. I didn't know why I came back home after dropping Nell off at the childcare centre. I didn't even remember driving back here.

When I was 14 and our family had just moved house, I had done something similar. I accidentally took the bus back to our old house and didn't realise it until after I had arrived.

I had been angry, because I wanted to stay at the old house. I smashed a window and climbed through it, and I remember seeing a man in the house. It's a vague memory, but I believe he was sitting on the stairway.

'In the attic we keep memories,' he had said to me, pointing at his head. 'Wanted and unwanted.'

I had been afraid, so I turned and ran. That had been a strange day, much like this one; a day of remembering loss and better times.

For a while, I stood silently in the attic. Light was sparse, and the attic was cold. Through my tears I saw boxes, most of them were full of Mary's old stuff: memories wanted and unwanted.

To those unwanted memories my mind wandered, taking me back to 2011, our small house on Greenhill Street in Stockport.

Mary stood in front of me, blocking my way to the door. 'Is it too much to ask, Richard?' Mary only called me Richard when she was angry; she knew I hated that name; I hated it to the point that I preferred being called 'Dick'.

I made a dismissive gesture and paced back into the room like an animal driven back into its holding pen. 'You're on about nothing!' I shouted.

But my shouting sounds like bad acting; it has never

impressed anyone, least of all Mary. She always responded to my shouting by shouting even louder or by
crying.

This time, however, she responded differently. She just
looked at me, and something in that look made me want
to give in immediately, to surrender to her uncondition-
ally.

So I caved; I stayed home like she wanted and didn't go
out for more drinks. I even made us some tea (I had mine
with aspirin), and when my headache was gone, I made
love to her softly and gently, just like we did when we had
just met.

But after she had fallen asleep, there was something
keeping me awake. I stared at the ceiling, looking for dis-
traction in the shifting shadows called to life by the head-
lights of passing cars, and tried to figure out what was
bothering me.

And just before I fell asleep, in that strange land of half-
slumber, where the real and the unreal tug at you at the
same time, I saw again Mary's face after I had shouted at
her.

She had looked at me in a way she had never done before. I had seen that look on other people's faces – those
of the homeless junkies that come out at night. They stare
up from beneath blue sleeping bags with a hunger and an
anger that makes me want to quicken my pace.

I realised that I'd been scared of her that night; for the
very first time, I had been scared of my own wife.

And that fear was with me again today. It first crept up on
me when I had come home to stare at the boxes in the
attic, and it was still there when I got into the office.

I tried to focus, but the numbers on my screen seemed

to flow into and through each other, until all I saw was a series of symbols in some pattern that I didn't understand, and my mind wandered.

There had been good times too, plenty of them. Mary had had a real sense of humour, unlike anything I had ever witnessed in the throngs of girls that risked pneumonia (and VD's) on any city night. When I met her, it had felt like it was decided by some higher authority that she would be mine. And although I had to fight hard to get her, I never gave up.

I'm a shy guy. I'm not much to look at either. I don't have a lot to chat about, and I'm not very exciting. I have no moves or lines, and my 'game' consists of staring down women until they get creeped out. My mates might say that all the girls want to get their hands on Dick, but I doubt they were ever talking about me.

But Mary, Mary was the opposite of me. She's that kind of girl that makes guys in the streets walk into lampposts. Everyone always secretly wondered what she was doing with a guy like me. In fact, I've asked myself that question more often than I care to remember.

But I do care to remember some things: the good things, like 14 March 2012: a cold Wednesday in Stepping Hill Hospital in Stockport.

Tears again. Of happiness this time. Amid the smell of sweat, fear, blood, and shit I held Nell. Little Nell, named after my Nan and Mary's mum; with that name we got two old birds with one stone.

I held Nell close to me, and I realised she was dearer to me than anyone or anything in my entire life had ever been. Her little hands grabbed my shirt and her little toothless mouth opened and closed.

Crying, I held her up for Mary to see. 'Look,' I said. 'She's smacking her lips just like Nan Nell used to.'

And Mary laughed. She was exhausted and broken. But when she laughed, she looked more beautiful to me than she ever had before. The happiness I felt was in part because I thought it was over now; she would stop. Whatever the hormones did to the maternal brain, they would at least make her more caring, less short-tempered, and less paranoid.

My mobile rang, taking me away from that sweet memory and back into the present.

I looked at it. The display lit up and showed an unknown number with the dialling code 0161.

I stared at it as it rang again, unable to move, scared. I could only look on as the ringing and the vibrating got louder. From the corner of my eye, I saw Amal looking at me from behind her desk. She seemed concerned for me.

Moved to action by her stare, I quickly picked up my mobile and touched the green telephone horn on the display.

'Yeah?' I said.

'Hiya,' a woman's voice said. 'Is this Mr Dick Clarke?'

My eyes met Amal's. She gave me a sympathetic look. I turned away from her to face the door to the office.

'Yes,' I said. 'It is.'

'Hi, I'm Sheila with the childcare centre. I'm just giving you a quick call about Nell.' My heart skipped a beat.

'Is she alright?' I asked.

'She's a bit sick. Nothing to worry about, I don't think. But we'll need you to come pick her up, Mr Clarke. Is that possible at all?'

I looked at the clock; it was 1:23 p.m.

'Yes, that's possible,' I said. 'I'll be there at two.'

'Great, love. See you in a bit.'

I hung up and turned to face Amal.

'It's Nell,' I said. 'She's sick, so I, uh, I have to go get her.'

She gave me a sympathetic smile and nodded. 'Okay Dick,' she said. 'Give me a call to let me know how she is,'

I nodded and managed to mutter a 'thanks'.

I felt tears welling up again, so I quickly grabbed my laptop, stuffed it in my bag and left the office. It was a fifty minute drive from here to the childcare centre. But since it was about Nell, I was sure I could manage in half an hour.

Even in the rain.

There had been no rain on that spring Friday in 2014; it had been one of the first (and last) warm days of the year, and I was on my way home to Stockport.

I had felt good all night thanks to good company and just the right amount of drinks. Back in the city, it had all been great. But when I left the bar and walked down to Piccadilly, I got that feeling again: that feeling that had been there for a few months now.

The first year after Nell had been born, I had nearly forgotten that feeling. Mary and I were exhausted all the time, but we also were very happy. There was a lot of love and support, even though Mary seemed depressed from time to time. But as the novelty wore off for friends and family and we grew used to having Nell around, it sneaked back into our lives.

The feeling is difficult to describe, but the word that comes to mind is 'hope'. Because I hoped that the lights were off when I got home; I hoped she would not be there waiting for me; and I hoped she would not wake up when I slipped into bed next to her.

On the train it always got worse. I would stare out of the window as the lights of Manchester faded from sight and made place for the dim glow of the sleepy towns south of the city, and I'd plan what I would say to her when I got home.

Just a night out with the colleagues, a night out after work, like everyone does from time to time. The type of night that you're not exactly looking forward to, but once you finally get there and get your hands on the first pint, it's all good.

I wouldn't tell her that everyone left early except for me and Amal. We hung around the bar in Spinningfields for three more hours after everyone had gone. We talked; nothing else happened, but Mary wouldn't like it anyway.

I had made the mistake of telling her about Amal be- fore – way back before Nell – and she had been suspicious for weeks. She didn't like Amal; she didn't like her because I liked her.

I got more nervous as I walked past the red brick houses with the white windows and the white doors on Old Chapel Street. And I got even more nervous when I turned right opposite of Edgeley Church onto Greenhill Street.

Home, and the lights were on.

I swallowed and walked up to the door, put the key in the lock and turned it slowly and softly. Maybe she'd just left the lights on and was already asleep. I could hear the television running some advertorials in the living room. I softly stepped inside and hung my coat.

'Richard?'

I winced.

'Yes, it's me.' I noticed I still slurred my speech.

Silence.

I walked into the living room, my muscles tense, ready to brave the storm. Mary had already gotten up from the couch and was looking at me in that special way, that mad way. I felt my balls shrivel. That was my body's fight or flight response. By staying, I chose the former.

'Who were you out with?' Mary asked.

'Ah, some guys from work. I sent you a message. Didn't you get it?' My voice was more high-pitched than it usually was. I had already lost this fight – if there ever was anything to win to begin with.

'Yes, I did.' She kept staring.

'Alright, sweetheart,' I said. 'So how was your night?'

'My night was fine until I saw this.'

She took her mobile from the coffee table and showed me a photo. In the photo were all of my colleagues – except me and Amal – standing outside of the bar with arms around each other's shoulders. Red faces, tussled hair, shirttails untucked.

The picture was from the Facebook of a colleague of mine she had friended. A comment was written below it:

#TGIF: great night out with the lads (and lasses!)
Cheers! See you Monday :(

It had been posted almost four hours ago. I looked at Mary and was silent. Her jaw was clenched shut and her eyes were wide open, staring daggers at me. When she opened her mouth again it was ugly.

'Were you out fucking that Indian whore?'

'Jesus Christ, Mary. Take it easy.' I looked behind me into the hallway. 'Is Nell sleeping?'

'Answer the question, Richard.'

'Of course not,' I said.

Suddenly, the madness went from her eyes and made place for sadness. Tears welled up and her face slowly turned red just like it always did when she was crying; I had seen it too often.

'Why do you lie, Richard?' She asked. 'Why do you lie to me all the time?'

I had learned a long time ago that Mary was a woman that did not require consolation when she was crying. She cried for the audience, whoever that might be. When Mary cried, it was always to justify the fit of anger that would come next.

If I had stepped up and tried to hug her she would have become fierce, very fierce. I stepped back instinctively.

'Think about Nell, Mary,' I said, fearing an outburst. 'She's sleeping.'

She sobbed. 'I try my best for our family; I sacrificed my career and my friends to make you and Nell happy. And all you do is lie and cheat.'

'Come on, you know it's—'

'Fuck you!' The mobile that she held a second ago flew past my left ear and smashed to bits against the living room wall behind me. I was lucky her aim was off.

In her room upstairs Nell started crying. I could hardly hear it over the sound of my heart trying to fight its way out of my body straight through my throat.

'I gave up everything for you!' she shouted through her tears. 'I even came to this shithole for you!'

'Mary, Nell—'

'No,' she said, seemingly regaining control. The mad look returned to her eyes and she took a few steps towards me. I believe I actually cowered.

'This is not about Nell; this is about you,' she said. 'That's what you like, isn't it? Everything should always be about you.'

She was silent for a second. I saw that her fists were clenched. She stood no more than a foot away from me.

'Mary—' I tried to back away but bumped into the wall.

'I can smell her on you, you know? That little slag,' Mary said, taking another step towards me. 'You stink of booze and whores. You're pathetic.'

She looked at me with contempt and hatred. For a second, I actually believed it would be best to lie and pretend that, yes, I had slept with Amal. It would be best to get on my knees and admit that, yes, I was pathetic. I should plead with her for forgiveness and say that if she would let me stay, I would try to be a better husband.

I wasn't at that stage just yet, but I couldn't find anything else to say to her; maybe there wasn't anything I could say. So I simply hung my head.

'You're pathetic,' she said again, while I looked at my feet.

I heard her walk away and up the stairway to little Nell's room. My heart settled down as she started consoling her. For now, it was over.

I felt sick.

'It's probably the flu,' Sheila with the childcare centre had said.

She told me that Nell – normally a bit of a rough one – had been quiet all morning. Sheila had taken her temperature and it had been a bit high. They couldn't keep her in the childcare centre or else it might spread to the other children.

When I stopped at the traffic lights on the intersection

of Wilmslow Road and Etchells Road, I looked over my shoulder at Nell, strapped in the car seat. She was a little pale but she looked back at me with clear blue eyes.

'How are you feeling, duck?' I asked.

'Yes,' she answered; her voice was a little weak. I smiled.

'Dick?' she asked.

It had disturbed me at first that she stopped calling me 'daddy' shortly after she had learned the word. In time, however, I had grown to like it.

'Yes?'

'Is Mary home?'

She asked that almost every day. At the childcare centre they had told me Nell talked about Mary a lot. She drew pictures of her too.

'No, love,' I said, 'Mary isn't home.'

'Why?'

The light turned green and I continued down Wilmslow Road.

'Mary is in heaven, baby.' Nell was silent. 'Do you miss her?' I asked.

'What's that?'

I stopped to let a few cars merge into traffic before me.

'Well, 'miss' is when somebody's gone and you'd like to see them again.'

'Oh,' Nell said.

She was silent. I felt some concern. Sheila was right; Nell was more silent today than usual. Normally, she would try to make jokes about poop or tell stories about animals that she thought looked silly; she must be really sick.

I looked back over my shoulder. She looked right back at me.

'So do you miss her?' I asked again.

She thought about it for a second.

'No,' Nell said. That must be a typical 'toddler no'.

'It's okay if you miss her, baby,' I said. 'I miss her too.'

That was true. It was hard to remember the good times, but they had definitely been there. Through all the hardships I had never felt as whole as when I did when Mary was still with me. And I had never felt as alone as I have since that night on 16 October 2014.

'No,' Nell said again.

That wasn't true. I knew she missed her; she drew pictures of Mary, talked about Mary, and asked about Mary. It bothered me that she wouldn't be honest. Of course, she had witnessed dozens of fights between us. She must think I hadn't liked Mary very much. I didn't want her to think that.

'Why don't you miss her?' I finally asked as I turned right onto Queensway, close to home.

'She's not gone.'

Yes, she is.

And with that realisation came the memory that haunts me every day: the memory that forces me to relive it all, to relive 16 October 2014.

It was about nine o'clock when I pulled up to the house. There were two patrol cars parked in front of it.

I felt like it should rain. It should rain and there should be thunderstorms. Everything should be in turmoil; the earth itself should scream and wail. And so should I...

But everything was calm, up to and including me. There was no rain, no thunder, and my mind had been clear on the drive home. In fact, I had never driven so carefully and full of self-control as I had done that day. But, every few seconds, two thoughts returned to me. They made me tremble and nearly choked the life out of me:

My wife is dead.

My baby girl is dying.

I parked and got out. There were blue and white police lines blocking access to the house like on television. The front door to the house was open.

On the door and on the walls of our house was writing, painted on in wide streaks of the pure white paint that I had bought to redo the living room. There seemed to be no pattern or method to it, but I could recognise some words: names she had called me in the past. But my eye was caught by what she had written on the front door in big, white letters.

It was my name, Richard; the name I hated.

On Greenhill Street, some people were watching from behind their curtains, others were standing in front of their houses or on the street corners. Edward from across the street even had his dog with him, pretending he was taking it for a walk.

They looked at me like people do when they're at the funeral of someone who was very close to you. That look is made of two things: pity and relief. They pity you, sure, but at the same time they're happy that it's not them; they're happy that they can go home in a minute, close the door, say 'isn't that a shame?', and then watch the repeat of EastEnders.

A policeman walked up to me with a sympathetic look. 'Mr Dick Clarke?' He asked.

I nodded and looked at the mad streaks of paint all over my house. The policeman followed my stare.

'The neighbours from across the street called us when they saw her painting. When we got here, they were both unconscious.' He cleared his throat. 'They were both... ah... administered a large dosage of painkillers, Mr Clarke. We found them in the attic.'

I cleared my throat. There was still that sense of calm. 'In the attic,' I repeated. I don't know why. 'How's Nell?'

'She's at the hospital, Mr Clarke; and so is your wife. Shall we bring you there?'

'Please.'

The policeman nodded. He motioned for one of his colleagues to follow us and then gently took my arm to lead me to the patrol car.

When we pulled out of the street, I finally started crying. I cried because it would never again be like it had been in the old house on Greenhill Street.

The new house was on Matlock Road. It was big; it was a standalone; and it had a garage and a driveway. It also had an attic.

I didn't use the garage, because it was inconvenient: I would have to go inside to open the door and then drive in, since I had no remote control. And besides, the neighbourhood was pretty quiet; there was hardly any trouble. You could easily leave a car on your driveway here at night.

I carried Nell to the front door. She held me tightly around my neck. I opened the door with one hand and quickly walked into the living room. There were some white stains on the hallway floor, probably yoghurt – Nell liked yoghurt. I'd have to clean that up.

'Alright, sweetheart,' I said, as I put Nell down on the sofa, 'I'm going to put you to bed in a second.'

'No,' Nell said. She looked at me with big blue eyes in her little, pale face.

'Yes, baby, you need some rest. I'll make you some soup.'

With some effort, I loosened her little hands from around my neck.

'Wait here while I get your bag from the car,' I said. She pouted when I walked away.

I got out of the house and walked back to the car. It was a quiet neighbourhood, but leaving a car unlocked with valuables inside is never a good idea. I took out Nell's backpack and my own laptop bag when I heard a voice behind me.

'You alright, Dick?' the voice asked.

I turned to see Mrs Hayes, the next door neighbour, walking her dog. She was a pensioner I paid to look after Nell on Mondays and Tuesdays.

'Not too bad, Mrs Hayes. How about yourself?' I said, as I shut the door and locked the car.

'I'm fine,' said Mrs Hayes. 'How's Nell?'

Mrs Hayes's dog, officially called Stewart but renamed 'Woofie' by Nell, started barking at something that only it could see.

'She's a bit under the weather, actually,' I said, raising my voice over the barking. 'I just picked her up from the childcare centre.'

In the corner of my eye, something moved.

'Oh, isn't that a shame, love?' Mrs Hayes said. 'I did ask myself, 'why is Dick back from work so early?' when I saw you just now.'

I glanced at the open door to our house and smiled at Mrs Hayes. The dog continued its barking, throwing in a growl from time to time and pulling wildly at the leash. Mrs Hayes motioned at Stewart to be silent, which the dog completely ignored.

'Yes, it's the flu or some such, I'm afraid,' I said. 'I'm just about to make her some soup and put her to bed.'

'You need any help at all, dear?' she asked.

'No, thank you, Mrs Hayes,' I said. 'I'm quite alright. And besides,' I added with a smile, 'you look like you have your hands full with Stewart over there.'

She sighed and rolled her eyes theatrically as the dog barked and tugged at the leash. 'Let me know if you need anything, love,' she shouted.

'Thank you, Mrs Hayes. See you later.' She waved goodbye and pulled the dog down Matlock Road.

I walked back into the house, closed the door and walked into the living room.

Nell was gone.

'Nell?'

I put the bags down on the sofa and looked around. She wasn't in the living room. My stomach shrunk.

'Nell?' I said again.

I hurriedly walked up to the kitchen at the other end of the L-shaped living room. She wasn't there, either.

'Nell!'

Panic. I ran back into the hallway and checked the toilet: nothing. I ran up the stairway, calling her name loudly. She wasn't in her room and she wasn't in mine; she wasn't in the bathroom, or the guest room, or the washing room.

Garage, I thought. I ran down the stairway, three steps at a time. I nearly busted down the door to the garage when I got there.

'Nell!' I shouted.

I looked around. Boxes, Nell's bicycle, tools, working table, paint—

I froze. The paint can was open.

I looked at the outside door that led from the garage

into the garden. There was a single word painted on it.

Richard.

That old familiar feeling; my balls shrivelled and my stomach seemed to collapse in on itself.

On the floor in front of the door was a smear of paint in the shape of a handprint. Small droplets of paint led from there to the hallway; the little white droplets that I had mistaken for yoghurt.

A thousand voices shot through my head in a split second. Then came a single voice. *Follow the trail*, it said.

This time, I moved slowly; I think it was because I didn't want to know anymore. I followed the trail of droplets from the garage, to the hallway, up the stairs, to the door that led up to the attic. There was a child safety lock on that door, which was placed high where Nell couldn't reach it; it was unlocked. Had I forgot to lock it this morning?

I opened the door and slowly went up the stairs to the attic.

'Dick?'

It was Mary's voice: so casual, as if she was about to ask me if I felt like ordering in tonight, or if I could pick her up after work. Tears filled my eyes. I had missed that voice; I was incomplete without it in my life.

I flew up the last few steps, carried by fear, desire, love, and hatred – all at once – until in the dim light of the cold and dark attic, I saw my wife again. For a second, I was happy; I was happy when I saw her.

My Mary was more beautiful than ever, more beautiful even than I remembered her. She wore the white dress that I loved the most, the same dress that she wore in my mind every day: not the wedding dress or the posh evening dresses, but the simple sun dress that was reserved for sunny days in the garden.

She sat on the floor in an awkward way, unanimated, as if she was a cardboard cut-out. And as I watched her, her face looked more and more like the pale, wax-like face I had last seen in a wooden box in the Stockport Cemetery chapel.

In her arms she held our little Nell, who sat on the floor in front of her. Her face was more pale than it had been before, almost white. Her beautiful blue eyes (how they had looked like her mother's) I could hardly see, since they were turned upwards in their sockets. Her mouth was open too, as it sometimes was when she was sleeping.

She was a dead thing now, my daughter; empty and lifeless.

In my mounting despair, I looked into Mary's eyes, as if searching for an explanation, but I saw only madness in those eyes that I had kissed a thousand times over. And even then I loved her. I could only ever love her – through hatred, guilt, grief, fear, and the tide of madness that mercifully washed over me to end my suffering and take my memories – both wanted and unwanted.

TOIL AND TROUBLE

Chris Ovenden

I'm not sure why, but I always seem to get lost in the Northern Quarter.

It's not like it's even that big, the parts I go to anyway. Just four streets off Piccadilly and a few running across them. Doesn't matter. Somehow between Port Street and Shudehill something goes wrong. I end up turned around, looking at a building I thought was someplace else and wondering how the hell I'm supposed to get to where I'm going.

Today is no exception.

I've been wheeling my bike around some side streets for about five minutes now, looking for this new bar I'd heard about. Pay for your time and not your beer, or something. Sounded pretty cool. I kind of wanted to check it out before it got too popular. You know, overrun with bearded guys bluffing about craft ale and raw paleo diets.

To be honest, I'm trying to find something to take my mind off Sam, mostly. I've barely been outside in days and this seemed like as good excuse as any to get out the house. Anyway, it's not like I'm averse to a drink in the afternoon.

I was lost pretty much as soon as I hit Thomas street: took a few wrong turns that I thought were right and I end up looking at this archway I could have sworn was about two hundred yards the other direction.

I'm just about to turn back when I notice this doorway on the other side of the street. Real narrow, wonky-looking thing, looks like it's pushed its way out from the buildings on either side but not made quite enough headway. There's a set of stairs inside, and a wooden sign swinging from a metal arm above the door that says 'Wytching Ways: craft conjuration for wayward wishes'. I figure it's a coffee shop or an art house, or whatever.

It's weird. I must have been up and down these streets a hundred times, but I can't remember ever seeing this place. I mean, I'm lost every time I come here, but everything always looks familiar. This place doesn't ring any bells at all. I feel this mad urge to run up the stairs and take a look around, like there's some alien force pulling me in. Maybe that's just the hipster in me I'm trying to repress.

In any case, it's just started raining, and I don't really like getting the bike wet, so I decide to give the place a shot: hang out here till the rain stops and I can carry on looking for this pay-per-time bar.

I sling the bike over my shoulder and jog up the stairs where another door opens out into a trendy looking bar area. It's a pretty nice space. Done in that kind of minimalist Scandinavian style: matte wooden floors and surfaces, raw brick walls with metal girders propping up the ceiling.

There's a large counter on the far side of the room and this hipster-looking guy just beside it, perched on a stool in skinny jeans and a checked shirt, flicking through a comic book. Thick square beard hanging off his jaw, finely waxed moustache, earlobe extenders. He's got that kind of long hair with the shaved sides, slicked back and tied in bun, jet black in contrast to his coppery beard. Got a pretty sweet sleeve tattooed down his left arm, too.

He doesn't notice me enter, and I start to feel a bit guilty about dragging the bike up into his space.

'Hey buddy. Do you mind if I bring this up here?' I call over to him.

'Hmm? Oh, hey. Yeah! Whack it wherever.' He hops off the stool and goes round behind the counter, tossing the comic onto the surface. I prop my bike against the nearest wall and then wander over.

'Sorry about that, fella. Was off with the fairies.' He has a slight accent – that kind of Northern-European lilt where you expect every other sentence to begin with 'for sure', maybe Norwegian.

'Get you a beer?' He's already back-pedalling into the adjoining room.

'Uh, sure.'

The wall behind the counter is covered floor to ceiling with shelves, packed with hundreds of glass bottles, maybe thousands. All neatly arranged into rows two or three deep, each one half-full of some brightly coloured liquid. Spirits, I guessed.

Over in the corner, there's this vintage looking coat stand with a single item on it. A long cable-knitted scarf with tassels hanging off its ends, kind of a greeny-blue. Turquoise, I suppose you'd call it. It jumps right out at me Looks just like the kind of thing Sam would wear. The kind of little gift I'd pick up for her after a fight, to say sorry, to make it better. I might have even bought her something similar a few Christmases ago.

I've got to get her out of my head.

I turn my attention back to the counter. There's a load of glass apparatus on one side. Like an old style chemistry set, with a few flasks actually bubbling away beneath the loops of tubing. The comic he'd been reading is on the other side of the surface, facing away from me. I turn my head to read the cover. It looks pretty trippy: a group of medieval soldiers are hacking away at this tree with a gnarly face carved into its trunk. I can't tell what's it was called. The name's written in these kind of scratchy looking glyphs. Like Elvish or something.

'It's Finnish,' the guy says, re-emerging from the back room, two bottle of beer pinched between the fingers of his left hand. 'Great fun if you can find it, about this God-guy who goes round granting wishes by singing songs and stuff.' He passes one of the beers to me, then grabs the book and flicks through a few pages to show me. Up close I notice his sleeve is done in the same art-style as the comic. Overgrown forests and lakes, all picked out in delicate line art, coloured in deep pastel hues.

'Real cool artwork,' he continues. 'You can't usually get it in the UK. I get them flown in from Finland.' He motions to a stack of boxes over in the corner. 'Got a friend out there.'

'Cool,' I say, Holding up the beer. 'Cheers!'

He clinks the bottom of his bottle against mine and we take a swig. It's nice, pale ale, quite hoppy.

I look back at the comic. A white-haired guy with a beard down to his ankles is waving a stick and yelling at some fish. I can't read the dialogue. All in Finnish, I guess. Even so, the lettering seems to resonate with me. I feel like I must have seen it somewhere before.

'So, what can I do you for?' the guy says.

I pause, mid-swig, not quite sure what he means. I've barely taken a finger out of the beer he'd given me, he can't be trying to offer me another. Did I need to pay for this one? He seems to catch my confusion.

'Hah, the beer's on the house, bud. I don't do drinks, unless you like your lager bewitched.'

'No. Yeah. Of course,' I say, putting my bottle down. 'D'you have a, uh, menu or anything?'

'Sure, one second, I've got one somewhere.' He leans over and slips a laminated sheet of card out from under the counter. 'Specials are on the board, and I'm all out of metamorphoses.'

I nod and glance round at a big black chalkboard on the wall beside me that's got 'Bottles of Envy – Half Price' scribbled across it. I look down at the menu and hope it makes a bit more sense. It doesn't.

It's split into four sections: Incantations, Sayings, Hexes and Metamorphoses, which I apparently can't have. I read through them again, trying to make sense of what I'm looking at.

'Are these like, drinks or...'

'Uhh, the envy spell comes as a tonic,' he says, pointing to the incantations section. 'I can do the strength and speed spells as a drink, but the rest are all over the counter casts.'

'Spells.'

'Yah, like, zap! Ooh, you're a newt.' He wiggles his fingers towards me, laughing.

I stare at him blankly. 'Sorry, buddy, you've lost me. What are we talking about?'

He holds my gaze a moment, a little smile creeping over his lips, then he looks past me, over towards the door.

'Sweet bike.' He points his beer over at my ride. 'I got a fixie myself, for nipping about town. Always fancied a ten-speed, though. You mind if I take a look?'

'Uh, no, go ahead. It's—' I turn to look at the bike and

he's already there. Like, crouched down on the floor next to it, checking out the rear derailleur and feeling the tire pressure. I look back behind the counter, but there's no one there. He's literally fucking teleported across the room.

'Great looking frame. Aluminium?'

'Uh... Steel.'

'Nice.' He stands up and grabs the top-tube, then lifts the bike a few inches off the ground. 'Pretty light. I bet she eats up the bumps.'

My head was staring to hurt. I closed my eyes and pushed my fingers into their sockets.

'So any thoughts on what you'll be having?' His voice comes from behind the counter. I open my eyes and he's already back there, cleaning a jar with a rag like some old-timey barkeep.

I feel sick.

'I don't...' I lurch away from the counter. 'I think I'm just gonna head. I'm feeling kind of off.'

'Look, just go with it, yeah? What do you want? Sky's the limit.' He taps a finger on the menu, still clutched between my fingers.

I stand there, feet rooted to the floor, half of me wanting to go, the other half desperate to stay. It's not every day you actually discover something. I mean, really discover something.

What did I have to lose?

'Yeah, sure, okay.' I say, looking down at the menu. I still have no idea what any of it means, but I figure it doesn't really matter. I let my eyes settle on whatever they want.

'Sayings. I'll have a future... saying. Is that like you read my future?'

'Sort of, only, instead of reading a future that's already written, I say a future and make it come true.'

'Right. Well, yeah that one, I guess.' I scan the menu for a price. 'What's that going to set me back? You take card?'

'No. No money.'

'So?'

'A memory.'

He produces a sheet of high-quality paper and a pen from under the counter and passes them over to me. Then he stands there waiting, as if I have any idea what he's on about.

'A memory,' I say.

He nods. 'You give me a memory, I'll cast you a spell. Just write it down as best you can. Doesn't have to be precise, it's the intention that matters.'

'Right.' I look back at the blank paper. 'A memory.'

I have no idea what to write. I mean, how could I?

I scribble down a few sentences that I figure might work: I'm fourteen and my parents just bought me a skateboard. I play on it all afternoon then fall off and crack my head on next doors driveway, spend the night in A&E.

I pass it back to him and watch his eyes dance over my handwriting. He smirks.

'Come on, bud,' he says, screwing the paper up and tossing it behind the counter, 'you want me to cast a spell, or what? I need a memory that means something to you. Something raw. Something powerful.'

'I don't know what you're asking for.'

'Well, tell me about yourself, what are the important things about you, the important events?'

'I don't know,' I say, trying to think of something interesting. 'I'm a student, I play bass.' The turquoise scarf on the coat stand winks at me over his shoulder. 'My girl-friend left me.' I laugh.

'Yeah? Oh I'm sorry, bud, recent?'

'Last week.'

He strokes a hand through his beard. 'What was she like?'

'Sam? She was great. Funny, beautiful. She was, you known, great.' I sighed. 'And horrible. I mean, we were horrible together. We clashed. One minute it's incredible, the next... I don't know.'

'Sounds rough,' he said. 'You had any contact since?'

'No.' I tried hard not to reach for the phone in my pocket: see if there were any new messages. 'I mean, she's tried to get in touch, but I've not picked up. We go through this too much, breaking up, getting back to-gether. It has to stop somewhere. I don't think we ever could ever really work out. Like, we're just too different, but when it was good, it was just... you know. I wouldn't take any of it back.'

The guy hands me another sheet of paper. 'Now that's our memory.'

I look at him, and then at the paper. He nods.

I can't believe I'm actually contemplating writing this stuff down. But then, if he really can get Sam out of my head, why not? It's not like being miserable is doing me any good.

So I start writing. Everything, more or less. Where we met, the colour of her eyes. The way she sang in the shower. The way she wrinkled her nose when she was mad. The way we laughed, the way we fought. The way we ended.

And, at his insistence, the way I sold my memories of her to a wizard.

When I'm done, I pass it back over for him to inspect and this time he grins.

'Perfect.'

He doesn't waste any time.

He shreds the paper into long thin strips, then takes a flask from under the counter and pushes them through its neck. He takes the flask over to the glass apparatus beside us and connects it up to the piping, sending a steady stream of bubbling blue liquid over my memory, and out through a little opening on the flask's side. It shoots up and round the curved pipes, through heated bulbs over tiny gas burners, then finally drips, thick and dark, into a bottle at the far end of the counter.

'Sweet,' he says, as the ink starts to peel off into the solution. 'Now, let's see about that spell.'

He turns and scans the bottles on the shelves behind him, tracing a finger over each one and whispering their contents to himself. All the while I watch my memory leak into the bubbling liquid swirling around it.

'Aha!' He finds the bottle he's looking for, snatches it off the shelf and tosses it in tight arc over his shoulder, deftly catching it in his other hand.

'Boom!' he says, slamming it down onto the counter. 'Love lost, heartache and longing. Sound like someone we know?' He unscrews the top and ducks down under the counter.

The bottle has a poorly drawn 'S' scribbled on its side in thick black marker and is filled with a translucent blue liquid, a barely perceptible vapour lifting off its surface as it sloshes back and forth. I lean in for a closer look and a faint scent drifts up to me: quite sweet, like cherries.

The guy emerges from behind the counter with a small leather wallet in one hand and what looks like a vape pen in the other. He opens up the wallet flat on the counter, then unclips a small glass container from the pen and cleans it out with a cotton swab.

'Just got this batch in yesterday. Oh watch out. Pretty potent stuff.' He says, noticing me leaning over the bottle and pulling it from under my nose. 'Wouldn't want you to singe an eyeball.'

'What is it?'

'This,' he says, taking a long glass pipette out of the wallet, 'is the good stuff.'

He pinches the end of the pipette and sucks up a small quantity of the liquid, then holds it up to eye level.

'Refined memories,' he says. 'Pure human emotion.' He pops the tip into the little glass chamber and dispenses the liquid. Then he carefully slides the pipette back into the leather case and screws the lid back on the bottle. Finally, he takes the filled glass chamber, snaps it back into the vape pen, and presses a button on its side to start it up. A blue light springs into life just beside his thumb.

'Just got to wait for her to heat up,' he says. 'Shouldn't take long.'

I look around, rather concerned that I might have walked into some kind of hipster opium den, and that the police will be bursting up the stairs at any moment. But it's just us. Us and the pen, and the memory juice.

'So, what kind of future you thinking? Promotion at work? Write a novel?'

I shrug. 'I dunno, what do people usually ask for?'

'Forget everyone else,' he says, laughing. 'What do you want? What's going to make you happy?'

I don't think anything really can make me happy, what with the stuff with Sam. I don't think I've ever really felt happy single.

'A girlfriend, I guess.'

He claps his hands together. 'True love it is.'

The little blue light turns green and he picks up the pen and pops the mouthpiece between his lips. He closes his eyes and takes a deep breath, like he's filling up his whole body, and he holds it.

When he opens his eyes they're a brilliant blue. I can't remember if they've always been that colour, but they're practically glowing now.

He puffs out a cloud of vapour, then takes another draw on the pen and his eyes flash brighter.

'You long for love, and love, you'll find. A love you lost and thought undone. Forgotten and ended, now forged again by fleeting feelings, freely traded to a merchant wizard.' His voice is rhythmic, musical almost, the words tumbling out of him in a thick blue mist. He takes another draw.

'A girl, you'll find, who wants for finding. And you'll fall for her as you fell before. Unwittingly willing, freely caught, under a spell already spoken, your love for her will be unbroken.'

He takes a final draw on the pipe and blows a series of rings towards me, chuckling as he does.

'That's it?' I wave the vapour out of my face.

'That's it.' He laughs, harder now, a blue cloud billowing round his head. I stare at him a moment, wondering if there's more. But that really is it. He just carries on giggling to himself. Laughing. At me.

A sudden wave of shame rushes over me. It was a joke. Just some stupid joke, and I was the punch line.

I feel like a proper twat.

'Alright, very funny,' I say, turning to go over to my bike. I feel my cheeks burn as they flush red. 'Good luck with that business plan.'

I don't bother looking back at him. I lift the bike onto my shoulder and head for the exit, a little wobbly on my feet. The vapour from his pipe is making me light-headed, or something. I lurch out the door and stumble down the stairs to the lyrical sound of his giddy laughter.

I'm not sure why, but I always seem to end up lost when I go to the Northern Quarter.

It's not like it's even that big, really. Just a few streets crisscrossing each other from Shudehill to Port Street.

Like today, it's somehow taken half an hour of wheeling around to get to this bar I've been looking for. Pay for your time not for your beer, or something.

It's just stopped raining, so I lock the bike up outside and head in. It's a pretty nice space. Got that kind of Scandinavian minimalism going on that seems to be popular at the moment.

I'm just about to head for the bar when some hipster-looking guy appears in front of me. He's got that kind of long hair with the shaved sides, tied back in a bun, cracking beard. Really blue eyes.

'Hey, bud, you do me a favour?' he says, already pushing something into my hands. 'That girl over there dropped this. I gotta run. You mind giving it to her?' He points over to a girl at a table by herself in the corner.

'Uh, sure. No worries.'

'Cheers. See you later, bud.' He gives me a wink and slips past. I try to get another look at him before he leaves, but somehow he's disappeared by the time I turn round. Just vanished, into thin air.

I look down at the bundle of cloth. A scarf. Soft blue-green wool, turquoise I guess you'd call it, knitted into ca-bles with tassels at its ends.

The girl he pointed out is sat staring off into space, kind of zoned out. I feel weird just going over, but then I've sort of obligated myself by taking the scarf.

'Uh, hey,' I say, leaning towards her eye line and wav-ing. 'Sorry to bother you.' She looks up.

'Hi.'

'Hey, sorry. Some guy gave me this, said you dropped it.'

'Oh! I didn't even realise I'd lost it.' She takes the scarf, and wraps it round her neck. 'Ah, thanks so much. I'd be gutted if I'd lost this.'

'No problem. Hey, cool comic.' I say, noticing the glossy book laid out in front of her.

'Yeah, it's pretty awesome,' she says. 'Really great art style.' She flicks through a few pages of green forests and lakes and knights. 'You into this sort of thing?'

'Yeah, kinda. What's it about, d'you know?'

'Hah, I actually don't. It's all in Finnish, I think.' She twists it round for me to see. 'You want to check it out?'

'Sure.'

'I'm Sam, by the way,' she says as I slide into the seat beside her, holding out her hand. I shake it.

'Alex.

'So, where'd you pick this up?'

'Oh, this guy gave it to me.' She says, flicking her hair out of her eyes. For a moment I'm engulfed in the sweet scent of her perfume, like cherries. 'Kinda hipster-looking guy with a beard. Not sure where he went.'

'He have, like, blue eyes?' I ask. 'Like, really, blue?'

She nods.

'I think that's the same guy who gave me your scarf.' I

glance round to see whether I didn't just miss him. 'So weird, he just disappeared.' I look back at her, and laugh. 'How did he do that?'

She shrugs and flashes me a smile. 'Magic?'

TRAVELLER

Craig Pay

I was eight years old when I first met Traveller. It was an early Saturday morning in June, 1996, Manchester city centre. Corporation Street was already busy with traffic. I was standing at a pedestrian crossing holding my mother's hand. We were waiting for the red man to turn green.

I remember hearing a sharp crack of noise like the air breaking. My ears popped and a woman seemed to fall out of nowhere, landing on her knees in the road right in front of us. She looked about the same age as my mother, with dark hair tied back in a long ponytail, scuffed jeans, a white shirt with the cuffs folded back at the wrists. Behind her, through a gap in the world, I caught a brief glimpse of what was still to come: flames and smoke, the sky full of falling debris. Then the vision was gone, and it was just a busy road again. The woman stood up and looked around. She seemed confused. I heard the squeal of brakes and two loud thumps: one as the bus knocked into her and another as she landed in the road thirty or forty feet away.

We had driven into town that morning for my mother to go shopping. She spent most of the journey explaining how she needed her little boy to be on his best behaviour, that I should stay close and hold her hand. All of these veiled threats were sugar-coated with a series of thin smiles and the promise of a trip to the pick-and-mix at Woolworths. She had been looking forward to this trip all week.

A huddle of people gathered around the woman lying in the road. I wanted to get away but my mother pulled me forwards. 'Just a quick look,' she said.

I remember my mother's hands on my shoulders, grown-ups all around us pushing and shoving, the buzz of their voices, the smell of perfume and sweat. I think I fell over – or perhaps I just wanted to see more, it's all a bit hazy now – I crawled between their legs on my hands and knees.

The woman was lying on her back in the road. Grazes along one side of her face. A split lip. Her clothes were ripped, but I couldn't see any blood. A man turned her onto her side, and her empty eyes stared straight through me. I wanted to look away but I couldn't. Her eyelids flickered. She focused on me, smiled, and said, 'Exactly fifteen years from now—' Then there was another noise like the air splitting and she was gone again.

In the aftermath of what happened later that morning – the police cordons, our evacuation to a car park outside Victoria Station, the distant sound of the IRA bomb as it exploded just after eleven – I guess that the woman who appeared, was knocked down by a bus and then disappeared again was simply forgotten.

I was twenty three and in the second year of a computing degree at UMIST when I met her again. This was 2011, just a few years ago by anyone else's reckoning.

I guess I'd dismissed those strange events of 1996 as nothing more than the vivid imagination of my younger self or perhaps some kind of post-traumatic coping mechanism to seeing the woman's body lying there in the road. But I must have kept the memory of that strange day buried inside me somewhere, and that's why I found myself standing with all those other people on Corporation Street on one sunny Sunday morning in June. Another yearly commemoration for the poor young family that died, the fifteenth anniversary this time. Would the people keep coming back year after year? Perhaps this was the last time?

The street was busy. People and flowers everywhere. A cluster of different clergyman standing next to the now-famous red post-box that survived the explosion even though it was only a few yards away from the truck. The clergymen were taking it in turns to address the crowd.

I tried to get my bearings, find the same spot where I'd been standing all those years ago. I checked the time on my phone. Waited. Nothing. I listened to the murmur of the crowd. Someone arguing in the distance prompted a few people around me to glance at one another and frown. Perhaps I had imagined it after all?

The shouting was getting closer. Then the crowd parted and a woman appeared: the same dark hair in a long ponytail, white shirt ripped and smeared in blood. She shrugged away a man's hand from her shoulder. He had been saying something about a hospital.

'I'll look after her.' My own words, spoken before I'd even realised I had opened my mouth.

I reached out to take her arm.

She pushed me away. 'Get off!' Then she actually seemed to see me for the first time. She hesitated. Smiled.

'It's fine,' I said to her. 'I remember you.'

'I know,' she said. 'You waited? All this time?'

'Well… I came back.'

She rubbed her fingers across her forehead. 'Yeah, of course.' She sniffed. Grimaced.

'You do need a hospital,' I told her.

'I'm fine. I heal quickly.' She pushed past me into the crowd, heading away towards the Corn Exchange, the old Victorian yellow-stone building over at Exchange Square.

How could I not follow? I caught up with her at the Wheel. She was standing there, looking up at it.

'I've been here before,' she said. 'But this is new. Has it been here long?'

'A few years. I dunno.' I removed my jacket and offered it to her. 'Here, take this.'

'What a gentleman.'

'No, it's just…' I nodded at her ripped shirt streaked in blood. 'People are staring.'

She took the jacket. Shrugged it on. 'Better?'

I nodded. 'Well, you still look like you've been in a fight.'

She laughed. Grimaced again. 'I've been in plenty of those over the years. Don't worry. I'm tough.'

Silence for a moment.

'Fifteen years,' I said. 'Why that long?'

'What?'

'Fifteen years… You came back here, or… or something. I don't get it. You haven't changed.'

'That's as far as I can go,' she said. 'One hop at a time. A little more actually.'

'I understand.'

'No,' she said. 'You don't understand anything at all. But you will.'

She needed a place to stay and she didn't have any money

so I volunteered my hovel of a flat in Levenshulme without thinking that she would actually accept, which she did, of course. She said money wouldn't be a problem for long. She'd soon have her own place. Pay me back anything she owed.

I said, 'But I haven't given you anything yet.'

She didn't say anything to that.

We grabbed the train. I paid for her ticket. Sitting there as the carriage rocked back and forth, I told her my name. When she told me hers, I said, 'Traveller? What kind of a name is that?'

'Well, it isn't the name I was born with, but it makes a lot more sense to me now. I'm not the same person I was when I set out.'

Which actually made no sense at all.

'I can move in time,' she said. 'Fifteen years either way with each hop.'

I gave her some kind of noncommittal response, then I asked, 'What about going backwards?'

'Sure.'

I didn't believe her of course. 'But that would mean you could change things. How would that even work?'

She leaned forwards in her seat. 'You want to know if I could go back and kill Hitler? My grandfather? Myself? Change history? What about paradoxes? That kind of thing, right?'

'I guess so.'

She sat back again. 'I can do whatever I like but there isn't much point because it doesn't affect anyone else.'

'But you can help a lot of people. Warn them about all the bad things that are going to happen.' Straight away I was thinking about a dozen different manmade and natural disasters: tsunamis and earthquakes, planes flying into buildings.

She shook her head. 'It doesn't work like that. Anyway, even given how horrific one sequence of events might be, how do you know that there isn't something worse that might happen instead if something changed? Do you know anything about relativity?'

'Special or general?'

'It doesn't matter, they're both off the mark. You understand how the universe looks different depending upon where a person is or how fast they're moving?'

I nodded.

'Time,' she said, 'is just like that.'

After a moment, I said, 'I still don't understand.'

She sighed. 'The universe isn't one long temporal continuum. It's an infinite number of physical locations, each one with an infinite number of points in time. If I go back and make a change I'm just embarking upon another variation through the many that exist in parallel. You're travelling and changing time right now with every decision you make, with every word you speak, right down to the decay of individual atoms in your body, altering the course of future history each fraction of a second but only in relation to your own experience.' She shrugged. 'As soon as you go back you change the future. You can't help it. Butterfly effect. But you only change the future for yourself and anyone else in your immediate frame of reference, not anyone you leave behind in another future. Now do you get it?'

'I... I think... No, not really.'

'You will, one day.' She rubbed a finger and thumb along the bridge of her nose and frowned.

'You look tired,' I said.

She laughed. 'I could sleep for a month.'

'What's your real name? The one you were born with?' The train was slowing. We were coming into Levenshulme station.

She shook her head. 'Nice try, but no, not yet. Too soon.'

In my flat, she said she needed a shower. I wasn't sure what to say.

'You always look cute,' she said, 'when you're not sure what's going on.'

Which seemed to be most of the time lately. I sat there on the edge of my bed listening to the sound of her in the shower.

There was a certain inevitability in the events that followed, and later, as we lay together naked on the bed, with our arms and legs wrapped about one another, I looked at her body: not a scratch from the bus.

I asked her, 'How old are you?' But she was already asleep.

'I hope it was okay,' she said, 'borrowing some of your clothes.'

Three days since we met and we were sitting in some swanky wine bar on the edge of the Northern Quarter near the Shudehill tram stop. We had two bottles of expensive beer sitting on the table between us. She had paid for the drinks using a new credit card which she was still holding, balanced between her thumb and her middle finger, twirling it end over end with her index finger. She was wearing my favourite *Flash* hoody. It looked a hell of a lot better on her than it ever had done on me.

'Sure,' I said.

'I'll buy some more this afternoon. Want anything?'

'How did you manage to get that so quickly?' I nodded at the card.

'You get good at this sort of thing after a while.' She tried to smile but it flickered and died on her lips. 'You have to.'

'Why don't you stay?' The words were out before I'd even thought about their importance or how they sounded like: 'Stay with me because I'd like this to become a more permanent thing.'

She stopped her credit card twiddling. 'I'd really like that.' She looked more serious, tired again. 'But I can only stay for so long. I'm sorry.'

I picked up my beer from the table. Put it back down again without drinking any of it. 'It's fine.'

'No, you see—'

'It must be pretty cool, zipping around all over the place.'

She shook her head. 'I always struggle with this part… I can't… It won't let me.' She stared at me for a while with her head tilted to one side. There was something in her eyes that I found disconcerting. Fear? Resignation?

'There's something inside me,' she said. 'That's how this works, a symbiote, biological but engineered. That's how I travel and it keeps me alive. Heals me.' Which would explain the bus if any of this was real. 'It gathers potential energy, like a battery, but after a while, well, I have no choice. It will throw me away from here, forwards or backwards, some random amount of time.'

I nodded. 'You could take me with you.'

Her shoulders sagged. 'This again.'

'What?'

'There's only one symbiote. You know that. It's me or

you.' She paused, looked panicked. 'What I meant to say—'

'Me or you? So there's a choice?' I stared at her. 'And you said "I always struggle with this..."' My skin started to crawl. 'Have we done this all before?' I looked around the bar. Back to her. 'How many times have we sat in a place like this?'

She didn't say anything, but I had my answer. I stood up and was out of the bar before I even realised what I was doing. I could hear her calling after me. Outside, dusk was falling. The sky overhead was streaked in Monet pinks and blues. Red-brick, three-storey buildings lined the street on either side. Narrow pavements. I carried on walking. Stopped after a while next to a low, multi-story car park. Nearby, the statue of a metal broom stood upright on a blocky, stone pedestal.

'You always want the same thing.' Her voice was behind me.

I turned around to face her.

'You want to take the symbiote to save me the pain of travelling.' She stepped forwards and took my hand. 'I can't do that to you. All those places and people, each time slightly different. Finding someone you really care about, only to be thrown away and when you come back they're gone. Travelling again and again, until you eventually find them. I always offer to stay with you for a month and you ask for two, but we never make it past six weeks because you know what's coming. We argue. I decide to leave anyway.'

'Perhaps this time you should let me take it?'

She said nothing.

'What's your name? Your real name.'

'Rebekkah with two K's.'

'Well, Rebekkah with two K's, I think I'm starting to understand.'

'Yes,' she said. 'It'll be bumpy travelling the first time, painful. You will end up in a different physical place to the one you left. You won't be able to control it. The first few times it will take you wherever it wants to go.'

We were back in my gloomy flat. She never did get another place. The summer weeks had slipped away between us. We did start to argue near the end, just as she said we would.

I could feel the symbiote crawling inside me, feathering its way into every muscle, every nerve and synapse. The exchange had been simple enough, the touching of hands and a look on concentration on her face, then the rush of heat and pain through the palm of my hand. I could already feel it pulling, wanting to travel.

'You have a new name,' she said. 'You're Traveller now, not the person you were.'

We kissed. Then she was gone, or rather I was gone. I found myself standing in a once-familiar place surrounded by people: Corporation Street.

I pushed through to the kerbside. Looked either way. Cars and buses. Old number plates. The smell of cigarette smoke. Somewhere in the distance I could the dull stutter of a heavy bassline from a high-street store: *Don't Stop Movin'* by some group whose name I couldn't remember. I could fix this. Was I too late?

'Excuse me,' I said to a nearby elderly man. 'Do you have the time?'

He frowned. Raised up his hand to peer at his watch. But I was already looking across the road to a young woman standing there at the kerb. She was holding the hand of a young boy by her side.

'It's just after nine,' the elderly man said.

'I know.' I looked at him again. Apologised. He muttered something under his breath about wasting his time. I thanked him but he was already walking away.

I stepped out into the road holding up my hands to the cars. The squeal of brakes. A horn sounded. I carried on walking. I could feel the symbiote twitching inside me as if it could sense the future shifting and changing with every step.

I saw the bus approaching further along Corporation Street. I stood my ground. Held up my hands. With a loud hiss of airbrakes, the bus pulled up. The driver was shaking his fist, mouthing something. Then the air snapped. My ears popped. Rebekkah appeared in front of me, kneeling on the tarmac.

She stood up. Looked around, confused. Then she smiled as she saw me. 'Two symbiotes?' she said. 'How did you control it to bring you here?'

'I didn't,' I said. 'It wanted to come.'

We grabbed each other's hand. Her grip was almost painfully tight. We pushed away into the crowd.

The cordons were up within the hour. The sound of police sirens in the distance. Someone shouting through a megaphone. Too late to do anything about the bomb.

We allowed ourselves to be swept along, heading towards the car park outside Victoria Station.

I still don't know what we did. Something subtle that expanded out. The flap of a butterfly's wings that became a thunder clap, rippling through all of the possible futures from that immediate point. Maybe it was the old man that I asked for the time? Perhaps he ended up inside Marks and Spencer and found the young family huddled there, hiding, and helped to guide them out? The bomb went off as usual just after eleven. This time, no fatalities.

Does any of this matter? Or was Rebekkah right all along? In all of the other parallels the young family still die, don't they? Travelling through time seems like a selfish business. The only person to gain any benefit is the traveller. A handful of lives saved against all those lost in the infinite number of other parallels? Well, I do feel as if I've made a difference, even if it's only a small one.

A month later, I was holding Rebekkah's hand as we prepared for our first attempted trip together. We had no idea whether this would work or not. We kissed, perhaps for one last time.

Then we closed our eyes and travelled.

UNTIL FURTHER NOTICE

Gerda Pickin

The museum will probably have to stay closed for quite some time now. The media are blaming terrorists, or neo-Nazis, although the CCTV footage would put paid to that if they released it.

Which they won't, because the truth is beyond unbelievable, unless you're someone like me.

I'm a 'security guard' or 'attendant', or whatever name they're calling us now, but I've worked at Manchester Museum a long time, and know the collections better than most of the curators here. That's because I'm not blinded by science. I've studied the ancient beliefs, and I know that you can't mess with these things. Look what happened to Egyptian civilisation once the rot set in.

I know there's no actual connection between the Egyptians and Iron Age Britain. Only some sort of conspiracy theory nut case would try to link them, probably with aliens from outer space as the go-between. It's those people that make me keep my own beliefs to myself. But I think I've been proved right, although what happened to that school party is nothing to gloat about. It's tragic, and it could have been avoided. So easily avoided, if they'd only have listened to me.

The curatorial staff, now, they at least afford you some respect. They've taken practical advice off me loads of times when they were setting up a new display. I'll see where maybe they haven't thought through the flow pattern of the visitors, or just how the lighting sits.

'You know the footfall patterns better than we do, Mike. Good call.' And they'd change something round, alter the ceiling spots, realign a case.

No, the curatorial staff have their areas of expertise, and they aren't afraid to say that there's things I might be better placed to judge.

Unfortunately, it wasn't the same for those student interns. They think because they've had three lectures on 'antiquity' and one on 'theming your exhibition for a modern audience' that they know best. Pity they've had to learn the hard way, the hardest way imaginable.

I did try to tell them.

There are things that your instinct tells you are wrong. Two notes next to each other on the scale played at the same time sounds jangly and irritating. Orange and green side by side make your eyes hurt if you look too long. Vinegar and chocolate together triggers your gag reflex. These are things your instinct will tell you shouldn't be combined.

Beyond those sorts of things, there are some much subtler 'wrongs'. People whose joints ache when the weather takes a turn for the worse. Lots of you will say 'touch wood', and some actually do it, when you say something that you want to happen but think you're tempting fate by mentioning it out loud. I knew a man who would never own, or even ride in, a green car, citing 'bad luck' as a reason.

Then there are the things that are lost to most of western civilisation today. The things that ancient peoples made sacrifices to try and prevent. The idols they decked with gifts and expensive oils and prostrated themselves before. Modern man puts those actions down to ignorance, scoffs at those beliefs. But look what happened to those ancient peoples when they let things slide. Egyptians, Mayans, Incas, Easter Islanders, Romans; there are lots of examples in history and prehistory if you bother to look.

But I digress. Lindow Man, who was discovered in a peat marsh near here, is a bog body 2000 years old who now belongs to the British Museum, but every now and then they let him come home to Manchester, and we display him with pride. He's always a big attraction, is 'Pete', and I like to think there's something more benign in his squashed up features when he's back where he belongs. He was a sacrifice of some sort, and it could be that his death saved his community from some Iron Age troubles they were having.

So he was being loaned to us again, and the curator decided to let the interns have a crack at designing and then putting up Pete's display this time.

The four of them met in the 'Green Room' (that's not the official name, but what we insiders know it as) to measure up the space and start planning their 'approach'.

'I think we should make him more relevant,' the only female among them said.

'Terry, how can a crunched-up brown leathery little munchkin be made relevant to anyone other than his long-deceased mother?'

'Terry's right, Will. We want visitors to see the man behind the wizened body. What do you think, Tom?'

'I think we should try to get a really modern, populist angle on it all. Not be constrained by conventional mores of museum display.'

'Okay, Martin. How outside the box are you prepared to go? We need to show some respect, or the academics will slaughter us.' It was obvious to me that this Will character actually wanted a job here after his internship, and didn't want to upset the curator by ignoring the tried and tested display policies of the department.

Terry, who already had a job lined up in her uncle's gallery in London (as she mentioned *ad nauseum* in the very limited time I had been forced to spend within earshot of her) was more than happy to rock the boat.

'What if we put together the "celebrities" of the museum? Display them all in one room simultaneously and let the public vote on their favourite?'

'Just which artefacts would count as "celebrities", Miss Know-all?'

Will could see that the others were drawn to the concept, and was making a last ditch attempt to stop them making fools of themselves (and by association, him).

Martin, who as the only local among them was more familiar with our collections, had already worked it out.

'Well, there's Neb-Sanu, for a start.'

'Neb-Sanu?'

'He's this 4000 year old statue that used to be in the Egyptian gallery, and had to be moved to the foyer because he kept turning around without anyone touching him. It was really spooky, there's even a YouTube of him doing it, and it made the news too.'

'I remember. They'd put him in the case and he'd mysteriously change position a little each day. Everyone thought it was some supernatural power until an engineer worked out that the vibrations from the road traffic outside were enough to shift him. Something to do with his base being concave. Or maybe it was convex....'

'Perfect. X-factor meets the X-files!'

'Brilliant.'

'We'll need more than two, though. Martin, anything else in the galleries spring to mind?'

Martin made a show of scratching his head and furrowing his brow before proffering a third 'celeb'.

'Worsley Man. He's another bog body, well, just a head, really. The archaeologists proved that he'd been bludgeoned, garrotted, and then beheaded. He's actually still got one of his eyes, which makes him quite memorable.'

'And creepy. We can add in one of the mummies, they're always popular, and maybe another statue from somewhere, and see which one has the most star quality, according to Joe Public.'

This had to stop.

'You can't do it.'

They all turned to look at me as if one of the doorknobs had suddenly spoken.

'I beg your pardon?' Martin seemed to be insulted that a mere uniformed staff member would dare to venture an opinion. I returned his indignant glare with a cool look of my own.

'You can't put Lindow Man, Worsley Man, and Neb-Sanu together in the same room.'

'Why ever not?' Terry's sarcastic tone set my teeth on edge.

'I imagine that, uh, Mike here,' Will peered at my name badge like some mole blinking in the sunlight, 'has been in the museum long enough to know that objects from different cultures and eras shouldn't be lumped together for the sake of novelty. It will mislead the public and confuse children.'

'But that's the whole point!' Terry was adamant. 'To shake things up, make people view things with new eyes.'

I couldn't help it, I shook my head. I'm sure that only made me seem like some dinosaur who would object to anything new. I tried to keep my voice level.

'Will is right, but it's more than that.' I must stay calm. They needed to believe that I was serious. And rational.

'Those three 'objects', the two bodies who were sacrificed and the statue that was able to move itself, they each have a power that was invested in them by the nature of their making. Both those men died hideous deaths in order to bring about something desperately needed by the living, and Neb-Sanu still has some dormant energy bestowed upon him in antiquity for a purpose we no longer fathom.' Despite my best efforts, I could hear my voice rising in timbre and volume. 'You don't want to bring those three vessels of malign energy into the same room. There's no telling what cataclysm you'll release.'

Each of them stared at me as if I'd pronounced that the world was flat and the moon was constructed of cheese. Martin broke the spell.

'Alien vs. Predator.'

'Godzilla vs. King Kong.'

'Luke Skywalker vs. Darth Vader.'

They all had a good laugh then, but I held my ground and just kept looking at them, calm, composed, sane.

'Thank you for the warning...' Tom sounded sincere. Had I got through? But then he could not keep the smirk from his voice when he added, '...but I think it's a risk we're prepared to take.'

'We could even use it as a strap line for the poster: 'Caution, Ancient Powers at work here. Who dares to cross the threshold?'

'No, you can't have celebrities and supernatural together, it won't work. It's either one or the other.'

'You're right. Keep it simple, like most of the punters, and make it a popularity contest.' They turned their backs on me and continued planning, the silly old attendant already forgotten.

So you see, I did try.

They put the cases in a triangle, another mistake, as it only served to enhance the combined powers. Needless to say, I had myself rostered well away from the Green Room.

Hundreds of ballot sheets were produced, and an online voting system was created by the IT staff, which could give an electronic tally. The idea was to add this to the ballot box numbers (which, incidentally, they presumed would be counted by us attendants, the cheek) to determine the 'winner'.

To make it something of An Event, they had decided that all four of them would personally conduct the Grand Unveiling, and I was saddened to discover that they had chosen one of the local primary schools to be the very first visitors when the display opened on Monday morning.

The rest is history. It made the national news, of course, with talks of terrorists and the like, but there will be no YouTube posting of the footage, not this time.

God knows when we'll be able to open the museum again.

WRATH AND DUTY

Rob Prescott

Even from outside the station the whine of the high-speed approach was audible, cutting through the low rumble of the traffic thrusters and combustibles. On the board, one string of red letters changed to green.

'That'll be him,' McAlistair said. She stood, glancing over to her partner, French. 'Come on, pick up your feet. Let's go give this Aziz guy a proper Manchester welcome.'

'Alright,' French replied. She pulled her hood back up to cross the acid-rain streaked street between the shelter and the station. 'You hold him down and I'll knock his teeth out.'

Executive Inspector Aziz sat in the back of the hovercraft as French programmed in the destination. 'Charming man, they've sent us,' she said as she worked.

McAlistair didn't reply. She looked back at Aziz, who was reading the graffiti on the station walls with the expression of an anthropologist contemplating cave paintings. She glanced to the wall, where newer political slogans jockeyed for position with gang tags and crudely drawn vulgarity. AUTONOMY FOR THE NORTH, one slogan read. STOP THE WARS, another. The largest simply read SECEDE! and was placed over a stencilled image of a broken crown.

'You know who he's gonna blame, too, right?' French said, looking up from the navigation computer. When McAlistair didn't reply she snorted. 'Doesn't matter if it's the Yard, Thames House, Westminster... London always blames the secessionists.'

'They're still suspects,' McAlistair said.

'So are the fucking Scots.'

McAlistair shrugged. 'So's half the bloody world.'

'So, maybe they shouldn't just assume—'

'Look,' McAlistair turned from the window back to French. The younger woman's face was set firm and slightly flush. 'We're running this case, so far, he's advising. We don't assume, right?'

French's jaw softened, almost imperceptibly. 'Right.'

'Right. So let's solve this thing. Are we bloody moving or what?'

'Sure,' French said, and hit the start up on the hovercraft. It thrummed into life and lifted the few feet above the pockmarked road.

The intercom buzzed and Aziz's voice came through. 'There's no signal back here. I need the details on the case.'

'Sorry about that, sir,' McAlistair said. 'Rain blocks the connection most of the time. All we have so far is an unattributed bomb threat to the spaceport.'

'I know that,' he said, his voiced tinged with impatience.

McAlistair continued without acknowledging him. 'Says that at 3am tomorrow terminal seven will be hit unless the government reverses the decision to move all services to the Central South-Midlands Megaport.'

'Wonderfully self-defeating,' Aziz said. 'How do these

people imagine the spaceport will function if they blow it up?'

'Some people lash out when they're pissed off,' French said. 'Sir.'

Aziz cleared his throat. McAlistair gave French a look. She shrugged, focused again on the traffic. 'The threat doesn't fit the behavioural templates of any known terror suspects and it's vague enough to come from any of a dozen active organisations in the city.'

'I had assumed you would have narrowed it down some more than that, Inspector.'

McAlistair sighed. 'The CSM Megaport is a bit of a touchy subject for a lot of folk round here,' she said. 'As well as the loss to the city, rumour is it could overshadow the Scottish hub and be used as a launchpad for further military ops in Ireland or Europe. So that's the anti-war groups, any of a dozen Irish groups, Scots Intelligence, Euro-Block agents as well as the usual Jihadi or anarchist organisations all with potential motivation.'

'And your local home-grown secessionists,' Aziz added.

'There's no evidence of any secessionist link to terror-ism,' French said. 'Whatever your London lot might keep saying.'

'None *proven*,' Aziz said.

'Eyes on the road,' McAlistair said.

French turned to argue with her, but the expression on McAlistair's face killed her response. 'Aye, boss,' she said, turning back to the traffic, her jaw set tight.

'Quite,' Aziz said.

'The terminal's been closed, traffic diverted and a full evacuation, bomb squad are combing through it now. We've still got four hours.'

'Stopping the explosion is secondary to apprehending those responsible for this,' Aziz said.

French turned her head slowly towards McAlistair.

'Eyes. Road,' McAlistair said.

She shifted in her seat to look back at Aziz. 'Sir, all due respect, but that bomb goes off the damage—'

'Will be contained,' he said. 'Contained, what's more, in a site scheduled for demolition within the year. It simply accelerates the timeframe.'

McAlistair chewed the words around in her mouth. 'Sir, we don't even know what kind of bomb—'

'I believe I've made my point,' Aziz said. 'Ah, finally, some reception.' He clicked off the intercom.

McAlistair shifted back in her seat. She could hear French seething. 'Look—'

'Don't want to hear it, boss.'

'Four hours. They'll find the bomb. We'll find the suspect. Just got to put up with this guy a few hours more.'

'A few hours. Right. But after that, you'll forgive me if I shoot him, right?'

McAlistair gave French a look. She glanced back, suppressing a grin. 'Sure, just get in line.'

The streets leading to the spaceport were thronged with protesters, held back behind barricades manned by a mix of heavily armed riot police and soldiers. The roads, thankfully, were kept open. Some effort had been made to drive the crowds back to a safe distance but from what McAlistair could see it had been met with resistance. Four ambulances passed them in the other direction, sirens and lights blaring.

A masked riot control officer waved their vehicle through, directing it to the small departures entrance, dwarfed by the eight-story cargo terminal that had grown up around and beside it.

'Christ,' French muttered as she released control to the autopilot for parking. 'This is a right shit-storm.'

McAlistair shrugged in agreement. She glanced over her shoulder at Aziz who was lost in his datapad and oblivious to the scene outside. She rapped on the window separating them.

'Hmm?' he said through the intercom.

'We're here, sir.'

'Good.'

The intercom clicked off.

Stepping out of the hovercraft, smoke and tear gas was heavy in the air. McAlistair felt her eyes start to sting almost immediately. The chants of the demonstrators fused together into a drone that rose and fell like a wave, rendering unintelligible the police loudspeaker that opposed it.

Aziz, to his credit, did not seem in the slightest affected by the gas in the air.

'This is Terminal Seven,' McAlistair said, her voice straining over the noise as well as the thick air. 'Mostly just cargo and penal ships these—'

'Hardly relevant,' Aziz cut in. 'I believe we have work to do?'

'Right,' French said. 'Bomb squad are already combing through the terminal. We should get in there.'

'Whatever for?' Aziz asked.

'It's not our job,' McAlistair said. 'Bomb squad have the training.'

'Exactly,' Aziz said.

'That said,' McAlistair continued, 'any evidence they

turn up is relevant.'

'I'm not so sure that anything your bomb squad can dig out while combing for explosives will count as evidence.'

McAlistair bit back her first response. 'Sir, all due respect, but the bomb itself is evidence. If we can get our hands on it we can find out who built it, how it got here, track its whole supply chain to the port. We could get enough on whichever group planted it to crack their operation.'

'Or we could get nothing,' Aziz said. His gaze wandered over to the crowds away from McAlistair. 'We need to round up suspects, whoever you think the ringleaders are of this lot, your local secessionists, whatever else you have. Interrogation of suspects is how terrorist organisations are broken, Inspector, not scavenger hunts.'

McAlistair searched for a response but couldn't find one.

'Are you fucking kidding?' French said, stepping forward until Aziz was forced to look at her.

'Excuse me?'

'Are you even fucking police? There's a bomb right there, in that building, which you want to ignore to go rough up some locals?'

'French,' McAlistair said, 'find the officer in command of crowd control – we'll need to liaise.'

'We need to be in the fucking terminal!'

'Not right now, we don't.' McAlistair turned to face French. She saw the younger woman bite her tongue and, after a moment just long enough to give McAlistair doubt, back down.

'Aye, boss,' French said. She stalked away across the terminal approach road.

'She's a problem,' Aziz said.

'I can handle her.'

'Of course I'd heard of the discipline problems being faced by our northern counterparts, nonetheless...' he trailed off.

'She's good police. Bit tightly sprung right now is all. Give her a task and she'll get it done.'

'So will a dog, Inspector.'

'That's hardly fair, sir.'

McAlistair held Aziz's stare as a hint of a smirk showed on his lips. She turned away, trying to compose herself. Was he trying to antagonise her?

'If you're quite calmed down,' Aziz said, 'we need to start rounding up our suspects.'

McAlistair turned back to face him.

'Look,' she said, 'I'm trying to be balanced and facilitate relations and all the rest of that bollocks but you're really not making it easy for me.'

Aziz briefly looked taken aback. The smirk returned as he opened his mouth to retort.

Then the terminal exploded.

Slowly the dull ringing in her ears gave way to other noises. Shifting rubble. Gunfire. Screaming.

McAlistair picked herself up, leaning on the side of the hovercraft. She looked up.

Half of the cargo terminal wall had collapsed outwards, fire-lit smoke pouring out of the wound. The passenger entrance, where their hovercraft had parked, seemed undamaged. Lucky.

French. Aziz. McAlistair couldn't see either of them. Shakily she stood up.

Aziz was standing to the rear of the vehicle, speaking into his headset while brushing dust from his suit. He looked over to her as she stood but offered no other acknowledgement.

The spaceport approach was a scene of chaos. The protesters had scattered, but the police line was broken as well. Again, McAlistair heard bursts of gunfire, a few streets distant. Some idiot local command must have ordered the attack. She saw French running back over towards the hovercraft and raised a hand.

'Shit, boss, you're okay?' French said as she reached her. 'The whole thing's gone to shit, command ordered the streets clear right after the bomb went off, fucking chaos out there.'

'I'm alright,' McAlistair said. She ran her hand over her forehead. It came away bloody. 'What do we know?' she said.

'Bomb went off three hours early,' French said. 'No warning, no nothing. Either deliberate misinformation from the call or something went wrong.'

'Anything from bomb squad?'

'No. Shit! They're still in there, boss, we gotta—'

'Slow down, we're not search and rescue. They'll be on the way.'

'But, boss—'

'Facts, right? That's what we need, not to get stuck down digging in the rubble.'

'Well put, Inspector,' Aziz said, walking around to join them. French stiffened. 'Local command seem to have things under control here for now.' He waved his arm in the direction of the gunfire for emphasis. 'So I suggest we retire to the on-site HQ to await the fruits of their labours.'

'The fuck does that mean?' French said. McAlistair didn't bother to correct her insubordination.

Aziz sighed, laboriously. 'We need suspects to interrogate,' he said, slowly. 'They will bring them to us while clearing the streets.'

'Still just want to rough up the locals?' French said. 'The bomb went off, we failed.'

'Not at all,' Aziz replied. 'For one thing it is far easier to convict a bomber who has bombed something that one who merely tried. We'll likely be able to get the death penalty for this, especially if any inside were killed.' Aziz turned and began heading towards the mobile command centre, set up further down the spaceport approach.

French stepped forward to follow him, but McAlistair intercepted her and grabbed her arm. 'Easy, not worth it,' she said. 'Not least 'cause I think he's just trying to rile you up now.'

'Yeah, well it's fucking working, Boss,' she replied.

McAlistair released her grip. 'He's not wrong about everything,' McAlistair said. 'The bomb's gone off, we need to find out who, how and why. Same job as before, just gotta focus.'

'Focus. Right.'

'What's your instinct? Think the call was a set up? The bomb just shoddy? Or maybe bomb-squad tripped it?'

French sighed. 'Okay,' she said. 'I get it. Calm me down with some nice logical thinking. Fine. Right, well first up I don't think bomb-squad screwed up. If they'd have found something they'd have called it in before they started to mess about with it, and they didn't.'

'My thoughts as well.'

'Shoddily made bombs don't end up in spaceports. Security here is tight, especially in the cargo area. No group that could get a bomb in there is amateurish enough to do so with a half-baked effort.'

'So that just leaves a set up.'

'Pretty much.'

French rummaged in her coat pockets for something, pulled out a pack of cigarettes and lit one up.

'Didn't you quit?'

'Yup. Want one?'

'Not funny. All right, let's focus. If it's a set-up, who? And why? What do we know?'

French took a drag of the cigarette while watching across the spaceport approach. McAlistair followed her gaze to Aziz entering the mobile command unit.

'Maybe this is crazy, boss, but hear me out.'

'It's crazy.'

'But hear me out?'

McAlistair sighed.

'I mean, think about it? Who kept us from going into the terminal? Who had no interest in evidence? I mean come on, who wanted to investigate this case without even looking at the fucking crime scene?'

'Look, he didn't even get into town until an hour ago.'

'Tell me that's not worth looking into.'

'It's not worth looking into.'

'Tell me it's not worth thinking about for five seconds!'

'Alright,' McAlistair turned back to French. 'Alright, let's say you've cracked it, Aziz is a plant sent by his shadowy London overlords to make sure that we don't suspect them of blowing up the spaceport and instead lock up some local knuckleheads thus sweeping the whole thing under the carpet. Why? Give me a motive.'

'I got two,' French said, with a grin. 'First, it discredits the secessionists. London's been itching to have something to pin on them for years and Aziz made no secret of who he wants to take the fall for this. Second, they get to push through the spaceport closure without any opposition. I mean, who's gonna protest the closure of a bombed terminal?' French flicked the half-finished cigarette away with a triumphant flourish. 'Tell me that doesn't make sense, boss?'

McAlistair sighed. 'It doesn't make sense. I hate to say it but if you take that half-baked conspiracy theory upstairs they'll take your badge. It's crazy. London doesn't need to bomb the spaceport to push through the closure, they just need to do what they were already doing.'

'Which is?'

'Ignore the protests and do it anyway. Come on, let's head over to the command post and see what's going on.'

As McAlistair and French approached the mobile command post, a group of armoured riot police shepherded a line of cuffed protesters along. McAlistair counted twenty in that group alone.

'Cells are gonna be bursting tonight,' French muttered.

McAlistair didn't respond.

Aziz exited the trailer accompanied by a uniformed military officer. They strode across to meet them. 'There are already around one hundred protesters in custody,' Aziz said. 'Military intelligence will identify the leaders and then we, or rather I, shall conduct the interviews.'

'Interviews?' French muttered.

'Military intelligence seems a bit severe, sir,' McAlistair said. 'Surely we should be handling this ourselves?'

'The Yard disagrees. After your handling of events up to now,' he indicated the burning terminal behind them with a nod of his head, 'you should feel lucky to still be involved.'

'Very, sir,' French said.

'Frankly this whole affair has been a debacle,' Aziz said. 'The Yard is already concerned about secessionist sympathy within the local police ranks, thus the military will be overseeing from now on.'

'Overseeing what?' McAlistair asked.

'You, Inspector. Given the scale of this movement that you've allowed to grow up in what some still laughable refer to as our "second city" the military will be directly overseeing the Greater Manchester Police until further notice.'

'You can't be serious, sir,' McAlistair said. She felt a tightness in her chest beyond that already caused by the smoke in the air. 'You're talking about martial law.'

'Terrorist attacks on this scale cannot be ignored.'

'Hold up a second,' French said. 'You don't even know that it was the secessionists – where's the evidence? You've got to have some kind of proof, or something, to—'

'No, I don't, Inspector.' Aziz held McAlistair's stare as he spoke over French. 'Your department is under investigation, immediate effect. You'll continue to assist me for now, pending a full review of which local officers can be trusted.'

'This is a fucking joke!'

'Save your breath,' McAlistair said. 'It's out of our hands.'

An hour later, McAlistair and French sat in the observation area to the interrogation room in the spaceport police station. A man in his early twenties was shackled to the table, separated from them by a one-way mirror.

'This is wrong, boss, so fucking wrong,' French said.

'I know.'

'We've gotta, I don't know, we can't just sit on our arses! They're taking over – it's a fucking occupation.'

French rummaged in her pockets and produced her cigarettes.

'You can't smoke in here,' McAlistair said.

'Want one?'

McAlistair sighed. Things had spiralled fast. 'Fuck it.' She turned in her seat and took the offered smoke, ignoring French's grin.

'Knew I'd break you. Even if it did take six years.'

'Yeah, you got me,' McAlistair said, leaning forward for French to light the cigarette.

'Here's trouble,' French said, nodding towards the window of the interrogation room.

Aziz entered the room behind the shackled suspect. 'Peter Byrne,' he said. His voice was distorted by the speakers. 'Twenty-three. Music student. Dropped out. Unemployed. No fixed abode. And now here you are. Quite the downward trajectory, Mr Byrne.'

The young man looked up. He was handsome, in a scruffy sort of way, though the large purple bruise around his eye and split lip spoiled the effect somewhat. 'Fuck you, man. I want a lawyer.'

'You don't have a lawyer, Mr Byrne. Lawyers cost money, and I don't think you have much to your name right now.'

'Aren't you supposed to, like, provide, or something?'

'I think the state is quite done subsidising your pathetic existence, don't you?'

'What?'

French leaned forward. 'He's not allowing him a lawyer? How's he gonna get anything? The courts will throw him right out.'

'Martial law,' McAlistair said, exhaling a near-perfect smoke ring – six years, maybe, but some skills you don't ever seem to forget. 'Old rules don't apply.'

'Shit.'

'Yeah.'

'What's your position in the secessionist movement, Mr Byrne?' Aziz asked, pacing slowly around the table.

'I don't have a 'position', and I'm not answering your questions until I get my lawyer, or, I don't know, a phone call or something?'

'A phone call? And who would you call?'

'That's... it's private, innit?'

'Your privacy was lost when you chose to affiliate yourself with a terrorist organisation.'

'Speak fucking English, man.'

French chuckled.

'You seem to be labouring under the pretension that you have rights, that you should be treated as a member of society. You don't. You lost that when you turned your back on us, and when you chose instead to give your loyalty to those who would tear down that society whose rules you now demand returned.'

'Turned my back on society? Fuck you, man. Your fucking society turned its back on me and mine long ago, only thing the government's good for round here is screwing you over.'

'So you lashed out, joined a group promising to look after you, your local interests, and then things turned violent.'

'Violence is the only thing you fuckers understand!'

Byrne was becoming increasingly animated, spinning in his chair trying to keep facing Aziz as he paced around him.

'Hmm,' McAlistair said. 'Aziz is actually not bad at this.'

'Just 'cause he made the guy mad, I don't know...' French trailed off.

'It's all just, you know, sucking the wealth and the life out of the rest of country so you can keep, you know, running shit from your fucking tower or whatever,' Byrne continued.

'Ah yes,' Aziz replied, 'I think I actually read that pamphlet. Not, I'm assuming, one of yours.'

'I don't write shit.'

'No, of course not. But you did read them, didn't you?'

'Man, everyone's read 'em. They're all over.'

McAlistair winced as Byrne spoke. She could see the line Aziz was pursuing. She stubbed out the cigarette. Her chest was already starting to ache.

'Stupid kid,' French said.

'Peter Byrne,' Aziz said, stopping his predatory circling and standing in front of him. 'You will be charged with the possession and distribution of terrorist propaganda.'

McAlistair wondered what Aziz and his Yard colleagues would make of the secessionist literature frequently adorning the station bulletin board. Nothing good, for sure.

'What?'

'Promoting terrorist organisations is a very serious crime. You can expect to spend at least a decade behind bars, if not more.'

'You're fucking kidding, right? Terrorist?'

'I am most certainly not kidding, Mr Byrne. Of course, should you show repentance for your crimes by aiding in our current investigation, I could make things look more favourable for you.'

'Hold on, man, this is going way too fucking fast. You

gotta let me talk to someone, please.'

'I'm letting you talk to me,' Aziz said. He leant forward over the table in what McAlistair assumed was supposed to be a sympathetic pose.

'Christ, he's got him,' French said.

'Alright, look, let's go slow, alright?' Byrne said.

Aziz straightened his back again. 'Time is of the essence. If you want to save yourself, tell me what you know.'

'Who the fuck even talks like that?' French muttered.

'There's this place, right?' Byrne began. 'I never went there, but I heard about it, right?'

'Spare me your denials and get to the point,' Aziz said.

'Right. Look, this place, they got printers and shit in the basement, routers and datahubs, all that shit, it's not one of the meeting houses, fucking idiot local cops don't know shit about it, trust me on that.'

'Thanks, kid,' McAlistair muttered.

'It's close, right, Wythenshawe, near the flood walls, some old estate, I can take you—'

'You most certainly cannot.'

'I... alright. I can show you, right? On a map.'

Byrne didn't lie. By the time French pulled the hovercraft in at the address he'd given it was already surrounded by a cordon of riot police, called in in advance by Aziz as they were on route. Behind the police a group of military types seemed to be in charge.

Getting out of the hovercraft McAlistair looked south. The column of black smoke rose against the dull grey dawn sky from the spaceport several miles at least. She wondered if the clean-up would outlast the fallout, physical or political.

'Gentlemen,' Aziz said, approaching the soldiers. 'Situation, please.'

'At least twenty inside, armed, some pot-shots already fired. We've secured the perimeter. Surrounding buildings have been evacuated. We are awaiting further orders.'

French got out of the hovercraft and walked around to McAlistair. 'You know this place?' she asked.

'Nah. The kid was right, it isn't on any of our safe house lists. Don't know how though – if half of what he said was right, it should have been flagged months back.'

'You don't seem too worried?'

'Doesn't seem much point to be anymore.'

McAlistair looked over to her younger colleague, trying to remember if she'd been as driven, as hot-headed, as optimistic, when she was her age. She sighed, feeling the pain in her chest again as she did so. Christ, there were only five years between them anyway.

'We've been pulling resources away from monitoring secessionists for months, boss,' French said. 'After the Quays attack it's all been about the Irish. Not too surprising something slipped through.'

'You call that something?' McAlistair indicated the tower of smoke to the south. 'We fucked up. Maybe Aziz isn't wrong about everything.'

French looked over to where Aziz was conferring with the soldiers. Her expression shifted. 'I don't know about that, boss.'

McAlistair gave her a quizzical look but before she could speak French was already striding across the street. 'Hey!' she called out.

Aziz glanced over to her, McAlistair saw his jaw clench. 'Inspector, please wait in the car,' he said.

'You're going to order a full assault? It's a residential

area, you can't—'

'Inspector!' The force of Aziz's shout stopped French in her tracks. He strode towards her. 'Inspector, you will wait in the car, you will do so silently. This matter, this operation, is out of the hands of you and your incompetent, likely corrupt, department.'

French moved to protest, but Aziz was not done.

'You've allowed a local gathering of dissidents to form into a cell to rival any of the foreign groups already running rampant though the north of England, threatening countless lives beyond those already lost in tonight's attack, and now you think to lecture me on what tactics I may or may not use?

'Perhaps you have not been paying attention, Inspector, but we are at war. At home, abroad, and now here. You may dislike my tactics, but given your lack of any alternative you may not question them. You are relieved of duty, effective immediate.'

McAlistair winced as she heard the words. Even from behind she could almost see French crumple inwardly. Aziz turned back to the officers as McAlistair reached her.

'Wait in the car,' she said, giving French a squeeze on the shoulder as she passed her. 'I'll keep an eye on him.'

'Are your men in position, lieutenant?' Aziz asked.

'Sir,' the soldier replied. 'Marksmen have their posts, windows and doors are covered. Riot cops will launch gas then breach, my men will hold the perimeter.'

'Ensure that none escape, lieutenant.'

Aziz turned to see McAlistair. 'Inspector, I think my feelings have been made clear.'

'Aye, sir,' McAlistair replied. 'But I'm still on duty, and last I heard that meant I was to assist.'

Aziz's expression tightened, as though trying to sense

out the trap. After a few seconds he gave up. 'Fine. Keep out of the way.' He turned back to the lieutenant and gave a curt nod.

The soldier allowed a brief grin to cross his face before strapping on the armoured gas mask. He turned back towards the house and raised an arm.

As the soldier's arm fell the riot police opened up with the grenade launchers, firing projectiles through the windows until their magazines were empty. A few shots were fired back from the house, each answered by the high powered rifles from the soldiers positioned in the neighbouring buildings. Smoke and gas poured from the windows of the house. The soldier turned back to Aziz.

'No,' Aziz said, replying to some question given via his earpiece. 'Not yet. Wait.'

McAlistair turned back to the house. She knew the tactic, had seen it in use before in the riots of her youth.

The first figures stumbled out of the door, hands held high. The cordon of riot police shifted in eager anticipation. The first to escape fell to his knees, vomiting from the gas. Almost half a dozen were out now.

'Okay, move in. Subdue all you find,' Aziz said.

'Sir, you've still got maybe fifteen—'

'I know what I'm doing, Inspector.'

McAlistair watched him. For a second she thought she saw the shadow of a doubt cross his face, but then it was gone.

'You don't know what's in there, sir,' she tried again.

Aziz did not respond.

The riot police advanced on the house, stepping past the prone figures who had made it out already. They disappeared into the smoke. McAlistair held her breath. She would have killed for a headset.

She counted the seconds as they passed, tried to picture the progress of the men inside. Entrance hall would be clear, back door probably into a kitchen, clear. Five more seconds, ground floor should be clear. Did the house have a basement? Twenty inside said it should. So they'd be dividing into two squads, one moving up, one down. Onto the stairs now and—

Gunfire erupted from inside the house. McAlistair heard the loud static burst from Aziz's headset as he winced from the shouts of alarm. More gunfire, sustained bursts.

Several shots came from the soldiers behind them, high powered rifles punching through the ancient brickwork.

McAlistair realised what Aziz had done.

'You bastard,' she said.

Aziz looked down at her with a smirk.

'Five armed men were on the first floor. Now there are none. Firing on a police officer is a capital offence.'

'And the police? You're supposed to be one of us, for Christ's sake.'

'I'm not supposed to be anything beyond efficient, Inspector.'

Aziz began walking towards the house. He took a small pair of goggles from his pocket and pulled them on as he did so but made no other accommodation for the gas still filling the structure.

'Shit,' McAlistair said. She took a spare gas mask from the riot police van and followed him inside.

Stepping into the house felt like stepping back in time. The house was much the same as the ones in Longsight she'd grown up in. The bodies by the windows, clouds of tear gas, and the growing sense of inevitability and futility all had changed little in the decades since.

At the foot of the stairs two of the riot police were pulling back a body from the stairs, one of their own. McAlistair didn't need a second glance to know the price he'd paid for Aziz's plan.

She entered the front room, transformed into an arsenal. Boxes of rifles, ammunition, and other weaponry were piled up around the old fireplace, opposite the sofa. Two more riot police pushed past her, one holding the other up. Downstairs, she knew.

The basement stairwell opened up into a large converted room, one that seemed to have been made up by knocking through into the neighbouring houses. The gas hadn't come down here as much.

Five men and three women were on their knees in the centre of the room, riot officers behind them. Two others lay motionless. Aziz stood before them, disinterestedly looking around the room. McAlistair approached him.

'This can't be it,' he muttered.

'You've got maybe a dozen new arrests then,' she said. 'On top of the hundreds pulled in from the street clearances, you think that was worth the lives you've paid?'

'There must be something else here. There must be.'

'He's lost it, boss.'

McAlistair turned around to see French enter the basement.

'French, you shouldn't be in here.'

'I know, I know, I've calmed down, right?'

McAlistair turned back to Aziz. He was pacing around the room now.

'Sir, what are you looking for?' McAlistair said.

He looked up and seemed to regard her for the first

time. 'There has to be something here. Has to be. Why defend this place if there's nothing here of value? There has to be something more.'

'Maybe 'cause it's their home?' French said. 'Maybe 'cause they live here, and you just coming in, crashing around, scares the shit out of them?'

Aziz looked at French for a few seconds. 'No,' he muttered. 'There's something here.'

McAlistair looked over to the other riot police officers, herding the captives upstairs. One gave a shrug, before turning to follow the others.

'It's you, isn't it?' he said, looking at French. 'Running interference, and I think if you hadn't come down here to gloat you might have got away with it.'

'Sir, there's nothing here,' McAlistair said, stepping forward to put herself between them. 'We should move, we can maybe get more useful information from these captives, but only if we move quickly.'

'No, I don't think so,' Aziz said. He looked past McAlistair to French. 'Where is it?'

'Where's what?' French said. McAlistair heard the hint of nervousness in her colleague's voice, and looked over at her.

'French?' she asked.

French took a step backwards. 'You're gonna listen to him, boss? Seriously? After this fucking massacre? After the fucking spaceport?'

They both caught the nervous glance she made towards the drywall. Aziz didn't hesitate. He strode across and, with a force that surprised McAlistair, kicked hard, breaking a chunk of it loose.

'Alright, fucking stop!' French shouted.

McAlistair looked back to her to see her gun in her

hand, pointed at Aziz.

Aziz looked across at French and smiled a quietly condescending smile. 'Inspector, there are thirty five riot police and a squad of armed soldiers right upstairs. I don't think you'll shoot me.' He planted another kick on the drywall, knocking more bricks loose. A hole big enough for a child to pass through was already present.

'One more kick, I swear...' French said, her voice trembling.

'Stand down, officer,' McAlistair said. Her hand rested on the grip of her own weapon, but she didn't draw.

'Bit late for that now, boss.'

'It's never too late. Put the gun away, we can talk about this.'

'I don't think we can, not now.'

'Tell me,' Aziz said, 'when the secessionists recruited you, did they not say it would end up like this? It always does, for people like you, doesn't even matter if they win in the end, those like you are always sacrificed.'

'Fuck you,' French said.

'It doesn't matter if it's your own command or people like me, people like you never live through the wars they start. What will I find behind the wall? The link to the bomb, perhaps?'

Aziz turned to face the drywall again. Above them heavy bootsteps could be heard on the ground floor.

'French, stand down, please,' McAlistair said.

'One more fucking kick...' French mumbled.

Aziz kicked.

The gunshot was loud in the confined basement. The bullet caught Aziz in the back, between the shoulder blades, the exit wound painting the wall in front of him a dark red.

'Shit, boss...'

McAlistair lowered her gun. She could hear the shouts and boots coming from above them already. 'Take me in,' she said.

'Boss...'

'Best be quick about it, or they'll kill us both.'

Aziz half turned back towards them before falling to his knees, blood dribbling from his mouth.

Slowly French aimed her weapon towards McAlistair. 'You know, you promised me I could shoot him,' she said.

'Sorry. I'm a bad person, I know.'

Aziz fell forwards onto his face.

The bootsteps above them had reached the top of the stairs. McAlistair slowly knelt, placing her weapon in front of herself, hands raised behind her head.

'Shit boss, I...'

'Forget about it. Got a smoke?'

WHEN THE SUN IS DEAD

Angus Stewart

There was some chatter about problems in the sky on the radio at first. I was wearing this flowered dress with a black silk inside and short little arms and I'd got flour stains and dough splotched on the tummy area and it was really bothering me because the dress was new, and I'd blogged about it on my channel and I'd promised a follow-up video, and the last thing I'd ever want to do is disappoint my followers. They're a voracious bunch. They've learned to expect so much of me. Like I said, mum had left the radio on and it wasn't really helping. She favours Radio Two, and though I can usually deal with said station, today all the music and patter was being replaced with urgent newsflashes. Big news about the sky, but did I listen? I've never been a listener. I'm a doer, and a speaker–hence this story.

Sometimes, my mum and I can't figure out which one of us was supposed to be the leader of our cosy little family unit. She's ruthless and clever and loving, but she has a poor head for a crisis. If too much goes on in there, it's over. I'm more the calm and collected type. So on my YouTube videos for example, I need to speak and be cheerful and focus and think of this endless stream of words whilst worrying about the framing and the camera angle and the lighting. It doesn't bother me though. It never really feels like work. Mum says that's because it isn't. But I get a ton of Adwords revenue, so what does she know. I've even almost got sponsors. Anyway, mum's the boss. When the first cloud fell she caught me looking out the kitchen glazing into the patchy grey sky hanging over our garden. I like our garden.

'What's that,' she asked.

'A squirrel?'

'No, look.' She pointed.

I squinted. 'I think that's a cloud falling.'

Mum shook her head. 'Clouds don't fall.'

'Well, look.'

Jeremy Vine babbled on about something. Mum paid attention, but I didn't. She said that we ought to take the cakes down to the fair a little early, but I hadn't started on the second batch. Never mind the second batch, Mum told me. We ought to cut our losses and go. Cut our losses. Do you hear the worry and nonsense you get out of this woman?

We own this red Honda Civic that we both have insurance on and I love to drive, because I just passed my test two months ago and still get a kick out of driving around, though not with that weird green L plate that some new-bies favour. My mum still doesn't really trust me with her little red baby, but her heart is in two places on the matter and I know how to play both ends.

She pulled off my green L plate to start with. 'I'll drive,' she said.

No. No. No. I had to deploy quite a lot of persuasion. Mum has crashed a car twice in her lifetime. Once going alone down a hill in Spain, once about twenty metres out of the driveway, drunk on a Friday night. The neighbours didn't forget. I never fucked up once in my lessons, nor on my test. I'm an immaculate driver, or so my record says. Mum has seven points on hers. Seven. Look at this woman. And she's telling me not to drive. I guilt her about dad. Dad didn't like her driving style much. I tell her I don't either, but I play it softer than dad would have, because I love my mother and I don't want to see her cry. But if I can load her brain onto three or more tracks of thought I'll overload it, and she'll pull back a little, and I'll have some semblance of control.

'Who'll hold the cakes?' asked Mum.

'You will,' I said.

I passed her the little white plastic Tupperware box. These were good cakes we'd filled it up with. We'd gone for a theme of good and evil, with half of the cakes on one side iced with white icing, and the half on the other side iced in black. Have you ever eaten black icing? It's delicious. It tastes kind of like what I think forbidden fruit would taste like, if it had a thick sugary texture. The white cakes taste good too but they aren't decorated as nice and need the black iced cakes beside them in order to look sufficiently awesome. I showed them all to my followers on YouTube and Instagram and tried to go on a spiel about the theme. It went like this:

Have you ever played Reversi, or Othello, or Go? I love them. They're all board games where you pick a side and flip over round counters coloured black on one side and white on the other. Reversi and Othello are the same game actually, but still. You get to pick a side: white or black. You try and take over as much of the board as you can. How's that for good and evil? Lightness and the dark, locked in battle, and one turns into the other, faster than the blink of an eye.

The fairground was quite a distance away from our house. South Manchester has a lot of nice parks – you should check out Fog Lane – but the Ferelli family who ran this fair today and a lot of the other big ones in the North-west prefer to do things way out in the open, where no-one can touch them. Mum had to hold the cakes and fret while the inevitable moment where I turned off the mo-torway that she didn't trust me on and onto the country roads that she really, really didn't trust me on drew nearer.

'Do you know how many children your age die on those country roads?'

I had to laugh. 'I'm not a child. I'm twenty one.'

Mum sighed. 'You're still young. And look – no, don't look – another cloud!'

So do I look or do I not look? Of course I look. Sure enough, there's another cloud, drifting slowly down out of the sky. This one's bigger than the last one.

'Turn on the radio,' said Mum.

This time I didn't mess around. Clouds aren't supposed to fall from the sky.

I only half-listened to Jeremy Vine this time, because I was trying to focus on the road. Some of the cars were moving very fast now. Getting out of Manchester and get-ting into the countryside we started to hear sirens, fading in the distance. Then the road became very quiet. Some-one muscled Jeremy Vine off the microphone.

'What was he talking about?' I asked Mum.

Mum was kind of cowering in her seat. 'He was trying to go back to regular programming,' she said.

'And they wanted more news?'

'Yes, they did.'

Mum sounded nervous and I wished I was a listener

like she was.

'Was it more talk about the sky?' I asked.

'Yeah,' said Mum. 'Stuff about the sky. But we're only a half hour from the fair. We'll get there in time.'

In time for what?

I thought about the flour on my dress and more clouds began to drop. It was quite a spectacle. Mum kept reminding me to focus on the road. And I don't blame her. It was nigh impossible not to look. This was incredible. We were losing our mixed cloud cover and sunlight for a perfect sheet of blue sky. And the shadows underneath the clouds thickened and narrowed and changed as they fell closer to the earth. Then just when I was finding this business fun and relaxing and I'd come to terms with the fact that the clouds didn't want to stay in the sky, Mum started shaking.

'What's wrong?' I had to ask.

'The sun's falling.'

I didn't want to see that. I drove and tried to focus on the ever-tightening road, and the fewer and fewer cars that drove down it. I focused so hard that it got hard to blink. The road busied up a bit as we skirted the edge of Stockport. I slowed for some traffic and glanced up. Yeah, no doubt. The sun had dipped a little. I thought about my followers and considered asking Mum to hold my phone and open the video camera and shoot some footage so I could pop it online somewhere, but I decided that would probably be too much for Mum – she'd have to put down the cakes – and anyway there were probably a million, million people already filming this sun as it sunk lower in the sky. Because the sun is the same everywhere, supposedly.

'Maybe it's afternoon,' I said. 'The sun goes down in the afternoon, so maybe it's that.'

Mum shook her head and glanced at me. 'The sun is supposed to set in the west. It never just goes straight down.'

Mum was right. And the men (and one woman too) on the radio were getting more urgent. It was kind of just one man – a news presenter with a Bangladeshi accent – trying to give us updates, but other people kept popping up in his ear, giving him new information. I think he must have had a machine in his ear too, speaking to him, because he got a bit pissed-off and tried to leave the studio once or twice. They didn't let him. The updates just kept coming. Ma flicked off the radio right at the moment when they decided to bring back a shaky Jeremy Vine. On any other day I wouldn't have been disappointed.

'Look out,' said Ma.

We were driving into a cloud. This was a small one that vanished right out of the sky and dropped down into the road in front of us. When the Honda hit it, it was thick and wet on the windscreen and everything went dark quickly, and Mum reached over my lap and flicked on the fog lights.

'Good idea,' I said.

The fog kept coming. Even a small cloud is a big, relatively speaking. It was so quiet in there. We felt like we were on another planet.

Then a car shot at us out of the gloom and Mum screamed. I swerved right and the cakes slid in their cuboid and I got us back on to the road. I reduced the speed and crawled along the hard shoulder, keeping a watchful eye on the road beside us for wayward vehicles. I could feel some cold sweat getting between me and the steering wheel.

'Let's get off the motorway,' said Mum.

On any other day that idea would have been unthinkable for her. But the sun was sinking lower.

'Here we go,' I said, at a turning near the bottom of Stockport.

We crawled up a ramp and over a bridge, and we were out of the cloud and off the motorway, on a silent country road leading east. The sun shot back into view, and now it was halfway down to the earth, bathing the horizon. The light it was giving it was rich orange and gold like you'd see in a sunset, but we weren't even halfway through the real day yet. The fair started at half past eight in the morning and was supposed to finish at five PM. And now this nonsense had shot the clock forward to seven in the evening.

'Are you sure the cake stalls will still be there,' I asked.

'We're going to keep going anyway,' said Ma, and she was clutching her cake box. 'This is for you. You wanted your cakes there at the fair, and you baked them, so there's no backing off now.'

Can you believe the courage of this woman?

'And they're on such a good theme,' continued Ma, 'it'd be a shame to put them to waste. Goodness and evil, evil and good.'

'It's better than Disney,' I said, swerving to avoid a vicar.

'Your followers get enough Disney,' said Mum. She paused for thought. 'Will you still be Instagramming these things from our stall?'

'I will if I can.'

'But will Instagram work, if, you know. The sun goes down.'

This woman. My own mother.

We arrive at the fair and I nearly crash again another five times. So much for my spotless record. As I navigate through the speeding Rover Jeeps and evacuating Renaults, Mum starts talking about Dad.

'He wouldn't approve of the mess you're making of this journey,' she said.

She was right about that.

'What do you think he'd do about what's happening right now,' I asked, voice dry.

Mum frowned as I parked and we pulled open the red car doors. She's funny when her face is crinkling up in thought. It makes her look kind of like a monkey.

'I think,' Mum said, 'he'd tell us to stay calm and wait for instructions from the Government or someone, or something. He was never too keen on hearing anything about misery and death.'

Mum passed me the cakes. Who said anything about death?

The evening light was turning into the red of a full-on English sunset. I slung the cakes under one arm and popped my phone out to take a picture – fifteen whole megapixels, which would be impressive if megapixels still meant something – and got a quite a good one with the big line of tents and farm warehouses, shot in silhouette. The colour of the sky came out perfect and the horizon was as straight as anything you can imagine, you should have seen it.

'Stick it online,' said Mum. 'People might be interested.'

That's when I remembered about my 3G and as we made our way through the mud and straw to the white tents of the food court I pushed the photo aside for later and opened up every social media channel that my processor could handle. Panic on Facebook and Twitter. Lots of videos and photos of different parts of the sky. Hilarious webcam footage of Jeremy Vine crying, forced from the studio, and the accompanying memes to follow. I preferred not to look at those. That's mean, I thought, and it stinks of panic.

'Don't forget to upload,' said Mum. 'I'm sure people really will be interested.'

I love my mum, always encouraging me. One day she'll understand how Adwords works too, I bet you. We round the corner into the clothing section of the fair and see that a lot of the stall keepers are leaving. Some are packing up their stuff, others are simply vanishing. We hear a lot of talk about there being lights in the main warehouse that will stay on a good month thanks to a spare generator, but Mum tells me not to pay any interest.

'We're here for cakes,' she says, her voice trembling. The shadows are getting long now. 'We'll get these to our stall and then we'll be good.'

Good? Good for what?

Mum's face is getting hard to see now. The light's really starting to go. I remember the solar eclipse that happened when I was young. It was some time before puberty, and mum and dad were still together and we were on holiday with their friends. Two of them, a husband and wife called Patty and Ronald. Patty and friggin' Ronald. Yes, it was that kind of holiday. When the sun went black the animals all stopped and the birds dropped from the sky and there was this huge silence that made me realise I hadn't ever noticed the noise before. Mum and Dad and Patty and Ronald stopped talking as well. We were all very quiet. Patty and Ronald ended up divorcing too, in their later years. But Ronald never died.

People at the fair start getting just about as morbid as my thoughts. Suddenly just about everyone wants to talk very loud about death. We sidestep one raggedy man who would rather have us talk about Jehovah. One other man tries something on my Mum and another taller man punches him to stop him and we say thank you and walk a little faster. Someone sees me browsing with my smartphone and they approach and proffer one of their own. Me and Mum peer in. They're streaming something that looks like a news broadcast, captioned 'Wiltshire, Kent'. It's time-stamped the same as us, live, but the sun's still up over there in Kent. Then it fucking rockets straight down and screen goes black and we all scream and I have to hold mum, panicking, as we lose our new friend to the darkness.

It may as well be night now. The sunset is as good as over. I can see Mum's face when I pull it close and there's the outlines of the tents as we stumble forwards through the gloom. Mum is quiet and crushing my hand in hers, but the screaming of others is growing louder. And I've still got the cakes under my arm, sliding in their box. Black and white, white and black. Mum's got one hand out in front of her, fingering the tablecloths. She keeps grabbing them and pulling and I can hear all the nice things on top as they clatter and fall to the ground. We work our way forward over the mud and straw, stall to stall.

In a few long minutes of walking the light is gone completely.

'Get out your phone and turn the brightness up,' whispers Mum.

I do and I try and the light is meagre, then someone unseen snatches it from my hand. My mother sniffs hard and I try not to cry. The screaming voices grow distant. I clutch the Tupperware box, and we feel our way along through the silent dark.

COLD METROPOLIS

Luke Shelbourn

Goldstein's face was a mess.

I hit him with the briefcase again, and his wife cried out behind me. TJ was resting his boot on her throat while she lay supine on the floor. A thought jumped into my mind about my own wife. I pushed it away on instinct. Goldstein started blubbing.

'Don't bitch to me. You're two weeks behind on payment already, you think this is gonna wash with Quinton?' I cracked him again with the briefcase. 'Well?'

Wordlessly, he gestured to the safe on the wall, his face smeared with blood and tears. I let him go and he hobbled over to unlock it. Soon enough, he brought over a heap of cash. 'It's all we have. It's a couple of grand short, I'll have the rest next month I swear.'

I loaded the money into the briefcase. 'Why'd you have to make me hurt you like this – you don't think I have better things to do? Next time, have the money ready for me.'

TJ was vomiting against the wall when I walked out of Goldstein's office. I'd worked up a sweat beating on the old man and the cold air felt good on my face. 'You been eating at that dodgy chicken shop again?' I said with a grin.

TJ spat into the pool of vomit and marched off to the car without a word.

The freight terminus where Goldstein's office was located was flooded with artificial light. It was just south of Wythenshawe, pretty much as far south as you can go in the city until you end up in Cheshire. Huge interstellar transport freighters sat in suspension above the industrial wasteland of the district. The roar from their stasis engines a constant background sound, the smell of their fumes aggressive, the smog thick and clawing. As the cold began to bite, I pulled my jacket closer around me. The freighters sheltered the terminus floor from the snow, but the cold was a stark reminder that it was falling above them. In the distance, where the carpet of freighters stopped, I could see terraced suburbs, dusted white as if there was an invisible portal to another world, a world even older and bleaker than this one.

TJ was waiting in the passenger seat of the car, staring out of the side window.

I got in. 'What's up with you?' I asked.

'Nothing.'

The lad hadn't been the business long. He was from a shit family, in a shit area. Spent most of his time in care before he was sixteen, and spent most of that time fighting off kids that didn't like the colour of his skin. I'd had him running little errands for me and Jimmy since he was twelve. Nothing serious, just a few drop offs here and there. Now that he was sixteen and sprouting some hard muscle, we'd started taking him out on heavier jobs.

He was a good kid, maybe too good for this kind of work, but he fit the mould well enough. He had no hope of earning money doing anything else. He kind of reminded me of my son. That was why I liked having him around – I only have photographs of my own boy now.

'You need to toughen up,' I said. 'If you're gonna get in a sulk every time we have to knock someone around at a collection this city is gonna to eat you alive.'

'Why'd you make me hurt the woman?'

I didn't have an answer he would like. She was Goldstein's pressure spot. We all have them, and almost everyone's turns out to be their family. But this was a lesson for another day.

I put the keys in the ignition, started the car and pulled out, heading for central Manchester.

The car sloshed through the shallow carpet of snow in the road. I was taking it easy on the accelerator – the brakes on the car were worn and speed in the snow was a recipe for an accident. The terraced social housing of Wythenshawe looked grey and filthy. The streets were mostly empty save for a few solitary figures wrapped up in dark rags, shuffling bent backed through the overcast gloom. On the corner, the burnt and ancient supports of a church sat derelict and roofless, only a few blackened bricks remaining. Inside the ruin, three locals were burning litter in a large metal waste bin.

It was payday for the many businesses that Quinton had a hand in, and Goldstein was our last collection. We picked up Jimmy from an industrial estate in Beswick, a bulging carryall bag in his right hand. He made TJ get out and sit in the back so he could sit up front with me. TJ complained until Jimmy spouted off about pecking order and the boy gave in.

As we drove Jimmy unzipped the carryall and brought out a ream of money, flicking through the notes.

'Good day?' I asked.

'Full payment without breaking a sweat. I hate it when they pay up too easy. Don't sleep right when there's no beatings to dole out.'

'You should have been at Goldstein's this morning. Took us half an hour to squeeze money out of the old boy.'

'You've always been the lucky one.'

TJ was quiet and pensive in the back seat. Jimmy started fiddling with the heater controls.

'It's knackered. Leave it alone,' I said.

'I'm freezing my balls off.'

'Leave it.'

'We should ask Quinton for one of those flashy hover cars like she has.'

I scoffed. 'Good luck with that.'

'You really think she is going to let you leave? You can't even get a new car.'

'I've paid my dues to this city and to Quinton.'

'People like Quinton are always hungry for more. You think she cares about dues? This city never stops taking.' The dial from the heater came off in his hand and he threw it in the foot well. 'You should ask her for a new car, at least you have a chance of getting that.'

'I think I'll stick with retirement.'

'Selfish bastard,' he said with a smile.

As we moved north towards the city, the buildings began to modernise. Public money didn't tend to seep out into to slums. It stayed central, stuck to the palms of corrupt councillors like Quinton. We parked up in a street just out-side Albert Square and left TJ to catch a tram home. Three was a crowd where Quinton was concerned.

It was midday and the square was busy with dead-eyed

municipal workers, trussed up suits enjoying their daily hour of respite from the moral gutter of local government. Advertising hoardings hung suspended by stasis modules around the courtyard, all of them businesses that Quinton took some kind of taste from. There was one for Goldstein's Freight just outside the entrance to the town hall. Jimmy tipped an invisible hat to it and shot me a knowing smile as we walked past. The town hall itself maintained much of its old-world look, its gothic geometry standing out stark against the modernity of the city centre.

An optics drone swarmed in front of me and projected holographic spam for some seedy escort agency on the pavement. I back-handed it out of my path and it clattered against the outside wall of the town hall.

'Not your type, eh?' Jimmy asked, with a grin.

I shot him the middle finger.

We entered the town hall and went up to the second floor. The receptionist acknowledged us without a word.

'The two gentlemen are here to see you, Ms. Quinton,' the receptionist said into the intercom. Then to us, 'Please go through.'

Natalie Quinton sat behind a huge walnut desk, in a room that was a monument to dripping wealth. Her glasses were perched half way down her nose, her hair tied back pristinely in a bun. Her face was fixed with a stern, professional look, morphing into a touch of disdain as Jimmy and I entered her office.

'Gentlemen, I see you have something for me. How I love the end of the month.'

'Goldstein was a couple of grand short. He said he'd get the rest to us next month,' I said.

Quinton flashed us both an annoyed look. 'I trust you

shall not let Mr Goldstein make a habit of it?'

'He's been motivated. He'll have the full hundred next time we're there.'

'Yeah, they knocked him around good,' Jimmy interjected. 'That'll be "motivation" enough for next month.'

I winced.

'Quite,' Quinton said, her dead expression betraying nothing. She exercised power from a distance, and didn't concern herself with the finer details of what kept her business associates under her fist. It was obvious enough that we were expected to do whatever was necessary to make sure payment was made.

She took the briefcase and Jimmy's carryall over to a large wall safe where she placed most of the money, reserving two bundles for me and Jimmy. Then she locked it and walked back over, holding out a roll of money to each of us.

'This is short,' Jimmy said, unrolling the bundle and leafing through the notes.

'I know,' Quinton said. 'I find myself out of pocket as well. I see no reason I should bear the burden of your shortcomings.'

'Goldstein wasn't even my—' Jimmy began.

'No problem,' I interrupted. 'We'll make sure we get the rest next month.'

'At which time you will both be recompensed. Jimmy, leave us. Malcolm stay behind a minute, I require a word with you about something.'

Jimmy nodded to me and left. Quinton gestured for me to sit at her desk.

'I'm glad you asked me to stay,' I said, absent-mindedly rubbing my upper arm. 'I have something I need to talk to you about.'

'Oh?'

'I want to talk about you letting me go.'

There was a short pause. 'I see.' She said it slowly, like she was tasting the words as they came from her mouth.

'I'm getting too old for this kind of work. I'll be sixty in September. I'm not far off old Goldstein's age. Jimmy is as fierce as he ever was, and TJ is coming up.'

She said nothing but sat looking at me as if she was expecting more. Her stoicism was slowly killing me.

'And it's my wife, you see. I need to get her out, take her somewhere quiet. This city… it isn't good for her condition.'

A little smile arched its way into the corners of Quinton's mouth. I regretted telling her the last part immediately – it was none of her business. Quinton always had a way of making you give up more than you wanted to.

'I'm sorry to hear about your wife, but your absence would leave me in a bit of a predicament. I don't feel I could trust Jimmy to do the job on his own, and I have… reservations about your young apprentice.'

'TJ is as good as anyone, but there are thousands of other young men in Manchester who would give their left arm to get this job.'

Quinton waved her hand dismissively. 'Yes, yes. I have no doubt that given an opportunity to exercise glorified thuggery for cash, all manner of miserable peasants would throw their hat in. But would you expect me to trust these vermin with my business interests?'

I didn't know whether I should feel flattered or defeated. 'Natalie, I've given my life to you and your empire, to this city. I've carried out your will to the last word for forty years. I've even neglected my family for this business. Please, let me retire, I don't have anything much left to give you.'

Quinton was silent a while. 'We may be able to reach an outcome that is agreeable,' she said finally, with a sigh. My heart jumped. 'The reason I brought you in here is that your young apprentice was arrested last week. One of my informants tells me they took him to the investigative headquarters in Monsall. When he got out I had him shadowed. Two days ago, he was seen with a suited gentleman in a café in Stockport. Did he tell you anything about it?'

My stomach knotted.

'No. They probably turfed him when they realised they couldn't make anything stick. He has a cousin in Stockport – it could have been him he was meeting.' My bluster was forced, and the part about the cousin was a bare-faced lie.

'Don't make excuses, Malcolm. You know what it means.'

'It doesn't look good, sure. But you've got the police in your pocket, what have you got to be worried about?'

'Granted I have most of them – I do so value venality in a person, it makes life so much more uncomplicated – but there are a few that cling to their false notions of duty and their counterfeit morality.'

'What are you asking me to do?'

'You don't need me to spell it out for you, Malcolm. If you want out, this is my price.'

I didn't have much to say. I'd known Quinton long enough to recognise that there would be no negotiating.

'It needs to be done by tomorrow. Come and see me afterwards and we'll tie up the loose ends. And don't mention anything to Jimmy – he's fond of the boy, even more so than you are. Send him in when you get outside. I need to apprise him of his promotion.'

I left Quinton's office and told Jimmy that she wanted

to see him, then sat down in the waiting area. I couldn't stop my hands from shaking. My road into this business was paved with violence. My road out was looking much the same. Fuck this city, and fuck Quinton. They never stop taking, just like Jimmy said.

Jimmy was in Quinton's office a good twenty minutes. He looked ill when he finally came out.

'Let's go,' he said.

'You okay?'

'Yeah, come on.'

'You not gonna congratulate me?'

'Congratulations.'

We didn't speak much on the car journey home. I was worried that Quinton had told him about the lad, but I put it from my mind after a while. She had nothing to gain from telling him.

I took the M60 northbound to drop Jimmy at his place, crossing the huge bridge over the Manchester Ship Canal. Jimmy and I had dropped a fair few bodies off the edge of it in our time – it was a good place to mock up suicides for people who got on the wrong side of Quinton. We'd throw them off in the early hours of the morning, sending them three hundred foot down into the frozen waters. If they broke through the ice they'd wash up in the centre of town a few days later, just another victim of the city and its levies. If they didn't, they'd lay there like gored snow angels on the ice, waiting for the morning for some horrified pedestrian to find them.

At the apex of the bridge, I noticed Jimmy was staring over the edge into the grey void.

'Take the next exit,' he said. 'I think I'll get some fresh air and walk back.'

Frankly, I was relieved. I needed time alone. There was a pub a couple of streets away. Once I had dropped Jimmy off, I went in and ordered a Johnnie Walker neat.

I told the barman to leave the bottle.

The car swerved slightly in the road as I drove back from the pub. The night was bitter cold, and the snow was falling hard. I lived up in Blackley, just before the relative flat of the city turned into rolling hills. This part of Manchester was still old, still poor and decrepit. There were no hover cars here or fancy billboards, just people slowly decaying, day by day, night by night.

I swung off the motorway onto Victoria Avenue, the road hugging the fringes of Heaton Park, a sea of dark punctured only by burning litter bins and bonfires, a Mecca for the destitute and the broken. On the other side of the road, red-bricked terraces glowed under the street lamps, their windows covered with rotting wood.

I bumped the car up the curb outside my house and shuffled to the door, happy that I could still walk in a straight line. The lights were off inside, a standby light from the TV the only thing illuminating the lounge. I flipped the light-switch.

Ameerah was in the chair I left her in that morning, her eyes open and red-rimmed, a smudged glass half full of gin in her hand.

'Hi sweetheart,' I said, bending down to kiss her.

'You've been drinking.'

'I have some news for you,' I said. 'I spoke to Quinton today. It looks like we are going to be able to leave soon.'

She laughed, sardonically. 'I'll believe it when I see it.'

'We could be out of here in a few weeks.'

'Okay,' she said, her eyes absent, no light or hope in

them.

'You don't believe me?'

'I believe you think it will happen. But good things don't happen to us, Malcolm. I came to that conclusion years ago.'

'We'll get out, I promise,' I said and kissed her again. She wrapped her arms around me and I felt her eyes dampen on my shoulder.

'I'm tired,' she said. She got up from her chair, and swayed as she made for the door. I picked her up into my arms and carried her up the stairs to our bedroom.

'I watched a programme on the TV tonight,' she said as I carried her.

'Yeah?' I placed her in the bed and pulled the covers over her.

'It was about the old religions. They spoke about this thing called sin. It was like a skeleton in your closet, things you were ashamed of.' She wiped a tear away from her eye. 'We have a lot of skeletons in our closet, don't we, Malc?'

'Go to sleep. Remember what I said.'

She turned onto her other side so she was facing away from me. I went into the bathroom and washed in the sink. I caught sight of my face in the mirror. An old face that I barely recognised stared back at me. It was hard not to have skeletons in your closet in this city. I had the feeling that I was about to add a huge shambling revenant to mine.

Morning announced itself, light percolating through the kitchen window. I'd sat at the table all night, drinking cheap coffee and looking at an old, framed picture of my son. He could have only been about six in the photo. He was sat with Ameerah, smiling into the camera lens, sheer glee on his little face. Ameerah was smiling too. I hadn't seen her smile like that for a long time. He'd been in the ground for thirty years, and the best part of my wife had died with him. I kissed the glass in front of his face and put him back on the mantelpiece, then went back to my chair. Looking at the photo up there, it felt like he was staring right at me.

I went back over and laid the frame flat.

I tucked my gun into my belt at the small of my back, slipped a switchblade into my boot, and rang TJ, telling him I needed him for a job and to be ready in thirty minutes.

He was sat on a wall when I came to pick him up, hands in the pockets of an old tracksuit. The lad lived in a bedsit down in Moss Side, some old hovel the council had converted into living space for unwanteds. He opened the door to get in the back seat.

'Jimmy's ill. Looks like you're promoted to the front seat, big man,' I said. I could feel my foot quivering on the accelerator.

He hesitated then shut the back door and climbed carefully into the front, like he was slipping into Jimmy's grave. The stale sweat that clung to his clothes hit me almost immediately. Poor bastard never had anyone teach him how to use a washing machine, never had a mother to tell him when he stank. He rubbed his face and asked me what was on the to-do list. He had a shadow of a moustache across his top lip: tiny black hairs interspersed with thin wisps of white. He suddenly seemed very young: a child playing at a man's game.

'Got some business out of town today, mate. Jimmy's

laid up with flu or something, so you're my right-hand man.' I could feel the cold burn of gunmetal against the small of my back.

He nodded without expression.

We drove out east across the city and into Stockport. The crumbling buildings there lay destitute, the sallow-faced underclass haunting their ruins, a world away from the towering wealth of the distant Manchester skyline. The Pennines loomed, growing larger as we drove towards them, white and steep.

'What's the job, so far out? There's only wasters this far outside the city.'

'Just a guy that needs talking to. Don't think we'll need to resort to any rough stuff.'

He fiddled with the fabric of his trousers and his leg jittered up and down. 'Seems like a long way to go. Quinton really got links this far out the city?'

'Seems so.'

We passed through Glossop and trundled onto the lower slopes of the Pennines. Hardly anyone lived out here anymore. The further we got from civilisation the more agitated TJ became. The roads were barely visible from the path because of the deep snow. Only the derelict houses gave any indication as to the centre of the street.

When we hit the countryside proper I had to slow right down to make sure I didn't run off course.

'Can I ask you a question, Malc?' There was a slight tremor in the boy's voice, his leg was jittering more and more.

'Sure,' I said, trying to maintain an air of calm.

'What did you want to be when you were young?'

I looked over at him, he seemed like he was on the edge of tears. He wasn't stupid. If there was any doubt about whether he was informing or not, it was gone now.

'Don't know if I can remember.'

'I wanted to drive one of those big freighters they've got over at Goldstein's. I wanted to get out. To get away. First from my old man, then from the kids at the care home, then from everything. The colonies couldn't be worse than this right?'

'I think maybe I wanted to be a footballer. Something like that anyway,' I replied, trying to change the direction he was going in.

'Even then I knew it would never happen. At eight years old I knew,' he said.

We crested a rise and on the other side of it the bluish, frozen white of the Ladybower reservoir stretched across the valley. When we hit the bottom of the descent I turned off at a barely-visible side road and trundled down to a copse of trees near the ice. The ice was thick, but it would be easier to hack a hole in the lake than dig a grave in the frozen ground. I parked the car amongst the trees and sat for a moment.

'Please don't do this,' TJ said. His voice broke and tears streamed down his cheeks.

'You shouldn't have talked.'

'I didn't have a choice. The prick who picked me up, said he was gonna pin all kinds of shit on me unless I gave him information. I didn't give him much, Malc. You've gotta believe me. You can talk to Quinton for me, tell her I'll keep my mouth shut.'

'Get out the car.'

'Please, Malc.'

'Get out the car.'

'Please, no.'

I got out and ran round to the passenger side, pulling

the gun from the back of my jeans, a sharp, metallic taste in my mouth. I flung open the door. He cowered away from me, trying to shimmy over to the driver's side. I grabbed his hair and tried to pull him from the car, my heart nearly beating out of my chest. He grabbed onto the handbrake. I cracked him in the side of the head with the butt of my gun and he let go, screaming simple, elongated vowels, his voice breaking into animal terror, the screams punctuated only by sobs.

I had to drag him down to the ice. He kept trying to claw his way out of my grasp, clinging on to tree branches and snow-covered bushes. By the time I got him to the edge his hands were slick with blood from the friction, tiny droplets splashing onto the ice, streaming in red veins across the surface.

I pushed him face down on to the ice, put my knee against his spine and pressed the barrel of the gun against the back of his head. He was weeping like a child

'I'm sorry,' I said. 'I have to.' My hands were shaking badly. Snow had started to fall, I didn't know when. A cold wind was blowing it across the frozen lake into my face. I gritted my teeth, tightening my finger on the trigger. Glimpses of his face arrived piecemeal behind the snow that the wind whipped up around us. It was stacking in his hair and on his face. A pool of vomit lay on the floor next to him, I didn't know if it was mine or his. The wind and the snow swirled around me, like I was at the eye of a frozen storm, the centrepiece of some whim of nature.

I could trade this city off for a boy, all I had to do was pull the trigger.

The city was obscured behind the hills and moors, but I knew it was there, waiting, hungering for its taxes and levies, a gaping maw that swallowed us all whole. I felt its hooks in me, operating me like a puppet, feathering my finger on the trigger. I looked down at the boy in front of me: the cities spawn, its living heritage, its discarded waste. He was nothing, a nobody, disposable to everyone he had ever known.

I thought of my son staring at me from a photograph.

The gun dropped to the floor, softly thudding as it nestled in the snow.

TJ sat in the passenger seat wrapped in an old blanket I found in the boot of the car. His trousers were red and wet, and he shivered with the cold. He hadn't spoken since I dragged him back to the car. We sat there for a long time staring at the lake as the new snow cascaded down to sit atop the old. I moved off when I realised that we might get stuck out there if the snow got much deeper.

We trundled through the roads for hours until the city moved into view on the horizon.

'I'm sorry,' I said. The words felt feeble and inconsequential.

He stared blankly out of the window towards the city.

'How did you end up in custody?' I asked.

'They brought me in for nothing.' He was still shaking. 'Just threw me in their car and brought me to the station, told me they were gonna pin all kinds of shit on me. Stuff I'd seen you and Jimmy do.'

'You should have called me.'

'Doesn't matter now, nothing does. If Quinton wants me gone, then it's only a matter of time. If you can't do it, someone else will.'

At the motorway I took the southbound exit.

'You're going the wrong way,' he said, panic finding its way back into his voice.

Goldstein's freighters hung black and grey in the sky to the south of the city, like an angry, metal cloud.

'You'll never pilot a freighter, but you might get to ride in one,' I said.

Old Goldstein gave TJ some of his old clothes. He looked ridiculous, like a teenager would do if he took to dressing like a pensioner.

'Is it going to wipe out that two grand, if I do this?' Goldstein asked, his face still swollen from the beating I had meted out the day before.

I took out the roll of money Quinton had given me and held it out to him. 'If you mention a word of this to anyone, let alone Quinton…'

'I get it. I get it. You'll do very unkind things to me. I'll have a shuttle ready to take him up to the freighter in ten minutes. Anything for a quiet life.'

The boy was sat on a bench, rocking back and forth. I went and sat next to him. We sat in silence, watching the freighters gently sway in the sky above us.

'I've never known anything else but the city,' he said after a while.

'There's nothing left for you here. There's nothing left for me either, if you want the truth. Things are different in the colonies.'

'What if they're not? What if this is all there is?'

'Whatever's out there has got to be better than this, especially for you. Goldstein's going to set you up with a job. You'll need to think of a new name, just in case.'

'Where am I heading?'

'He hasn't told me. Better that he doesn't – if Quinton finds out I let you go she'll put my balls in a vice.'

I got up to leave.

'Malc?'
'Yeah?'
'Thanks. You didn't have to do this.'
'Yes I did.'

It was dark by the time I got back on the M60 and the roads were quiet. I was going through the story I was going to tell Quinton in my head. It didn't have to be extravagant: TJ was laying at the bottom of the reservoir, with a bullet-sized hole in his head, end of.

At the top of the bridge over the Manchester Ship Canal there was a police cruiser pulled over on the hard shoulder. Two officers stood to the side of it: one at the railing, leaning over the wall and looking at the ice below, the other stood beside the car talking on the radio.

I recognised the one near the railing from a job me and Jimmy worked a couple of years ago. He was on Quinton's payroll. Victor was his name, bent as they come. He knew this spot as well as Jimmy and I did.

Something inside me rose to the surface, some subconscious feeling of wrongness. It felt like someone had reached inside my chest and gripped my innards in a meaty fist.

I pulled over just in front of the police cruiser and walked back to them. Victor recognised me once I was close enough. 'Malc, what are you doing here?' he asked.

I pushed past him to the railing and peered over the edge to the ice hundreds of feet below. I could hear the other copper talking on his radio, and could vaguely make out Victor trying to say something, but the words didn't register. Down in the sea of grey, through the murk and the falling snow, a stark, bloodied figure lay on the ice.

I turned and grabbed Victor by the throat. 'Who's

down there?'

'You're making a big mistake.'

I pulled the gun from the back of my jeans and hit him with it. 'Tell me,' I screamed.

I heard the safety catch click on a gun behind me, pushed Victor away and jumped sideways. A gunshot burst and pain ripped through my left shoulder. I brought the gun around as I fell and pulled the trigger, braining the copper that stood behind the door of his cruiser. Gore splashed against his cruiser. A bullet hit the tarmac close to my face and hot grit flew into my eyes. Blinded, I emptied half a clip in the direction of the gunshot then pushed myself to my feet with my good arm and ran towards my car for cover.

Another shot flared. More pain ate into the right of my abdomen and I fell in a heap at the back of my car. I couldn't see shit and, somewhere in-between falling and hitting the floor, I'd dropped my gun. I felt for it on the ground but found nothing but grit and snow.

Something smashed down onto my searching hand, and I felt fingers break. A blunt force crunched into my face. I fell backwards.

A heel dug into my throat and stayed there pinning me down. 'Nothing personal, Malc.' Victor said.

I swung my free arm, caught the back of his standing leg and pulled as hard as I could. He fired the gun as he fell and I felt the right side of my head go hot as the bullet ricocheted of the tarmac. All I could hear was ringing.

I climbed on top of him as quick as I could, pressing my weight against his arms and torso, and pulled the switchblade from my boot. He struggled, trying to shake his gun arm free. I plunged the blade into his navel and dragged it up through his abdomen until I hit the ribs. Hot guts spilled out against my hand and his garbled screams filled my ears, the fight fleeing from him quickly. I yanked out the blade and pushed it hard into the left quadrant of his chest. He went limp.

I dragged myself into my car, trying to rub the grit from my eyes. Victor had taken my right ear off, and there was a bullet in my shoulder. Neither of them worried me as much as the slug in my stomach.

Or the body on the ice.

I wiped blood from my face and drove hard for my home.

I almost fell as I got from the car, tears already forming on my eye lids as I smashed through the fence in front of my driveway.

'Ameerah,' I shouted as I burst into the house. The curtains were open, and a bowl of cereal lay half eaten on the kitchen table. I shouted for her again, but no one responded. I dragged myself upstairs to look for her. All the rooms were empty, our bed was made and uninhabited.

I stumbled to the window and crumpled against it, weeping. Outside I could see the overcast and starless void carpeting the frozen wastes, the street lamps dulled by white nimbus' made of snow, the distant skyscrapers towering above the city all wreathed in light, the gluttonous heart of the North. This fucking city.

In the window's reflection, a figure moved into the room. Jimmy stood there, the grey metal of his gun aimed at my head.

'You were right,' I said.

'About what?'

'This city never stops taking.'

Up in the sky, outside the window, a hole cracked in

the clouds and the light from the stars shone through, just for a moment. Then, as soon as they had appeared they were gone again, the gloom of the city's canopy encasing the cold metropolis once more.

ONCE UPON A TIME
IN THE NORTHWEST

Sam Tein

It was a perfect splodge. The pie had flown in a graceful arc rotating perhaps twice before hitting the old flinger square on the nose. The base crust collapsed on impact, but the top, the top gained traction and continued to roll sideways, leaving a graceful streak of meaty gravy that trailed off to the guy's ear.

Uproar followed when the crowd saw the points awarded. Ten for the accuracy of course, but the judges being too traditional, marked the splodge down for the off-centre spread. Even so, the nine-point-three marks assured the contestant the win he so richly deserved. Just as well, as some in the crowd were becoming a bit ugly toward the judges. The knockout stages had been well worth the watching, but the final they produced was a really exceptional finish.

I made my way over to the press box to interview the young winner. 'Congratulations. That was a splendid contest. My name is Tein,' I said, showing him my press accreditation. 'I would welcome the chance to interview you for the Flinger's Gazette.'

He seemed amenable, but before I had the opportunity he was hauled aloft and carried off toward the beer tents by a group of burly youths. He would soon be incapable of answering questions. No matter, I would find him later. Hopefully, the booze would loosen his tongue and make him less secretive about his recipes and ingredients. In the meantime, I thought, I could write up my notes on the day's events so far: the procession of the hives through the streets and the Abbot's opening address to the games. I thought it would look well as part of my report on the festival. I had written down his speech verbatim.

'It gives me great pleasure as Abbot of Numank to welcome one and all to this holiday. However, I must ask you all to remember the reason we celebrate the blessing of the hives at this time. Our predecessors called this period of the year "Spring" which for them signified the rebirth of the world following the cold period they called "Winter". Our forebears believed this natural period of regrowth also represented the promise of resurrection. In our way, we do the same, for we have also come through the tragedy of the old wars to this simpler existence. So, in accordance with tradition, I now declare the Festival of the Bees open. Let the games begin.'

He was new, only appointed toward the end of last year. I was glad he hadn't resorted to any details about the wars. People were fed up of the recriminations of the past. Nowadays, children were not even taught of the causes of the famine and resulting conflicts: the collapse of bee populations worldwide; the eventual discovery that microwaves disrupt bees' delicate brains; and all so humans could text their mates across a room.

After the opening, I naturally made my way to the Pie Flinging field. There is a lot to be said for the other events: cake, flan, and the like, but in my opinion, nothing can beat the sight and sound of crust on face.

By chance, somebody caught my eye as I started toward the beer tents. I was sure I had seen the unmistakable bulk of Grutt 'Hard Crust' Broggwaller. The interview could wait. If I was correct, a one-to-one with Broggwaller would be a real scoop for my report to the *Northwest Pie Flingers Gazette.*

It was one of those rare days for Numank: warm and sunny with no sign of the grey overcast skies that deposit endless mizzle, the bane of pie flingers in the North West.

Closing the distance between us, I could see his trademark leather bag. Oh, it was Broggwaller alright. What surprised me was, I hadn't noticed his name in any of the professional fling-offs, nor in any of the exhibition matches. In fact, he was heading off Castlefields toward the overgrown desolation of Deansgate. As we skirted the twisted metal and concrete of Thilton mound, I managed to catch up with him but kept a few paces behind. We walked in this manner for some time, through the Chin sector and across what was once Picky Square. The Plaza still stood defiantly despite the damage. At all levels, I could see the dregs of humanity desperately thrown together by the need for shelter. Windows, the glass long gone, had washing hanging or banners declaring clan loyalties. Some had children dangling their legs in the warm sunshine. I knew a day didn't pass without somebody falling, or more likely being thrown from that rat-infested structure. At the top, the now useless phone masts were peering precariously over the edge.

Finally, we came to the old warehouse sector, which had fared better in the wars, suffering only superficial damage to its massively thick, red-brick walls.

Grutt had glanced my way on a few occasions and

seemed unconcerned with my attentions, but as he ducked into a tavern he nodded and indicated I should join him.

'May I buy you a drink Mr. Broggwaller?' I asked, handing him a glass of local ale.

'Happen,' he said. He took the glass and quaffed a good portion of the foaming Bee's Slash, nearly draining it. Apparently, the brewer knew a thing or two about piss taking, especially today. Naming a beer after the trigger to the wars that nearly brought human life to extinction. Who says Numanker's are miserable bastards with no sense of humour? Still, ancient history now.

Grutt observed me over the top of his pint as he took another slurp.

'I thought I saw you sniffing around, Tein,' he said, waving his pot in my direction. 'Looking for a story for that rag of yours, eh? I never understood why you stopped flinging to write for that chip-wrapper of a paper. How's your throwing arm by the way?'

'I keep my eye in. Look, when I saw you strolling away from the fair what was I supposed to think? What are you up to and why the sudden interest in my arm?'

'That's for you to find out, but if I let you tag along, just make sure you paint me in a good light, else I might have to look you up. In the meantime, keep then coming.' With that, he slammed his empty glass on the table and nodded toward the bar.

For all the apparent welcome in Grutt's voice he seemed in a dark mood, so I did as I was told and ordered another round. Maybe the ale would put him in a happier frame of mind, and then I might find out the reason for this diversion away from the Pie Flinging.

Soon I had plied him with four or five glasses, which he sluiced down in rapid fashion, lining up the empties in front of him on the table. I was still sipping my first, it was heady stuff. As he took another mouthful, something happened at the door behind me. Almost immediately, people started to leave. Some even left before finishing their drinks so, whatever the cause, it was serious. As though with one mind they just upped and left through the nearest door.

Grutt remained steadfast, although his face changed almost imperceptibly. I decided to risk a look in the direction of the main entrance and I too felt the sudden urge to leave. As I started to stand, I felt Grutt's hand restraining me. 'Stay where you are lad,' he said.

The cause of this mass exodus was simple, at the entrance, stood two apiary monks weighing up the situation. They were huge mean-looking buggers, all due to the honey, I suppose. By the look of them, someone was in for a good kicking, and their options had dwindled to either me or Grutt because the room was now empty apart from the four of us. I considered the wisdom of the choice of ale I had bought, for there in front of me were six glasses, each emblazoned with a bee taking a piss on a monk's head – the barman had been the first to leave. apiary monks were known to be sensitive types.

They strolled over to us, full of menace. One, the meanest looking, had the three yellow and black stripes of a sergeant on his arm and very big boots. The other wore no insignia, but the uniform was unmistakable. As they drew closer, I saw his collar studs: Queen Bee with Abdomen and Stinger. This was a Major, a rank rarely seen outside monastery walls. Grutt seemed nonplussed.

The sergeant reached for a chair and pulled it out for

the Major, who sat down next to Grutt. He gave me a cursory glance dismissing me as something he may have stepped in. Grutt was evidently well known to him and they exchanged a few guttural sounds. My knowledge of the old tongue is scant, but I was just able to make out what was said.

'So, Grutt, you up for it then?' the Major asked.

'As I'll ever be,' Grutt replied, punctuating his words with a belch.

'Let's be at it then,' said the Major.

The sergeant stretched out this hand to take Grutt's bag, but Grutt snarled 'Leave it for the lad,' nodding in my direction.

The sergeant shrugged and growled at me, 'Fetch it, sonny.'

Now, generally I would have taken exception to this 'lad' and 'sonny' business, being well into my thirties. However, arguing with an apiary monk, especially the sensitive ones, usually leads to pain and discomfort, so I let it pass and grabbed the bag. 'Oh, okay,' I said, happy to see the boots walking away.

We were ushered away from the bar and into an alley at the back of the tavern. Waiting was a hive car, an armoured personnel carrier. Grutt stepped in, but I was shoved unceremoniously through the door. I was grateful it ended with a shove and not the usual stomping.

During the journey, Grutt and the Major were deep in conversation, but I heard nothing of that as the sergeant kept me distracted with the occasional friendly kick to the shin. After some time, the car stopped, and I was chucked out.

The hive car drew away leaving us in an area of Numank I was unfamiliar with. Judging by the devastation there must have been a massive battle here: most of the buildings were flattened. Directly in front of us was what appeared to be the ruins of a large stadium. Grutt started walking toward it.

I tried for information. 'What the hell are we doing here?' I asked.

Grutt said nothing but just kept walking.

I followed. What choice did I have?

When we got within two hundred yards of what I now realised was old Menarena we were suddenly surrounded. There were twenty or thirty men, each holding a cudgel or roughly fashioned spear.

'Oh aye, and what do you think you're up to then?' said one, evidently the leader by the look of him. He carried an old baseball – no, cricket – bat. His clothes were somewhat smarter than the rest and he oozed authority. It was the sword at his belt that actually gave away his status. Only someone who commanded would risk being caught with such a thing. The monks took the carrying of even basic pre-war weaponry very seriously. We had fallen into the hands of Backtechs, rebels who wanted a return to what they called the "Golden Age". Basically, we were in the shit.

'Name's Grutt,' Grutt said.

'What, you?' the leader said.

'Yep, me,' said Grutt, reaching for something inside his jacket. In his hand, was a common Pork Growler. He hefted it once to feel the weight and then let fly. Thirty paces away one of the rebels felt the impact smack in the middle of his forehead. He dropped like a stone.

'My credentials,' Grutt said, nodding in the direction

the pie had taken.

The leader turned in time to see his man crumple to the floor face first.

'Follow me,' he said.

We were led past the stadium into the ruins of an old train station. In its time, it must have been quite a complex. I counted at least twelve bays. Some even had the burnt out shells of old vehicles that they say used to travel on iron rails. The rails were all gone now of course – ripped up for the valuable metal they contained. We were shown to a room under the concourse.

'Wait here,' the leader said. 'It'll take a while to sort out who you're going to fling against.'

He posted two of his men at the door and left, followed by the rest of his men, some of who were dragging the man Grutt had felled earlier.

I was up to my neck now and could only hope to ride the whirlwind I had inadvertently stumbled upon. I could see no good end to what was coming. Grutt had apparently become involved with one of the high-priced death match events where all comers pay vast amounts for the chance to face living legends like Broggwaller. The losers could pay with their lives, but if they won through and beat the champion they would have overnight fame and be made for life.

Food and drink had been provided, so I ate and Grutt drank till he fell asleep. Even in his drunken stupor it was hard not to admire the man. Swarthy and muscular, barrel-chested, with the neck of a bull and arms like a gorilla. I knew his reputation as a master flinger and could easily believe the fantastic stories I had heard about the horrendous injuries and even decapitations he was said to have inflicted.

When he came round sometime later, he eyed me suspiciously though I doubted he remembered much of the day we had spent together. He reached for some ale and took a mighty swig. Setting the jug back on the table, he wiped his sleeve across his mouth, smiled at me and looked down at his boots indicating I should do the same.

I saw what I thought was a trickle of piss coming from the bottom of his trousers. My initial reaction was disgust. However, when the liquid started foaming and turning a dark brown colour, I was shocked. I looked up, his finger was casually placed across his lips. When he saw he had my full attention, he opened his mouth to reveal a hidden orifice. It was a small funnel and, looking closer, I could now trace the faint hint of tubing under the skin of his neck, which he pulled slightly, revealing its prosthetic makeup. With a glance of his eyes he indicated it ran through his clothing to the side of his boots. Judging by the stained wet patch on his trousers, it ended just short of the turn-ups. As a further demonstration, he took another manly gob full and sure enough some seconds later it leaked out at the bottom of his trousers and was absorbed into the rough ground of the chamber.

He smiled again and gave a barely perceptible wink as he let his head rest on his folded hands, as though in a tired state of satiated drunkenness.

'Don't say a word,' he whispered from the corner of his mouth, barely audible over the noises from the corridor. 'Stay close, and for fuck's sake act dumb, that way we may get out of this alive.'

No need for acting on my part – I was already dumbfounded by this turn of events. For one, the stranger in front of me had changed from the rough, coarse drunken brute of his reputation into a well-spoken sounding bloke that would be welcome in any society. For two, I had already sussed that we were in a tricky situation, though I thought the discovery of my true identity was the danger. Now it seemed that the danger had been doubled as the two of us had something to hide.

Keep quiet? Ha! I doubted I would ever speak again after this.

Over the next ten minutes he burped, wheezed and farted out an incredible tale of his undercover existence as an agent of the apiary monks. Later he would tell me more but, for now, whatever happened I must not let his bag out of reach. Soon they would come for us to provide the main entertainment in the arena.

I hugged the bag closer and managed to glimpse through the partially open zip an array of fine hardened egg-washed pastries still in their foils. He had come prepared at least. There was a final, tumultuous applause from the crowd that drowned out anything that had gone before, and I gathered that the contest had reached a final conclusion. Grutt looked up and glanced a warning then raised himself from his chair and leaned heavily against the nearby wall.

The door swung open and two rebels entered. One addressed Grutt: 'Please follow us Mr. Broggwaller, we are ready for you now.'

Grutt stumbled across the room and as he reached the pair, he leaned against the nearest rebel, the leader from our encounter before. He glanced in my direction and slurred, 'I think I'm a bit pissed. Can the boy carry me bag? He's harmless and he won't be no trouble.'

The leader turned to me and barked, 'You there, carry the bag.'

Somehow, the rebels managed to assist Grutt down

the narrow passage that led to the lights and noise beyond. I followed as best I could, straining under the
weight of the bag all the while hoping I wouldn't disgrace
myself.

We entered the arena to a roar from the assembled
crowd. Everyone had been prepared for Grutt's appear-
ance and every man jack of them stood and applauded
him. Grutt, taking his cue, appeared revived, soaking up
the atmosphere of the audience waving his hands to the
crowd and slowly turning to show his appreciation of the
plaudits.

We crossed to an area that had been marked out for
flinging. It was in the shape of a hexagon. I immediately
noted the ancient rusty barbed-wire fence that encircled
us – eight feet high and covered with cruel-looking, razor-
sharp, wheel spinners – too high to jump and with no
chance of climbing. We were imprisoned with no escape.
I started to feel giddy.

At the nearest apex was a table that had been set up
for Grutt's use. I placed the bag on the table and faced
what must be Grutt's opponents. There were three of
them, each standing at one of the apexes opposite and
some twenty paces away. They stood next to tables of
their own, which were piled high with various forms of
confection.

The leader himself announced the competition and introduced the contestants to the crowd. No surprises
there. It was to be to the death and, should it turn out that
Grutt fell, then the others were to fling it out to the end.
No mention was made of my fate. I sensed I was considered crust-fodder, not expected to survive the opening
salvos, my only role apparently to set out the great man's
stall. The odds seemed overwhelming and I couldn't see

how we could possibly escape, but Grutt seemed calm. I could only wonder at the man I stood beside. He seemed utterly fearless and even appeared to be looking forward what was to come. I shook my head and arranged his pies on the table.

Money was exchanging hands furiously amongst the crowd. In a specially erected stand, there were perhaps two hundred spectators. They were the toffs of society – the rich and famous that the sport has attracted. None of them knew a thing about the game, the finesse, their only interest was in seeing a blood contest and winning money, fortunes perhaps, on the outcome of men's lives. The rest of the audience consisted of ordinary people taking advantage of the free entertainment on offer.

I became euphoric at the selection of pies I was arranging. Wertferler's Blackcrust Meat Porkers, solid and heavy, Randolf's Cruststingers with their razor-sharp crimp and Mrs. Mirtiflow's Scragg End Pasties corners honed to a point, to name but a few. No expense had been spared in the contents of the bag. They had all been modified with indents so that they would fit comfortably in the hand. During the final accolade Grutt shouted, heard only by myself above the deafening noise, that we had to stay alive until the monks found them. I began to hope.

Reaching for the last of the contents of the bag Grutt shook his head. 'Leave those,' he said, sternly. I looked down, the bottom of the bag was layered with Scrigharp-pen's Rough Cast Anti-personnel Eccles Cakes. Hope was turning almost to optimism.

Each man held his choice of pie for the first fling and awaited the signal to begin. Grutt held a Wertferler in his right hand. His left was hovering close to, but not touching, the Cruststingers – he intended to compete in the spirit of the contest regardless of personal danger, a true competitor. My neck hairs stood up with pride that I if I fell in the mêlée to come, it would be at the side of a crusty of the old school. He did, however, nod toward the pastries and whisper that if things turned nasty I should be ready.

The leader locked the gates to the enclosure from the inside and remained in the caged area. His role it seemed was to act as a referee, though his only function would be to start the contest and let out the eventual winner. He went through a farce of requiring the contestants to act in the spirit of the game as though this was a casual, Sunday-afternoon contest.

Grutt belched out, 'On with it.' A menacing guttural command that the rebel leader took as his cue.

Shouting, 'Fling your crusts!' he started to run to a neutral area.

He hadn't taken two steps before the Wertferler hit him the back of the neck, caving in the back of his skull. He fell, sprawling headlong into the dust, and soon a dark stain developed around his head. He never moved again. It was an appalling breach of play: Grutt had loosed his pie even before the word 'crusts' had left the guy's lips. He never had a chance.

The three opponents froze, stunned at the callousness of the kill, but before they even had time to look back in Grutt's direction another pie was hurtling toward the middle contestant. The look on his face was a picture of abject horror.

This time, the pie appeared poorly thrown. It was aimed to the side of the target, missing the fellow by feet.

His face turned to a smile as he realised he would survive the exchange. The smile soon turned to a gasp as the Cruststinger took out the legs of his table sending his arsenal of pies spilling to the ground. Most of them broke open, making them useless and leaving him with the one pie he held. By this time, his comrades had realised the deftness of Grutt's throw and had cast their pies in our direction. They were skilled, but the element of surprise was lost. The big difference in a death match is the contestants are free to move anywhere within the hexagon. Of course, if you move too far then your ammunition is out of reach, which would be stupid. We both dodged the attacks with ease, the pies shredding themselves harmlessly as they hit the almost impenetrable fence.

Grutt's thinking then became apparent. The ruthless attack on the leader now made sense. He held the only key to the gates and, since he was no longer in a position to unlock them, we were effectively isolated. The cage was now our protection, not our prison. Those on the outside would be helpless to affect the outcome of the match and since they were now leaderless would also be thrown into confusion.

The middle man decided not to throw his pie, realising that if he did he would be entirely defenceless. He was effectively out of the contest and looking his demise in the face.

Grutt looked at me smiling. He was thoroughly enjoying himself – all pretence of being drunk had long gone. He picked up a Mirtiflow. It was evil-looking, more like a boomerang than a pasty. Grutt eyed his other two opponents who had also re-armed and were now dodging about though never actually committing to an attack. The one on the right, a young 'cook', seemed the most nervous. Earlier, I had seen him strutting about, catching the eyes of the expensively-draped women that furnished the tiers above. He had looked lustily at several of the single women and, in return, their eyes had raked over his firm, muscular body. He must have skill though to have reached the final of the competition and Grutt wasn't about to underestimate his opponent, just because women found him attractive.

To the left stood a young rebel. His horror at the crusting down of his boss was still playing havoc on him. He had the look of one determined to take revenge and seemed to me to be paying too much attention to my direction.

Grutt didn't hesitate. The Mirtiflow was loosed, its curvature ensuring a wicked attack, visibly bending in the air between the release and the target. The man in the middle, thinking himself safe, looked down to see the pasty had pierced his torso just under the rib cage and blood was pumping from his chest. He sank to the ground and fell on his crumpled crusts.

Again the other two were taken aback at the callous manner that Grutt had dispatched their supposed colleague. He had been the least dangerous and yet was cut down without even the offer of quarter. They knew one of them would be next. It was the speed of the attacks, the ferocity of the flings and the terrifying accuracy that would strike fear in anyone. For my part, I could only admire this hulk of a man.

He shouted, 'Eccles cake!' at me, and at first I was bemused. Surely, he knew I could take no part in this – I was technically a non-combatant. He knew his stuff though. His two opponents flung, both directing their shots in my direction. Fortunately, I was alert to this possibility and managed to duck both attacks, though one rebel winged me on the left shoulder, the sharpened crust of his pie tearing at my shirt and drawing blood. Grutt's instruction made sense now. I rolled and reached for an Eccles cake from the bag and tossed it in his direction. Catching it easily, he let out a 'What are you waiting for?' and hurled it high, high into the air, clearing the fence where it arced down toward the spectators.

The nitro in the Eccles cake exploded in an air burst, sending the tiny, hard-baked currents screaming toward the crowd on the seats. Chaos erupted among the stand as the high rollers realised they were in the firing line, the panic causing many to lose their footing. A scrambling, tumbling tangle of dinner jackets, torn evening dresses and bodies were sent scrawping down the terraces toward the barbed fence. The screams from those that provided the cushions for those from the higher levels was pitiful. Everyone in the stadium was now aware that death and destruction in the form of 'Hard Crust' Broggwaller stalked them. No one was safe.

Most of the spectators ran, but the rebels outside the cage were desperately attempting to force the lock on the cage to get at Grutt. Several were trying to attack him through the fence, but everything they threw ended in a shredded mess that never flew more than a few feet inside the fence. Some of the more intelligent were attempting to climb over the struggling mass of spectator's bodies so they could attack us from above. Grutt looked at them and dismissed the threat for now. It would take several minutes for them to reach a position, by which time he intended to finish the contest.

I had been attacked and bloodied. Grutt had seen this coming and knew I would be entitled to defend myself which was why I had tossed the Eccles cake and why I now held in my hand a Randolf's Cruststinger. Some of my subscription readers will know I am not unfamiliar with the sport, having won the North-West open championship three times in my previous existence as a professional flinger. I was in no mood to stand as a target while someone took pie shots at my person without at least fettling a crust. I tested the Cruststinger, feeling its balance. It was perfect and fit my hand like a glove. I flung it, discus-like toward the rebel that had bloodied me earlier. It took him in the groin where I had intended and, although not a killing strike, he doubled up. To his credit, he refrained from crying out in pain. He looked up in my direction, eyes bulging and anger straining out from every muscle on his face. Another Randolf severed his head from his body – Grutt's fourth throw, accurate and deadly.

Rebuking me with a 'Stop messing about,' Grutt tossed me another Eccle's cake, nodding toward the rebels that were opening the gate with some success. At the same time, he took a Mirtiflow and took aim at the young cook.

The crack of the lock snapping distracted the poor sod from Grutt's attack so he never saw the Mirtiflow coming. Otherwise, he would have been killed outright. As it was, it hit him a glancing blow, knocking him senseless and sending him sprawling to the ground. Grutt, his blood up, had already reached for another Randolf to finish him off on the ground. I reached out, turning him toward the gate with my left hand and flinging with my right. The Eccles cake exploded in the gate's upper structure sending barbed shrapnel and currents into the mass of the rebels.

Several died immediately. Most were either blinded or too seriously injured to carry on their attack. The tailenders, three in total, rushed us, arms held back, each with a weapon of some type in his hand. Grutt took out the first with the now redirected Randolf. I dodged to the right, casting a hastily obtained Blackcrust right in the face of the furthest. His last memory would be it hitting him square on the nose in a perfect blot, the delivery caving in the front of his face.

The remaining rebel turned tail and ran. Grutt's Eccles cake exploded over his head before he reached the gate and he fell to the ground his skull a ruined mess. The contest was over.

The scale of the carnage we had inflicted was almost biblical. Most of the rebels were dead or soon would be if they were lucky. I turned to look at Grutt and he stared back, resolute.

Shortly after, the monks arrived, and they soon rounded up the Backtechs. One of the well-to-dos demanded the Major arrest Grutt and me for the deaths we had meted out to the crowd.

Grutt stepped in before the Major could respond. 'Count yourselves lucky you're not sucking on the sharp end of one of these,' he said, raising a Cruststinger.

The toff backed away into the waiting arms of an apiary monk and was escorted to a waiting wagon. The Major followed and busied himself with some paperwork. It seemed that Grutt was in charge. For my part, I was grateful he was. I thought we would both be marched off for a quick trial and an even swifter death for the terrible bloodshed we had inflicted on the spectators. The mystery of Grutt and his position within the apiary structure had deepened.

I expected to be carted off with the others for getting involved and possibly ruining the operation. Instead,

Grutt actually thanked me for befriending him and shook my hand, saying, 'I owe you one.'

We parted as crust-mates.

I never saw him after that. I was taken back toward Castlefield in one of the Hive cars and let out just outside the part of the city wall formed by the collapsed Manky Way. I made my way back up Deansgate and arrived just as the closing ceremony was about to start. The young flinger, the one I saw win earlier in the day, had to be helped to the podium by two of his mates. He collapsed to the floor just before the Abbot placed the medal round his neck. No interview from him, then.

There was one thing that puzzled me – as the lad was helped to his feet, I noticed an unsightly wet patch at the bottom of the Abbot's trousers...

WATERWAYS

Ekaterina Fawl

The 'Rainy City' name is a lie. Statistically, Manchester gets less rainfall than the rest of the country, but, shielded from harsh winds by lines of green hills and blessed with enough bodies of good, soft water, it always stays wonderfully humid.

The River Irwell hugs Manchester from the west and curls through all its vital points. Small canals shoot away from it and fan through the body of the city: Bridgewater, Rochdale, Ashton. The river Medlock snakes out to meet them. No spot within the Mancunian Way is more than half a mile away from open water. There are reservoirs to the east and river Mersey to the south – the whole area is perfectly, beautifully defensible.

It's no Amsterdam, but coastal cities on this planet are a write-off anyway. Humans will sink them long before the first wave gets here.

Jamil, sentimental little spawn, thinks this is the most important place on the planet. This is the birthplace of their science, such as it is. This is where they began to understand sentience. He gets cloudy-eyed at the thought, as if he's watching a child learn to swim. One time, he showed me the maths they teach to their young here. I cracked a joke: maybe we should take the whole place out then, if it's so close to being dangerous. He didn't talk to me for hours after. He's over it now.

'You love it here. Look at you, you flipping love it,' he says in English. We only converse in English when we're above water. I don't even know what his native language is: I can't tell his ethnicity because of the mods. They gave him brown eyes – creepy, but I'm adjusting. We only know each other's human names and human faces. I have no idea what he used to look like, or if he was male before the mission.

'Maybe I love it a little,' I say and watch my feet tread the canal towpath. Foot protection is culturally mandatory here, but flip-flops aren't that painful to wear. It's a rare sunny day, and the surface of the water shudders softly, radiates moisture. My new skin sucks it in, humming, happy. The gravity is still punishing, though it feels subjectively easier by the water's edge, knowing we could simply dive in if our bodies gave out.

I love the busy streets, perversely, like I love walking on the ground in double gravity. The constant stream of humans, a torrent of speech in several alien languages, occasional eye or physical contact, barely tolerable but easier every day. My brain revs up at the challenge just like my muscles do, coils tighter, stretches, grows.

I love the open spaces west of the Irwell, where the lay of the land reveals itself so readily and I can really plot and plan. But these little pockets of calm by the still, dark water, these secluded places where the canals turn and curl, they're like home.

It doesn't look like home, of course not. But it feels... solid, not like an alien world at all, just like a world, a place to live in.

We've made our daily training into a ritual. We call it

patrolling, but we flatter ourselves. We don't have re-sources to establish any kind of hold. We're only here to taste the water or, as the humans say, put feet on the ground. Everything looks different from the surface. Our mission, apart from maintaining data relays, is to make the first mistakes so the next team doesn't have to.

We begin at Islington Wharf and follow the towpath to Deansgate locks. My grand plan is to walk by the river all the way to Victoria station and take the train back to the main relay. It sounds horrific – we'll be sealed inside a car-riage, no access to outside moisture, with only the perspi-ration of our fellow passengers to rely on – but it's only a few minutes, and humans are very wet. I'm sure we can do it.

We'd made it to the river once, under heavy, lush rain. The few humans around were busy shielding their faces from streaming water and we dove in right from the bridge without anyone noticing, swam for miles along the bottom, returned after dark and slowly made our way back through the locks.

Honestly, that's the only thing I want to change here: canal locks need to go. Silly nuisance.

The route is familiar now. At first the canal is wide, edged with small dwellings. The water swarms with fauna: fish, ducks, geese. The birds are terrified of us but the humans don't get suspicious. Humans stroll, jog, cycle along the path, sit on the benches, fish in the canal, si-lently revel in its generous quiet beauty.

The canal ducks under a few streets, into the dark dirty tunnels; the air is very wet there, yet unpleasant, too thick with local flora for us to enjoy. Then, in the city proper, it follows a neat little street past a tiny park that looks like a tree museum amongst the brick and concrete.

Here humans tend to clump together and interact with abandon, buzzed or calmly content from eye contact and body proximity. A lot of them hold hands.

'We should be a couple,' I say in a flash of inspiration. We're not cleared to engage humans beyond minimal ritualised interactions. But if we tried posing as, well, as anything other than two blank-faced, average specimens walking side-by-side, at least we could gauge our aptitude at imitating a social construct. If we're good, we'll get more leeway.

'Don't you think it's too risky?' Jamil asks. 'We don't know how sexually valuable we seem to humans. What if one of us is substandard? That would be culturally inappropriate, right?'

'Oh,' I say, trying to sound indifferent. Our throats are heavily modded; Jamil carefully monotones everything he says, but I'm often at a wrong pitch. 'Which one of us?'

'We look vastly different. One of us must be...'

'We're different genders! They're a dimorphic species, we're supposed to be like this!'

He shrugs his angular shoulders and ducks his head. I listen to his flip-flops slap and feel the fleshy implants on my chest heave up and down – probably as strange to him as his brown eyes are to me. I'm the one with the xeno training, it's my job to be open-minded and tolerant. I shouldn't get angry.

'I don't want to push our luck until we understand them better,' he says. 'Maybe you do, that's your field, and I'm happy to defer to you, but let's discuss it first. You can tell their genders, right, but to me their mating strategies look completely random. That's why I think there might be a pattern we're missing. Shape, size and colouring clearly aren't factors... and did you see those two? I think they're different races.'

There's something in the way he says it – even in English there's that shuddering gravity to the words I remember from the old chronicles. I realise his eyes must have been pristine, untainted red. Human eyes don't come in that colour.

'So that's why they had to replace your eyes, huh,' I say, because I'm not a subtle person. Open-minded and tolerant but not subtle. 'I didn't know they started letting your kind into the program. How are you doing with that in the camps, by the way, are you keeping your precious bloodlines pure enough?'

I'd love to see his real expression under the layers of synthetic skin, fat and muscle. Except they cut out most of our mimic plates to attach these faces, so I'd only see him staring at me blankly with dark, artificial eyes.

'All I'm saying,' he intones, 'is I like it here, there's a lot of work to be done, and I don't want to be extracted. But if you think it's a good idea, let's do it. Let's hold hands.'

'Shove your hand up your roe slit,' I say with relish. 'But not right now, that would be culturally inappropriate.'

We keep moving south, picking our way through the desolate part of the canal, a littered, stinky stretch between quiet, blind cliffs of the office blocks. I usually enjoy this bit – we're always alone here, and we don't have to check our gait and posture.

Whatever else is going on in Jamil's pointy head, there's one thing we both know: we both trust mission control completely. We volunteered for this, got cut up and reshaped and stranded here without support, with only emergency extraction between us and any catastrophic failure. They wouldn't have picked us if we weren't right for the job or if we couldn't get along. Besides, who else am I going to talk to on this planet?

'You're doing great with the gravity,' I say, not entirely truthfully. His legs are wobbling badly, and he's eyeing the water surface like he's already planning to plant his face right into it. 'Let's treat ourselves, get a drink at that pub.'

We sit on hard, slatted chairs. Folding our bodies lessens the pressure, but not enough to really feel rested. Still, there's water right by our feet, under the wooden decking, and there's a new, unseen before view: a jumble of wildly-unmatched buildings. And there's humans all around us, close enough for us to eavesdrop on whole conversations. Jamil copies their postures, slides from one type of slump into another. I'm mulling over the interaction I had with the bartender. He smiled a lot. I'm sure I've nailed it.

'I know you're frustrated,' Jamil says.

I grunt my assent. 'I have so much work, there's thousands of years' worth of data to process, and you don't have any opportunity to do what you do. But you could help me. They're an introspective species, so there's a lot we can learn about their social structures without direct... what?'

I can see the seams of Jamil's face, fake-human muscles straining to accommodate the contortion of fear where the stumps of his mimic plates are. His hand shoots over the dusty, wooden table to grab mine. 'Behind you. Just one,' he says. 'A runner.'

Deep space travel, alien worlds – you could live hundreds of years, see and do it all, but nothing really touches you quite in the same place, with this primal intensity. Of course it's a runner – a heavy would have collapsed under its own weight here – and nothing ever feels as real as the gaze of your natural predator lingering on the back of your head.

There shouldn't be any Verans on Earth, I think in panic, and then, wait, why not? This world is still unclaimed. There's only me and Jamil and a crate-full of easily self-destructible equipment. Maybe we have backup somewhere in another hemisphere – neither of us would know. But, until Homeworld makes a move Earth will sit here, up for grabs. There could potentially be anything here right now.

Any number of anything.

And we have no weapons.

The Veran is modded to look like a human male. He's five tables from us, staring at Jamil, waiting for my me to look at him too. When I acknowledge him with a nod he smiles, tips his head back and pours half a tall glass of amber-red beer down his throat. He doesn't even pretend to swallow the way humans do. I guess this is meant to intimidate us.

He crooks his finger invitingly, and we both get up and go. He can't compel us, we'd bred that out of our species centuries ago, but somehow this seems the most sensible thing to do.

'Don't you two look delicious?' he says when we're stood to attention by his table. 'Shall we walk?'

He slowly wades through the pub's patio, making us retrace the way we came, steps into a narrow alley and picks his way between burst rubbish bags, kicking his heels a little in obvious revulsion. His smell for rot is keener than ours. But, I would imagine, he wants a secluded spot for this.

'So, my heroes of the vanguard, have your glorious leaders made a decision yet? Will they thrust out their chinless little faces and try to take this system?'

I don't know what to do.

No, I do. Of course I do. I'm supposed dive for deep water, report and wait for instructions.

'Yes they will,' I say, and only then realise that Jamil is still holding my hand, because he digs his soft nails into my palm. I slip my fingers free. 'The announcement will come soon. We're going to report that we've issued you a warning, so I suggest you withdraw if you can.'

It's not really a lie – annexation *is* being considered. I might even be commended if he buys my bluff.

I can tell now that there's a definite pull every time his eyes meet mine. Something soft inside me shudders and swells to his will. Our two species don't have casual face-to-face contact anymore. There's a module during off-world training which I don't like to recall, but it had never felt like this. I can resist, but the sensation is unsettling.

It stands to reason – we've been breeding out our weakness, why wouldn't they have tried to improve their strength?

The Veran leans on the brick wall next to some incomprehensible writings. We're just out of sight here – the giant plastic bins block the view from the street. It's just as difficult for him, I remind myself – this gravity hurts him as much as it does me. Our ancestors are from the same world, he's only a runner, not that much bigger than me, and we're no longer his dumb prey.

'I could,' he says. 'Withdraw, that is. This is my fourth insertion. I might do a few more before I retire. My surgeries are fully reversible – yours aren't, though, are they? I'm curious, what do your glorious leaders do with you after an insertion? Do they just kill you?'

'No, we don't get killed, beast,' says Jamil. 'We're going to settle here and live with the humans.' His grating voice is as colourless as ever, but it makes me feel as if my whole body snaps back into alignment. I thought he might faint or offer his chest to the predator unprompted, but he's holding it together.

The Veran nods. 'I hear Castlefield is the place to live. Or Didsbury. I don't know if it will work though. Are you going to sleep in bathtubs forever? And at what point are they going to take your kill switches out? When the first wave arrives? Or… never?'

I don't know. It's not a question you ask. The switch is the last safety in case we really mess up; it's not supposed to be tripped if we do our job. Really – and that's why you don't talk about it – it's there for traitors. If you're not planning treason, why would you ask?

'I had one of yours under interrogation for a few hours once,' says the Veran. 'Until the signal came through and your glorious leaders pulled the plug. It's not dramatic or anything. You just plop on the floor. Sixty litres of sludge, give or take, takes about ten minutes to fully liquefy, and then you're water.'

He holds a pause, letting us absorb the mental picture. I know exactly how the process takes place, but he uses English words and Earth measures and it doesn't seem as familiar and clean as it was in my training materials.

'I know your glorious leaders aren't listening right now,' he says. 'Your tech is still a bit shit like that. Ours, however, isn't. Once we have a mesh in orbit we can block your signal for good. That's what you want, really, isn't it? Then you can settle here, splash in the rain, sit around in beer gardens, do all that dumb crap that's not about float-ing in lines, spouting slogans. You just have to keep being your adorable, bumbling selves. If you stall the next phase of the invasion – simply don't be too efficient, keep asking for more time to research the place – that'll be enough. If we take this world without having to waste ammo on your miserable little ships I'll set you free, personally.'

His smile is viciously natural and human-like. Veran's faces are a lot more agile than ours, their bone structure better for modding. Makes sense – humans are land carnivores too.

'If you aren't ready to see past your brainwashing, I guess you could try to make my job harder.' The smile fades. 'But I honestly can't imagine you'd slow me down much. I could just eat you both, but they'd only send more snacks, and, obviously, that wouldn't be a problem at all, but we're in the same business, we understand this life, and this is the best offer you'll ever get.'

'We will never live under Veran tyranny again,' I say. Because I'm sure I'm supposed to say something like that, for the record. When our reports are filed something like that definitely should be in them.

The Veran smiles wider, enough to bare his teeth, and for the first time I see a flaw in his disguise: human teeth are thicker. His have been made white and matte, but they're still a set of softly serrated blades.

'It won't be "Veran tyranny". That's what you little wrigglers can't comprehend. It'll be the natural order, the food chain. It'll just be life. This place will be a wilderness preserve; the humans won't notice any difference.'

'Unless you use their star for a launchpad,' I say. I've seen burnt-out star systems in the chronicles.

'Well, that can only happen once at most,' he says with a low, amused growl. 'Have you thought about what this city will look like after your glorious leaders have finished with it? I've infiltrated other planets you've annexed, so

I've seen it. Have you? Is that on the propaganda curriculum? When they put the sentries into the canals – what's the reach going to be on this planet?'

'Half a mile,' I say, dry-throated. I've thought about it. I've sent out detailed plans for installations.

'The layout would need to change a bit,' he makes a show of glancing around, at the angles of the buildings we can see though the mouth of the alley. 'I suppose it'll be around Fountain Street where you'll line the humans up for the evening counts, though this is a dense area, so you might need a different setup. You know, I stood in those lines for a month once, undercover. Shouted my name, flashed my regs, watched those *things* slither around the walls. Your guys burnt tunnels right through, riddled it, for ease of sentry access. And that's hardly the worst thing you did. It's the little details that stick in my mind, like watching a juvenile slobber over some broken rocks that used to be its home, and knowing exactly what it's feeling, thanks to the mods. How long have you been here? Can you read human emotions yet? Have you seen how they weep?'

'We won't kill them if they comply,' says Jamil. 'We'll nurture their development. *You'd* eat them.'

'If you cared about this world, you'd look at the human's population stats and recognise that we're the best thing for them. They desperately need a predator.'

I'm imagining what our report to the Homeworld will look like. *The agents have encountered a Veran. They were confused and intimidated, and there's disturbing information that the beast was nearly able to compel them.* Whether or not we tell Homeworld about the sedition attempt we'll come off as shifty, close to being compromised. Our whole mission will seem on the edge of failing.

I don't even think the Veran really wants us to work for him. He's trying to use us to send a message to the Homeworld: the Verans want Earth for themselves, but they wouldn't mind striking a bargain if they can take it peacefully. The Homeworld talks big about never bowing to our ancient enemy, but as long as it's all kept on down low they'll gladly sell the whole system to the Verans. It's only got one half-way good planet, and even that's too big, and only seventy percent open water. Me and Jamil might be ordered to handle the deal, since we've already made contact. We'd be ordered to build rapport, to get a better price.

But if we could establish a position of strength – or at least make things messy... I turn to Jamil and pull my face into a quizzical expression.

'Oh, absolutely, Helen, do what you do,' Jamil says.

I sweep the Veran's legs from underneath him and plant his face into the nearest clump of garbage. He gags; I use that moment to deliver my best kick to his hip joint. It's been reinforced for this gravity so I don't break anything, but there's some give, he'll be off-balance.

He springs up, barely swaying, and goes for close combat. I'm surprised he still has claws, well, intellectually surprised, they don't phase me. He swipes them at my face to make me raise my guard and then folds his claw points to a spear and aims the killing blow, right into my rib opening, through to my heart.

I let him. My ribs had to be fused together to hold against gravity. I have a breastbone now, like a human, and he'd need a hammer to break it.

He doesn't expect such resistance, and I think he injures his wrist, because he jumps back and guards for a moment, letting me pound at his shoulders, shins, elbows.

There's too much muscle layering every weak point for my strikes to have much effect.

He tests my knees with a vicious kick. My joints there are completely synthetic and hold fast. He goes for my chest again and I guide the strike to my armpit, through the soft prosthetic flesh until his claws sink into the knot of tendons that hold the implants up. His hand gets stuck in them long enough for me to hit the nerve cluster at his neck. He doesn't crumple like the training manuals promised, but he shudders and I know it hurts.

He goes for the usual vital points again and again, trying to find a way through. He can't kill me, I think, giddily. He doesn't know how to kill me – I'm too heavily modded, and he expects to win with a killing blow, like always.

He pulls back to regroup, puzzled. He's shredded enough of my muscle to bring me down eventually, but he doesn't realise that yet. He can't see how badly I'm bleeding – my blood is clear, instantly soaked up by layers of human clothes. He can't even smell my blood over the stench of garbage. I just need to keep my stance steady.

'I guess you're the heavy in the relationship,' he says.

'I guess I am. Do you miss yours?'

'Mine would protect me,' he pants and makes a dash for Jamil. If I was the defender Jamil would be safely tucked behind my back, but he backed in the wrong direction when the fight started and now he's flinching by the wall a good ten paces from us.

I don't really know what the Veran's plan is. Perhaps he thinks he'll stun me with grief if he manages to rip out Jamil's guts. Jamil turns and flees. Of course, neither of us will ever be faster than a Veran runner, but that's not the point of this manoeuvre.

Verans can't smell water, and he had no need to memorise the layout of the canals unless he knew we were here and considered us a threat – which no Veran would.

He jumps on Jamil's shoulders, and my freaky, brown-eyed science guy does probably the only good move he has – he goes down like an autumn leaf, rolls forward and slams the Veran's head into the ground.

They're almost out of the alley and onto the towpath, a narrow stretch of the canal under the railway, over-looked only by a small tower with no visible means of ingress. There's only few feet to the water.

I charge the Veran, and he slashes his claws at my throat. It's a pointless move – he'll have broken half his fingers on my neck plates. Then I realise: he's dazed and fighting on instinct and muscle memory alone. This is how he's been killing humans. Of course he already hunts humans, what else would he survive on?

I have enough momentum to lift him off his feet and throw us both toward the edge. The weight is too much, stupidly too much, and my right kneecap finally breaks. But the momentum carries us over and that's it, we're in the water and I've won.

I stop bleeding. Water flows into my wounds, nourishes me. My muscles loosen up and begin mending. But the Veran grabs at the canal edge and hold us above the surface – he could still escape me.

Jamil limps up to us, carrying a dirty piece of brick. He slams it into the pressure point on the Veran's wrist, precisely as described in the training manuals.

The beast chokes on a scream and lets go. We sink. He still thrashes, but water robs him of his speed. He slashes frantically, but it's not enough. His attacks slow down and then stop. His eyes roll back and blood vessels begin popping, black against white.

I glance up and sign a question. Jamil is crouched at the edge, keeping lookout. 'No,' he signs in reply. 'Witnesses.'

I gorge up a glob of oxygen, pry the Veran's mouth open and force the air down his windpipe. He convulses against me, briefly conscious, and starts fading again. I hold him still, fingers on his pulse point, and wonder if letting him die is actually my second preference.

When his heart rate drops I look up again, and Jamil is gone. Well, nothing for it. Humans are communal, so they'll rush over if they see two of their own crawl out of the canal. Worst case scenario, we'll both get caught and I'll get extracted. Second worst case scenario, I'll get away, while the Veran gets caught and dissected in a variety of ironic and fun ways. The Conglomerate will be embarrassed, and the Homeworld will commend me.

I scrape some moss off the stones, skin my hand against them until my suckers are exposed, cling to the wall and heave us both out.

Jamil isn't far, just by the corner. He's interacting with humans like nobody's business, keeping three of them from entering our towpath, their eyes glued to their mobile phones. I think he's asking them for directions.

I drag the Veran back into the alley and punch him in the chest until his heart starts again.

'...act of war...' he garbles through the water streaming from his mouth.

'Yes, put that in your report. We told you. Earth is ours.'

He glares at me, unbelieving. 'You attacked me. If your masters don't choose to back you, you'll be sixty litres of sludge by morning. They'll kill you tonight, in the water, in your sleep.'

'Why wouldn't they back me up? This story will be great for morale back home.'

'I'm not alone here,' he rasps. 'We'll catch you on dry land. We'll—'

'In the Rainy City, yes, good luck. You know why I didn't kill you, apart from I don't want your corpse poisoning my water? I want you to tell the others. You don't hunt in my city. Now go.'

The Veran twists away, leaps over the canal and makes for the high ground. He's badly hurt, I think – it's not just his injured hands, he's hunched over like he's nursing an internal injury. He'll need to feed soon.

Yes, good job, human female Helen. Good job.

My clothes are already dry when Jamil walks back to me. I didn't heal up fully, and my skin itches and aches for more water. He takes off his jacket and dunks it into the canal. 'Dropped it!' He flashes a wide smile at some unseen onlooker as he pulls the cloth out, sodden. He drapes it over me, waits a few seconds for my body to suck in all the moisture, does it again. 'Come on, go into the water,' he says.

I'm in a lot of pain. I have at least one ruptured bladder. I don't know what I'm going to do about my knee. But I don't want to go into the water right now. I'm too weak to shield, and the moment we're both below surface he'll know what I'm thinking.

'Please, you have to or you'll get worse, Helen. We have to go. We need to report immediately.'

I have to trust him. Who else do I have? I might as well tell him, in terms I can choose and control. 'We've started fighting for Earth. We've forced the Homeworld's hand. Our claim is now public,' I say. 'Unless they destroy our reports and extract us. That's possible, but is this better?

What did the Veran say – maybe we need more time to research the place. I don't know what's best.'

Jamil jerks his legs in contemplation, something humans don't do – I'll have to point that out later.

'Earth is on a swift technological path,' he says. 'We can buy them enough time.'

We both know what happens to plucky upstarts who fight back, so I say nothing else.

I let Jamil help me to the water and drop into the canal, right where we'd fought. I can't walk anywhere like this – my clothes are in tatters, and my nearest spare set is under Ducie Street bridge. Jamil slides in too and leaves me where I sink to check the relays and send the report. I fall asleep right away, so I barely hear him.

I drift by a pub after sunset and wake up enough to turn over and see the lights, take in water-muffled sounds. Then that goes past, and there are only black walls, sometimes pierced with bright windows, occasional silhouettes of trees, shadows and voices of people passing by, alien constellations above. Then I butt my head against a lock and can't climb over it, so I have to sleep there.

Jamil finds me sometime in the middle of the night. We twine our limbs to suspend ourselves deep enough for best comfort. My leg doesn't bend at all but he doesn't mention it, simply adjusts his grip. 'Report acknowledged and we're still alive, pretty good, don't you agree?' he thinks at me.

I blow some water into his face. He gives me his wide human smile in return.

Just have to do what we do, I suppose. It'll all work out.

BIOGRAPHIES

EDITOR BIOGRAPHIES

Craig Pay writes speculative fiction short stories and novels. His short stories have appeared with a number of different magazines and anthologies. He runs the successful Manchester Speculative Fiction writers' group, and enjoys Chinese martial arts.

You can visit Craig at **craigpay.com**

Graeme Shimmin was born in Manchester, and studied Physics at Durham University. After his successful consultancy career enabled him to retire at 35 to an island off Donegal and start writing his novel *A Kill in the Morning* which won the YouWriteOn book of the year, and was shortlisted for the Terry Pratchett Prize.

To find out more, visit **graemeshimmin.com**

Eric Ian Steele is a produced screenwriter and soon-to-be-published novelist. He has written many screenplays including the feature film *Clonehunter*, which was released in the USA, Canada and Japan. His short stories have appeared in print alongside those by Neil Gaiman and Kim Newman, and he is a published zombie poet.

Eric's website is **ericiansteele.wordpress.com**

WRITER BIOGRAPHIES

Die Booth lives in Chester, England and enjoys painting pictures and exploring dark places. Die's debut novel *Spirit Houses*, an action-packed tale of possession, betrayal and excellent Scotch, is available online and a single author collection of short stories is due out in 2016.

You can visit Die at **diebooth.wordpress.com**

Matthew Bright is a writer, editor and designer who often has to debate in which order. His short fiction has appeared in *Nightmare Magazine, Queen Mob's Teahouse, The Biggest Lover* and *Cairo by Gaslight*. He is also the editor of the forthcoming anthologies *The Myriad Carnival* and *Threesome*. He lives in Manchester, England with his partner John, and pays the bills as a book cover designer. Matthew's dog has a taste for eating valuable hardback books.

Find Matthew at **matthew-bright.com**

Bryn Fazakerley was born in Manchester, in 1984. Introduced by his uncle to science fiction at an early age, he remains to this day a raider of the city's second-hand bookshops. Shortlisted for the 2014 MMU Novella Award for his story *By the Victor*, Bryn has also had work published in *Nous* magazine. He is currently in the final stages of writing his first novel, *Departure Point*.

Bryn's website is **brynfazakerley.wordpress.com**

Ekaterina Fawl lives in Manchester and has had several short stories published. He has been attending Manchester Speculative Fiction since soon after it began.

Her twitter is **@ekaterina_fawl**

Katy Harrison was born in Stockport and raised in North London. She received a MA in Creative Writing from MMU in 2009 and is currently working on a novel. She has a tendency to collect tattoos and facts, and harbours a strong interest in all things Japanese.

Her twitter is **@spikykaty**

Sarah Jasmon lives on a canal boat near Manchester with her children. She has had several short stories published, is curating a poetry anthology, and has graduated from the MA Creative Writing programme at Manchester Metropolitan University in 2012. Her first novel, *The Summer of Secrets*, was published in 2015.

Sarah's personal website is: **sarahjasmon.com**

Chris Ovenden teaches philosophy at the University of Manchester, UK. When he isn't marking undergrad papers, he writes speculative fiction about robots, time-travel and possible worlds. His work has been featured on DailyScienceFiction.com and EveryDayFiction.com

You can find Chris at **chrovenden.wordpress.com**

Gerda Pickin is a writer and musician residing in Scotland whose stories have been published in numerous anthologies and one chap book. Still awaiting representation, the stories continue to flow regardless, an almighty itch that needs constant scratching.

Gerda's music is at **soundcloud.com/gerda-pickin**

Steve Palmer is the author of nine speculative-fiction novels and has had many short stories published. He lives and works in Shropshire, UK.

Steve's website is **stephenpalmer.co.uk**

Rob Prescott lives and writes in Manchester where he works as a corporate drone. He has been attending Manchester Speculative Fiction since 2014. This is his first publication.

Contact Rob via **manchesterspeculativefiction.org**

James J. Ridgway is a science fiction writer and global education consultant. He says, "Attending military school in the 1980s taught me how to survive the end of the world, but not what to do in the meantime". He lives and works in Manchester.

Contact James via **manchesterspeculativefiction.org**

Luke Shelbourn works as a project officer for a youth charity in Manchester, UK. When teenagers aren't trying to decapitate him with dodgeballs, he dabbles in short stories ranging from hard-boiled noir to cosmic horror. This is his first publication.

Contact Luke via **manchesterspeculativefiction.org**

Angus Stewart is from Dundee. He was runner-up in the *Ink Tears* 2014 flash fiction contest, and has been featured in *Nous* magazine. He has self-published two novels and two collections of his writing.

Angus's blog is **dustsymbols.tumblr.com**

Sam Tein is new to writing, but is no spring-chicken, having spent a long and successful career designing electronics. He tries to find the humorous side of the weird, dystopian and sometimes nightmarish worlds he creates

Sam's website is **www.samtein.com**

Quentin Van Dinteren is a Dutchman who moved to Manchester for the weather. He distributes his time between writing scary and exciting stories and working as a lawyer to support his expensive hobbies.

His free role-playing game is at **www.stage-rpg.com**

ACKNOWLEDGEMENTS

The editors would like to thank:

- Everyone who submitted a piece for consideration. We had to make some tough choices, and there were stories we really liked that were not included in the final anthology.
- Luke Shelbourn for volunteering as assistant editor.
- Chris Ovenden for reading submissions.
- Everyone who has attended the Manchester Speculative Fiction Group meetings and helped make it such as success.
- Madlab, who have given us somewhere to meet and always been helpful.
- Our long-suffering families, who may now believe we aren't having an affair after all.

FINALLY

Manchester Speculative Fiction Group was established in 2010 for writers interested in writing science fiction, weird fiction, slipstream, horror and fantasy.

Since then it has had many successes: two members of the group have had novels published so far, and others are on the way, having gained deals or agents. Several have won writing competitions and had short stories featured in magazines and anthologies.

We meet twice a month in Manchester's Northern Quarter to discuss each other's work.

New members are always welcome. To find out when the next meeting is, check our website:

manchesterspeculativefiction.org

21921976R00163

Printed in Poland
by Amazon Fulfillment
Poland Sp. z o.o., Wrocław